The Stones of Ailsa Craig

A Novel

David S. Florig

To Ann,

David S. Florig

David S. Florig

Book Cover design by David S. Florig.

Ocean Park, Maine.

Library of Congress Control Number: 2023911372

ISBN: 9798988554554 (Paperback)

ISBN: 9798988554547 (ebook)

　　　　1. Fiction – historical – general　　2. Fiction – multiple timelines　　3. Sport & recreation – winter sports – curling

BISAC: FIC014000 Fiction/Historical　　FIC080000 Fiction/Mulitiple Timelines SPO081000 Sports & Recreation

Printed in the United States of America.

10 9 8 7 6 5 4 3 2 1

www.davidflorig.com

Dedication

To my wife, Nancy, who put up with an awful lot as I wrote this story, and who faithfully read, and re-read the manuscript. And, of course, to all of those who love *The Roarin' Game*. Good Curling!

Acknowledgments

Writing a book is an enormous and challenging undertaking. It would not be possible without the support, encouragement, and yes, constructive criticism from many, many people. Thanks to everyone who was a part of creating this book.

Very special thanks to Tara Peterson, 2022 United States Women's Olympic Curling Team member and three-time United States champion, who answered the request of a complete stranger and wrote the Foreword. You can follow Team Peterson on Twitter at *@TeamPetersonUSA* and on Facebook at *facebook.com/TeamPetersonUSA*.

Thank you to Eve Muirhead, gold medalist at the 2022 Winter Olympics; Nina Roth, two-time Olympian representing the United States (2018, 2022); and Jamie Sinclair, three-time United States National Champion, who provided much-appreciated Advance Praise.

To my curling teammate Jim Ford, who read a very early draft and offered valuable insights and suggestions, and to my trivia teammates Paul and Scotte Mason, who also read an early draft and offered their comments and encouragement.

My thanks also go to the many curling clubs and associations throughout the United States and Canada who helped publicize *The Stones of Ailsa Craig*, including Belfast Curling Club, Broomstones Curling Club, Bucks County Curling Club, Chestermere Curling

Association, Curl BC, Curling Club of Houston, CurlSask, Detroit Curling Club, Diamond State Curling Club, Grand National Curling Club, Itasca Curling Association, Lone Star Curling Club, Mayfield Curling Club, McIntyre Curling Club, Mount Washington Valley Curling Club, Nashville Curling Club, Ogden Curling Club, Palmetto Curling Club, Rutland Rocks Curling Club, USA Curling, and Wine Country Curling Club.

Foreword

I never imagined writing a Foreword to a book, although I had imagined curling in the Winter Olympics for years. When David approached me out of the blue saying that he had written a novel with a curling theme and asking if I was willing to read the draft, I immediately said, "Yes." I am, after all, both a curler *and* a voracious reader – and there just aren't many novels about curling out there. And, I really liked the story. I readily agreed to write this Foreword.

I started curling as an eight-year-old when my parents signed me up for the junior program at the St. Paul Curling Club in St. Paul, Minnesota. I didn't care for the sport at first. It was so difficult, I didn't have any friends at the club, and the only thing that I liked about it was the snacks that were served during the break time. Eventually, I befriended some other kids and actually started to enjoy myself.

After one or two winters of learning the game, my sister Tabitha and I were placed on a junior competitive team and we would travel to weekend tournaments (better known in the curling world as bonspiels) throughout Minnesota and Wisconsin. My absolute favorite bonspiel was held in Centerville, Wisconsin every year – but it wasn't the curling itself that I loved that weekend, it was all the fun events that occurred during the bonspiel. My claim to fame was winning the karaoke contest on Saturday night. I always sang Gretchen Wilson's "Here for the Party." (And I still love that song!) The hosts of the event also put together scavenger hunts, trivia games, and other fun activities to keep the kids occupied when we weren't curling. (Or maybe to keep us out of trouble).

I continued to compete – most of the time with my sister – and my team continued to get better and better. We finally won a Junior National title in 2009. This led us to our first Junior World Championships that were being held in Vancouver, British Columbia. This was the year before the 2010 Winter Olympic Games, and this event was a trial run for the Olympics. Standing in the Olympic venue, being treated like an Olympian, was when I had my first glimpse of what my future could be. I knew then and there that if I dedicated myself to this sport, if I put the time and work into it, I could make that Olympic dream come true.

Curling took me to Scotland, Switzerland, China, and Japan before I was even twenty-one years old. I was able to form great friendships with my competitors that have lasted to this day. I did all of this traveling and competing while I was studying biology at the University of Minnesota. Because of my desire to have dual "career" paths, curling helped me build character and it shaped who I am today. It taught me grit, it taught me time management, it taught me that hard work pays off. Sadly, I knew that at some point I might have to choose between school and curling because it was becoming more and more difficult to do both.

I was accepted into the Doctor of Dental Surgery Program and was able to stay up with my studies while also being a member of the U.S. Curling High Performance Program the first year it was initiated. However, the time came during my second year of dental school when I had to make the hard decision to continue to my degree or continue curling. I simply couldn't commit to the rigorous training, travel, and competition schedule and learn hands-on dentistry at the same time. The choice was tough, but ultimately obvious for me – I chose to step away from curling.

So, I sat on the sidelines and watched and cheered my sister and my previous team from afar. I graduated from dental school in 2018, but a few months before graduation, I took a week away to travel to PyeongChang, South Korea. I watched and cheered for Tabitha, Nina, Becca, Aileen, and Team USA as they competed in the Olympics. As I sat there in the stands, hearing the roar from the crowd, I got goosebumps. I had imagined this moment so often, but I had imagined being on the ice, not in the stands. It was then that I knew that I wanted to be back, in the Olympic stadium, in four years, but this time as a competitor, not as a spectator.

Four years later, that is exactly where I was. I was a member of the United States Olympic Curling Team headed for the 2022 Beijing Olympics! When I reflect on my Olympic experience, I remember vividly walking down the ramp to enter the opening ceremonies with my fellow Team USA athletes, and walking amongst some of the greatest of all time, such as Shaun White and Chloe Kim. It was the thrill of a lifetime.

We played our hearts out, but we didn't finish high enough to earn a medal. Losing our last round robin game and failing to qualify for the medal rounds was heartbreaking. The disappointment of falling short of our goals and big dreams was tough. It was four years of a commitment to countless hours of training, stringent diets, regular workouts, and time away from home and work. For it all to come down to one shot, in one game, is overwhelming.

Fortunately, I was able to come home to my husband, my support group of family and friends, and my job, and think about something other than the outcome. I was able to keep my mind busy instead of re-living a missed shot here or there and wondering, "What if?" However, sometimes falling short of goals can drive an athlete forward. My team didn't achieve the result we had hoped for in 2022, so we decided to give it another go in 2026. Milan, Italy watch out – here we come!

Tara Peterson
2022 United States Olympic Curling Team

Preface

When I first had the notion that I would write a novel, I didn't really know what kind of story to tell. It was my wife, Nancy, who suggested that I construct a story about curling, which I had become obsessed with after first trying it at sixty years old. *The Stones of Ailsa Craig* was born.

Curling is certainly a niche sport, known primarily for being featured on television every four years at the Winter Olympics. Most people are unfamiliar with it, or know it only as a curiosity. For those people, I suggest reading the Appendix first, which provides a primer on the game's history, how it is played, the equipment it is played with, and the surface it is played on. A little understanding of the game will help provide context to the story.

The Stones of Ailsa Craig is a work of historical fiction, which can be a tricky genre to both write and read. The story toggles back and forth between present-day Belfast, Maine and 1800s Scotland, particularly the Scottish island of Ailsa Craig, which is home to, among many other things, the best curling stone granite in the world.

As with any work of historical fiction, some of the characters are, or were, real people, while others are entirely fictional. For example, Alexander Thomson really was the lighthouse keeper on Ailsa Craig for three decades, and Genie Francis (star of the soap opera *General Hospital*) really did live and own a store in Belfast, Maine. All of the historical records and newspaper accounts of events cited are factual. For the rest, you can decide for yourself.

David Florig
Ocean Park, Maine

Chapter 1

The Loneliness

The end is very close now, and it is finally safe to tell my story. All of it; or at least as much as I choose to tell.

The worst thing about Molly's death, for me, was the ensuing and all-consuming loneliness. It was the last day of November in 2020, four days after Thanksgiving, when I was left alone after just twenty-five years of marriage. *Glioblastoma multiforme*, the utterly merciless, indiscriminate, and ruthlessly efficient brain cancer which had been diagnosed in March, killed her eight months later, at only forty-eight years old, despite surgery to remove the tumor, six months of radiation, and chemotherapy. If the damn cancer hadn't killed her, the treatment most assuredly would have. The hospice nurse told me on the morning that Molly died, "It won't be long." She was right. I sat beside Molly and held her hand for the final six hours, waiting, until death mercifully and quietly arrived that afternoon. I don't think Molly knew that I was there with her, but I can hope that she did.

At least she died at home. It was the one thing that Molly had absolutely insisted upon, and made me promise to her, claiming that her spirit, or ghost, if you will, would remain close by to watch over me. There was simply no way that I would have ever broken that promise to her, so she died very quietly in her own bed with me and our dog, Bozo, by her side.

Molly had assured me repeatedly, and at most only half-jokingly, over her final weeks that I would most definitely need some watching over when she was gone. Now, I'm not really sure about spirits or ghosts – and I don't think that Molly actually was either – but having her silently and benevolently looking out for me after she was gone probably wouldn't be the worst thing, if that's how she really wanted to spend whatever there might be of an afterlife.

———◦○◦———

The first sign that something was wrong appeared while Molly was on one of her many trips to Augusta to meet with state representatives, or the governor, or their staffs, or to meet at one of the state's many regulatory agencies. Molly was in Augusta to advocate for state funding for bicycle lanes in Maine's Fiscal Year 2021 Budget. She knew the names of just about everyone in the state government. She memorized them and she used them. I think that, at any given time, she could name every state representative, state senator, their party, what their pet projects were, and where their districts were. During the budget meeting with a state senator whom she had known for years, she addressed him by the wrong name – not once, but twice. No one said anything at the time, but on the ride home, Molly's program director, Julie Smith, mentioned it to her. Molly didn't realize that she had called Senator Bailey by the wrong name and was appalled and dumbfounded that she had made such a careless mistake, especially with someone encumbered with a much-larger-than-warranted ego like a politician. Soon thereafter, the headaches began.

Molly and I took our last bike ride together on October 12, 2020. It was a chilly, but beautiful, fall day in Belfast, Maine, where we had made our home, with the leaves at their most varied and colorful, swishing in the breeze, before they would fade and fall. Molly's ride was slow and unsteady, without the grace and athleticism with which she rode before the cancer hit. By then, we knew that her fate soon awaited us, each of us trying to prepare for it in our own private way. Neither of us tried to strike a bargain with God. We didn't bother to pray for miracles, for by now we knew that none were forthcoming. Molly seemed much less afraid of what awaited her than I was, or so she acted. I was terrified.

Ten days before the end, it was an unusually warm and sunny day for November. Molly, so pale and fragile, asked me if I could take her out onto the porch and sit with her. I helped her into the wheelchair which she now needed. I put a blanket on her lap and wheeled her out onto the front porch where we had spent so much time together. We sat there silently, warmed by the sun, staring across the lawn towards Belfast Bay. There were no more plans to make or dreams to share. All that was left for us to do was to wait.

After her cremation and memorial service, which was attended by hundreds of people that Molly had worked with, shop owners, bicyclists, our friends, and even a few politicians, I took her ashes to Acadia National Park on Mount Desert Island. Molly had told me that she would like to have her ashes scattered at the spot where we had sat atop Cadillac Mountain that summer in 1987 when we worked together as counselors at a sports camp on Sabasticook Lake. I put her bike on the bike rack of what had been her car, but which was now mine. Bozo rode in the back seat. Molly's remains were on the passenger seat next to me. I drove to the top of Cadillac Mountain and got out of the car. I immediately knew the exact spot. How could I not? I walked toward it, trying to be as inconspicuous as I could be while carrying the box of ashes. I got to the spot and sat down on the smooth pink granite. I talked to Molly, sometimes in a whisper and sometimes just in my head, for a long time, staring out over the islands toward the horizon. Finally, I told her that I loved her, opened the box, hoped that no one was watching, and let her go.

Two weeks after the memorial service, I got a call from Julie Smith, who had succeeded Molly as the Executive Director at *Bike with ME*, the nonprofit where Molly had spent her entire career. Julie had worked under Molly for six years and was a natural to take over as the head of the organization. She asked if I could meet her for lunch sometime that week. We agreed to meet on Friday afternoon at Darby's, a 150-year-old restaurant downtown.

Julie and I chatted for a while, sometimes about Molly and sometimes about how things were going at *Bike with ME*. For more than twenty years, I had been doing most of *Bike with ME's* legal work *pro bono*, both because I could and because they were always on a tight budget, which would have been crushed by outlandish legal fees. I handled their contracts, easements, rights-of-way, charitable organization filings, and regulatory compliance. I thought that maybe Julie wanted to meet to tell me that with the changes at *Bike with ME*, they were going to get a new lawyer.

As it turned out, Julie didn't want to engage a new lawyer, she wanted to ask me for an unusual favor. She wanted to know if she could have Molly's bike – not to use, but to hang inside of the front door to *Bike with ME's* office. Julie and the staff wanted it as a reminder of Molly and as a tribute to her twenty-three years as their Executive Director and leader. I told Julie that I thought it was a wonderful gesture and told her that even Molly might have approved of the idea, albeit grudgingly. Truth be told, it was exactly the kind of idea that Molly would have had if she were in Julie's position. I told Julie that I would buy some bicycle hooks, bring the bike by next week, and help to hang it.

I then told Julie my news – that I was retiring as an actively practicing lawyer, a decision which turned out to be a horrible mistake. At almost fifty years old, with no mortgage, no children, proceeds from Molly's life insurance policy, a 401(k), and the proceeds from my partnership buyout at the firm, there was really no reason for me to keep working, or so I thought. I'm not one of those people who loved, or even really liked, being a lawyer, so now seemed like the perfect time to make my escape. I assured Julie, though, that I was going to keep my law license active, be named *Of Counsel* to the firm – a largely ceremonial title bestowed on some retired lawyers – and continue to work *pro bono* for *Bike with ME* if Julie wanted me to. She assured me that she did, although the work slowed and soon ended after a lawyer was elected to the board of directors and offered up his firm as *pro bono* counsel instead.

As Christmas approached, the "I just wanted to see how you were doing" phone calls slowed to a trickle. It was winter, the days were short and the nights were long, Christmas was quickly approaching, and people had their own lives to live. For most of December, the sun set before four o'clock in the afternoon in Belfast, making for long stretches of darkness after less than nine hours of daylight. A widower for barely three weeks, for the first time in my life, I spent Christmas alone. I hung Molly's Christmas stocking in its usual spot over the fireplace, between mine and Bozo's. I know that it was silly, but I bought a Christmas card for Molly and placed it inside of her stocking. The only presents under the tree were treats and toys for Bozo.

On New Year's Eve, I stayed home, as Molly and I usually did. We weren't really party people, and we enjoyed reliving the outgoing year and making plans for the new one while sitting together in front of the fire, always with a bottle of champagne. With Molly gone, there were no plans left to make and only a horrible year to relive. I allowed myself a bottle of *Dinner*, a double IPA from Maine Beer Company in Freeport, because it was Molly's favorite, and because drinking an entire bottle of champagne by myself seemed wrong in many ways. Champagne is for happy times and for celebration. There was absolutely nothing left for me to celebrate, and happiness was now a completely foreign emotion to me.

I went to bed well before the waterfront fireworks started and the year turned. Bozo slept on the floor on Molly's side of the bed, as he had done every single night since he first came home with us. He, too, seemed to be feeling the loneliness and loss. We all tend to anthropomorphize our pets, especially dogs, ascribing to them feelings and emotions like we have. Do they love us simply because we feed and shelter them, or for deeper reasons? Do they have any human-like emotions? Do they know grief, loss, and sadness? Do they actually smile? We want the answers to be yes, of course. Whether they have those emotions, though, I really don't know. What I can say is that Bozo *acted* sad and lost after Molly was gone. He ate less, he wagged his tail less, he seemed less excited to head out for his walks, and he had lost most of his interest in playing with his toys, even his favorite tug o' war rope. I think that he was just waiting for Molly to come home.

I woke up on New Year's Day and Bozo was dead. I touched him – he was still warm. If a dog can die of a broken heart, that's exactly what happened. A week later, for the second time in less than a month, I drove to Cadillac Mountain with a box of ashes, where Bozo was once again united with his beloved Molly.

Retirement was really tough for me. I found myself with little to do and with little that interested me. What few friends I had were still working, the winter days were short and the nights were long, and Molly and Bozo were both gone. Molly was the one that I did things with and had planned to always do things with. It had never occurred to me that one day I might have to construct a life without her. I was lost, floundering, looking for answers where there were none, and desperately wanting time to move backwards. I could feel myself slipping into a place where I had never been. It wasn't a depression so much as an absolute emptiness, a drifting, a feeling of disconnection.

January 22, 2021, was my fiftieth birthday, and it would have been Molly's forty-ninth. It had barely been seven weeks since she had died, but already I had spent Christmas, New Year's, and now our birthdays, alone. Other than to go food shopping, I hadn't really gone anywhere other than to Molly's memorial service, my meeting with Julie Smith, and the two trips to the top of Cadillac Mountain. I had never developed any really close friendships in Belfast, despite living there for a quarter of a century. Almost everything that I did, or wanted to do, had been with Molly. Now, I was alone.

Even though Molly was gone, or maybe because she was gone, I felt that I needed to know her better. I wanted to talk to her. I wanted to ask her about all of the things which I had neglected to ask when she was with me. I wanted to learn everything that I could about her. I decided that I would research her family tree. Maybe there were answers there.

Chapter 2

Darcie Ross

D arcie Ross was widowed on a Saturday afternoon, on the 16th day of June in 1888, at the age of only twenty-two. She had been married to Murdock Ross for exactly eleven months. Darcie and Murdock were married in St. Andrew's Cathedral, on Clyde Street on the northern bank of the River Clyde, on July 16, 1887. St. Andrew's Cathedral, the oldest Roman Catholic Church in Glasgow, had long been the parish for Darcie and her family. The Right Reverend Monsignor Alexander Munro officiated the wedding. It seemed as though all of Scotland was celebrating, even the thistle and the bluebells.

In accordance with the old Scottish tradition, Darcie and Murdock were hand-fasted with strips of tartan cloth from their respective clans, literally having their hands bound together during the wedding ceremony – the origin of the term "tying the knot." Darcie stood to Murdock's left, another old Scottish custom from the days when warriors would often bring brides back from their battles, keeping their right hands free to fight off anyone trying to prevent the taking of the bride. Darcie wore a wedding dress which had been sewn by her mother.

Darcie and Murdock were, of course, led into the wedding reception by a bagpiper. At their reception, they drank whiskey from a quaich, or two-handled silver dish, for good luck, using both hands, yet another Scottish wedding tradition. By using two hands, the person drinking from the quaich let others know that he or she was not holding a weapon, a vital piece of information to share should the bride and groom happen to come from rival clans.

As it should be for every bride, it was the happiest day of Darcie's life. She danced with her mother, father, brothers, and cousins. Everyone sang and celebrated the union. The whiskey flowed freely. She rejoiced in being married to Murdock, as he did to her. Everything was perfect and by God's grace always would be. Darcie's father delivered the toast to the bride and groom:

> *May the best you've ever seen*
> *Be the worst you'll ever see.*
> *May a mouse never leave your girnal*
> *With a teardrop in his eye.*
> *May you always keep hale and hearty*
> *Till you're old enough to die.*
> *May you always be just as happy*
> *As we wish you always to be.*

Darcie and Murdock had known each other for fifteen years, ever since they were just children in primary school. They had been fast friends before coming to the somewhat surprising realization that they were in love. On one knee, while presenting Darcie with a bouquet of red roses and a ring, Murdock proposed. Darcie didn't have to think twice. She was rarely seen without a smile after the engagement. Her parents were thrilled when Murdock had asked for their permission and blessing before asking Darcie to marry him. They had known Murdock for years, and may have known that the two were in love even before Darcie and Murdock themselves knew.

After the wedding, Darcie worked as a spinner in one of Glasgow's many woolen goods factories. She and Murdock lived in a small home near the River Clyde, close to where both of their families lived, and often spoke of a larger home filled with children. For his part, Murdock found steady work with Barclay, Curle & Company in Whiteinch, one of the premier shipbuilders in what was then the shipbuilding capital of the world. Murdock was working below deck as a painter aboard the paddle steamer the *Princess of Wales* on the morning of June 16, 1888. The *Princess of Wales* was a 216-foot-long, 600-passenger ship which had been built by Barclay, Curle & Company to ferry passengers between Southampton and the Isle of Wight. The ship left port in Glasgow to perform speed trials in Skelmorlie, on the northern end of the Firth of Clyde. The paddle steamer had been launched for the first time just three weeks earlier, and the final preparations were underway for her to be put into service, although that would never come to pass.

At 1:00 p.m. on the afternoon of June 16th, the *Princess of Wales* was sliced in two when the much larger and faster steamer *Balmoral Castle* rammed into her starboard side. On board the *Princess of Wales* were sixty people – crew, guests, and workers. One lifeboat was deployed from the *Princess of Wales* and all of the women on board were safely hurried ashore to Skelmorlie. Most of the others on board were rescued by nearby boats and yachts and were also taken ashore. While the bow section managed to stay afloat long enough for the people in the front of the ship to be rescued – which was most of them – the stern section of the *Princess of Wales* sank in a matter of just seconds, taking with it a dozen painters and joiners. All were rescued save for three – George Paterson, Colin Muir, and Murdock Ross – whose bodies were never found. The remains of the *Princess of Wales* rest on the floor of the Firth of Clyde to this day under seventy meters of water.

News of the disaster arrived in Glasgow late in the afternoon. It was not long before Darcie learned of it, too, while she was visiting with her parents and tending the garden with her mother. She waited with her parents for any news about Murdock. None would come. A formal inquiry into the disaster found both pilots – James Barrie of the *Princess of Wales* and James Parker of the *Balmoral Castle* – to have been negligent in the piloting of their respective ships.

After the inquiry, word of the pilots' misdeeds reached Darcie Ross, but she did not care. Fault was of no concern to her, because assigning fault was never going to change anything about what had happened that afternoon in the Firth of Clyde. She had never loved, could never love, and would never love, any other man. In an act that bespoke both guilt and kindness, Barclay, Curle & Company quietly presented Darcie Ross with £50, along with their deepest condolences, representing approximately one year's wages for Murdock. Darcie was grateful for the gesture, although money was of no consolation to her at the time, and she bore no malice toward the men who presented it to her.

Whenever Darcie went outside after the accident, whether it be to work, to mass, to market, or even to see her family, she wore black, just as she was expected to do. Everywhere she went in Glasgow, especially St. Andrew's Cathedral, where she and Murdock had been married, she was reminded of him and of the still raw and incomprehensible fact that he was gone. Not wanting to stay in Glasgow with its ever-present reminders, and not wishing to be forever known as "poor widow Ross," barely six months after the sinking of the *Princess of Wales*, Darcie left Glasgow alone for the seaside burgh of Girvan, South Ayrshire, on the west coast of the mainland, to try somehow to start afresh. She found a room for let a short walk from the Sacred Hearts of Jesus and Mary Roman Catholic Church in Girvan. Her parents begged her to stay with them in Glasgow, but Darcie knew that she had to leave.

Darcie Ross was steadfast in her Catholic faith and found a great deal of comfort in its rituals and liturgy. For as long as she could remember, she had faithfully attended mass at St. Andrew's, first with her family and then with Murdock. Her faith was a part of her, and she would not abandon it just because God, in His divine and unknowable wisdom, had called Murdock home. She found a measure, even if only a small one, of Saint Paul's "peace that passeth understanding" when she attended mass.

Many of the young men of Girvan were quick to notice the newest resident in their town. Some would, on occasion, try to strike up a conversation with her, never with any success. She was still living in her grief, the glint in her eyes dulled by loss. Sadness, fatigue, and the now-distancing memories of a life full of nothing but love and possibility had replaced the unbounded promise of a life and a family with Murdock. She had no interest in the young men of Girvan, nor in any other young men, for that matter. She longed to be alone, so that she could remember, pray, and try to somehow understand.

Darcie refused to wear black after arriving in Girvan, even though Murdock had been gone for barely six months. She had worn black whenever she went out in public in Glasgow, and she had come to utterly despise it. She hated having complete strangers staring and whispering as she passed, and she hated even more being the object of their pity. To her, they were invading a space which was not theirs, but hers alone, and she resented the intrusion. If there was grieving to be done, she would do it, alone, without the unwanted company of uninvited strangers. When she moved to Girvan, her black mourning clothes were all quite intentionally left behind in Glasgow.

Although Glasgow was fifty miles away, it didn't take long for people in Girvan to find out about Darcie's past. She could once again feel the stares and the pity when she walked the streets or attended mass. They were the same stares and pity which she had tried so desperately to leave behind in Glasgow. She longed for someplace where she could be alone.

Never did she speak to anyone in Girvan of what had happened in Skelmorlie on the afternoon of June 16, 1888, except for Father William O'Shaughnessy at the Sacred Hearts of Jesus and Mary Church on Harbour Street. Darcie took great comfort in the church and one of the first things she did upon arriving in Girvan was to begin attending mass. She always lit a candle and said prayers for Murdock.

Father O'Shaughnessy, who had served as priest at the church for nearly twenty years before Darcie arrived, was gentle and warm and seemed somehow to understand her pain, although there was no way that he could possibly know. She didn't sense pity from him, but rather a shared faith that God would take care of her through her struggle, just as He was now taking care of Murdock. Father O'Shaughnessy grew immensely fond of Darcie, and she of him, and they often walked the church grounds together or simply sat in its garden, sometimes in complete silence and at other times reflecting on God's unending love for His children. A few times, Darcie even talked to the priest about Murdock. Never did she ask the question to which neither she nor Father O'Shaughnessy had any answer – "Why?"

Darcie talked to Father O'Shaughnessy about her childhood in Glasgow. She spoke of going to mass at St. Andrew's, a parish that Father O'Shaughnessy assured her he knew well and loved very much. She told him of her time in school, her many friends, including Murdock, and of the wonderful teachers they had. She spoke of playing plainy-clappy, peever beds, marbles, hide-and-seek, tig, and of skipping rope on the streets, sidewalks, and yards around her house. She told him about the picnics her parents took the family on by the banks of the River Clyde. She most enjoyed talking about her mother and of learning to garden, cook, sew, and dance from her. There was an unmistakable joy in Darcie's countenance when she spoke of her childhood and of her family. Those were the only times that Father O'Shaughnessy ever saw her smile.

When Darcie arrived in Girvan, it was inhabited by 5,000 people, with many of the men working in the coal and fishing industries and many of the women finding work weaving cotton for businesses back in Glasgow. On her way to and from the mill, where she, too, had found work on the cotton looms, and on her walks to the market, the shops, and mass, she could see the island of Ailsa Craig across the firth. At night, she saw the light from the Ailsa Craig Lighthouse tower.

Chapter 3

The Memories

M olly and I met in the summer of 1987, when we were both still in high school and working as camp counselors at a sports camp on Sabasticook Lake in Newport, Maine. She was from New Hampshire, I was from Massachusetts. As it turned out, we shared the same birthday – January 22nd – although I was a year older. It took only a week until our first kiss, and we knew that we would spend our lives together, as most teenage couples imagine that they will. Only for us, unlike most others, it turned out to be true. Neither one of us was ever again with anyone else.

On one of our rare days off at camp, where we were on duty for sixteen hours a day, we got up before sunrise and drove to Acadia National Park in my orange, third-hand Honda Civic. We stopped above Bar Harbor and looked out over Frenchman Bay and the Porcupine Islands; went to Sand Beach, Thunder Hole, and Otter Cliff; hiked around Jordan Pond and took in the spectacular views of South Bubble and North Bubble, twin hills on the west end of the pond; and then rode past Eagle Lake. Finally, we drove to the top of Cadillac Mountain, the tallest mountain on the eastern seaboard and, during the winter months at least, the first place in the United States to see the sunrise. By the time that Molly and I reached the top of the mountain, though, the sun was getting low in the west.

Cadillac Mountain, along with the smaller mountains of Acadia, was formed tens of millions of years ago. The glaciers and the elements worked away at them for eons to carve out their shapes. At the summit of Cadillac Mountain, smooth, pink, granite rock, some still showing glacial striations, was exposed by glaciers as they repeatedly advanced and retreated across Maine.

As we sat there talking atop Cadillac Mountain, Molly asked me, "What do you want to be doing in ten years?" Without really stopping to think about my answer, I said, "I'm not really sure, but I'd like to be doing it with you." I couldn't help but notice that she smiled.

Molly and I didn't want to leave Acadia, perhaps recognizing that we were experiencing one of life's moments, but we finally headed back to Sabasticook Lake as the sun set. We decided then and there that if we ever had the chance, we would live in Maine. Fortunately for us, that chance came, and we seized it. After Molly finished college and I finished law school, we were married on Saturday, August 27, 1995, on the shore of Sabasticook Lake, where we had met eight years earlier. The wedding was small, very informal, and perfect in every way. Molly was the most beautiful bride. For my part, I was the happiest and luckiest groom. All four of our parents, many of our aunts, uncles, and cousins, and a few friends from childhood, college, and law school, celebrated the day with us.

We settled on Belfast, Maine, as the place where we would make our home together, both because it was on the majestic Maine coast not too far south of Acadia, and because we could both make careers there. If the conditions are right, you can even see Cadillac Mountain to the northeast, forty miles from Belfast. Belfast, like many, many cities and towns in Maine, takes its name from a place in Europe. Maine has an Athens, Belgrade, Bristol, Cambridge, Denmark, Edinburg, Frankfort, Limerick, Lisbon, Naples, Norway, Paris, Poland, Scarborough, Stockholm, Sweden, Vienna, and Wales. The small city of Belfast, more like a town, really, sits on Belfast Bay, an inlet of Penobscot Bay, and the Passagassawakeag ("a sturgeon's place") River. Even with fewer than 7,000 residents, Belfast still manages to be one of the twenty largest cities in Maine.

Belfast's history, or at least that brief part of it that begins after Europeans systematically began displacing the indigenous people who had made it their home for thousands of years, begins in 1770, when Scottish and Irish families from New Hampshire migrated and settled there. The history before Belfast was settled by Europeans is all too typical of American history and the displacement of native people. In 1630, two Englishmen were granted title to the land via what is variously known as the Muscongus Patent, Waldo Patent, or Lincolnshire Patent. They were granted the land, even though it belonged to the Penobscot and Abenaki people, to establish a trading outpost, mostly for the thriving fur trade. Some historians claim that the Muscongus patent was of great benefit to both the Europeans and the native people, although it is difficult to picture exactly how there may have been a truly mutual benefit. As typically happened, the Europeans simply treated all of the land as their own.

The City of Belfast claims that its name was chosen through a coin toss, although it does not say what the alternative name would have been – Londonderry, perhaps, according to some sources. It has been more or less continuously inhabited by the European settlers, except for a few years when the original white settlers fled the town during the Revolutionary War, fearing British soldiers. Most returned soon after the war was over and still more followed shortly thereafter.

Access to an unending supply of timber and to a tapered waterfront naturally led to a thriving shipbuilding industry in Belfast, along with a vibrant and profitable maritime trade. In the 1800s, upwards of one-third of the men in Belfast worked in shipbuilding or maritime trading. Using timber shipped down the Penobscot River from Bangor, which was then the lumber capital of the young country, Belfast produced hundreds of three, four, and even five-masted schooners. Belfast's shipyards turned out some 150 vessels in the 1840s, but by the 1870s only fifty-five, by the 1880s only thirty-one, and only eleven in the final decade of the 1800s. Shipbuilding was clearly on the wane. Downtown Belfast, close to the working waterfront, burned down twice in the 1800s – once in 1865 and yet again in 1873. After the second conflagration, most of the downtown was wisely rebuilt with bricks and mortar, rather than wood, and many of those buildings survive today, housing retail businesses, offices, art studios, restaurants, and lofts. Molly's office was on the second floor of one of them.

As the 20th century began, the shipbuilding industry had largely lost its foothold and Belfast's economy was transitioning to the harvesting of seafood, such as lobster, herring, and scallops. The development of more efficient and affordable refrigeration methods made seafood from Maine, in particular lobster, a viable and quite profitable commodity to ship to the growing populations as far away as Boston, New York, and Philadelphia.

Lobster, Maine's most notable seafood, was not always the popular delicacy that it is today, however. When Europeans first colonized New England, lobsters were so ubiquitous that they would often simply wash ashore, leaving piles of them along the beaches. Because they are not the most attractive creatures, lobsters were considered to be "the cockroaches of the sea." Colonists would gather them from the shore and use them as a free source of fertilizer and fish bait.

Since lobsters were, however, also a cheap and abundant source of protein, in the seventeen and eighteen-hundreds they were often fed to enslaved people and to prisoners as a cost-saving measure. By the end of the 19th century, though, Maine lobster had become an increasingly popular indulgence for people living away from the New England coast and for tourists who were vacationing in Maine, and the lobstering industry began to thrive. Today, 100 million pounds of Maine lobster are harvested annually, with Belfast contributing its fair share.

After World War II, Belfast's economy again pivoted, this time to the poultry industry. At one time, the two largest poultry processors in Belfast were being supplied with hundreds of thousands of chickens each week from Waldo County farms. Virtually every farm in the county, of which there were hundreds, was raising chickens for the Belfast poultry processors. Chicken was the uncontested king in mid-1900s Belfast.

In 1948, the city decided to hold Broiler Day, which was so successful that it inspired a second, even larger Broiler Day in 1949. The second event attracted some 2,000 people, including the governor and a host of "celebrities from the poultry world," who together consumed 3,000 pounds of chicken barbecued over an eighty-foot-long pit. A Broiler Queen was crowned, chosen on the basis of poise, personality, and appearance. The first Broiler Queen, sixteen-year-old Betty Perry, wasn't even from Belfast, but rather from the neighboring town of Lincolnville. Governor Frederick G. Payne himself placed the cardboard Broiler Queen crown atop her head. Betty Perry later gushed that it was the most wonderful day of her life. Molly and I arrived in Belfast a few decades too late to enjoy Broiler Day.

Being named Broiler Queen made Betty Perry famous. It lifted her out of deep poverty, where her mother had sewn dresses for her, quite ironically, from chicken feed sacks. Her family was so poor that they used newspapers for wallpaper. After being crowned the first Broiler Queen, Betty Perry toured the country with the other Maine queens – the Potato Queen, the Blueberry Queen, the Lobster Queen, and Miss Maine, although Miss Maine wasn't technically a queen. Why Susie Knight, the 1949 Maine Sardine Queen, did not get to tour with them is unclear, since the Maine sardine industry was nearly as large as the lobster industry at the time. It is quite likely that Betty Perry was the first Mainer to appear on television, promoting, of course, Maine broilers.

Molly stumbled across a story about the Broiler Festival and the naming of a Broiler Queen one time in *Down East* magazine and she gave it to me to read. When I was finished, we talked a little about the festival and the article and what the city must have been like back then. Later that night, Molly looked up from her book and asked me, "Do you think that I could have been a Broiler Queen?"

This struck me as one of those questions which was really just meant to be a conversation-starter, not a serious question, so I said, "Well, you have the poise, looks, and legs for it, but I don't know about the personality part." Apparently, that was not the answer that Molly was hoping for. She called me a rather unflattering name and went back to her book. I frequently gave the wrong answer to those kinds of questions.

By 1950, six million chickens a year were being processed in Belfast. While chicken processing was great for the city's economy in the 1950s, it came at an enormous cost to the city and to the environment. For years, all of the unused parts of the millions of chickens – feathers, guts, beaks, talons, and blood – were simply drained, completely untreated, directly into Penobscot Bay. Homeowners along the waterfront routinely raked chicken feathers from their lawns. Recreational sailors and boaters were advised to stay away from Belfast because of the sheen of omnipresent chicken fat floating on top of the water. Belfast was given the nickname "Schmaltzport," "schmaltz" being German for "fat."

All the while, Broiler Day continued to grow and grow. In 1951, 10,000 people attended and devoured 16,000 pounds of chicken. Broiler Day then expanded to become the multi-day Broiler Festival. In 1955, it took a crew of 130 people to barbecue 26,000 pounds of chicken over a new 200-foot-long concrete pit. A conveyor belt was constructed to transport the barbecued chicken from the pits to the throng of broiler-starved festival-goers. By the 1960s, the festival included fireworks, boxing matches, bands, political speeches, and car shows. Every ambitious politician in the state knew that it was best to attend and offer a few heartfelt words.

All good things must eventually come to an end, and so, too, did the Broiler Festival. By the late 1970s, a changing economy, recession, stricter environmental laws, and cheaper land and labor costs in the south killed Belfast's chicken processing industry. When Penobscot Poultry closed its doors in 1988, the poultry processing industry was gone from Belfast for good. The death of the poultry industry caused an exodus of people leaving Belfast to look for work elsewhere. The end of the poultry industry and the loss of population did, however, create an opportunity to remake the city's culture, with an ample housing stock and affordable prices, empty commercial buildings, and a magnificent coastal location that no longer reeked of chickens.

That was the Belfast that Molly and I moved to. One that was constantly changing and adapting, but not getting bigger. A small city that reinvented and re-imagined itself as the world changed. Molly and I were part of the generation that helped to create a very different Belfast.

Molly took a job as a Program Director with *Bike with ME*, a nonprofit organization advocating for bicyclists, building and maintaining bicycle trails and bicycle lanes throughout the mid-coast, educating people about bicycle safety, and working with state and local governments to enact bicycle safety laws. I had just finished law school and was an associate at a four-person, general practice law firm in Belfast. Within three years, Molly had risen to the position of Executive Director of *Bike with ME*. It took me, on the other hand, more than six years to become a partner at the law firm.

Bike with ME's office was on the second floor of one of the 19th-century brick buildings on Main Street, above a clothing boutique. From Molly's office, she could watch the locals and the tourists shopping, going in and out of restaurants, and walking their dogs. She loved watching the sometimes chaotic scenes being played out below.

Molly was a fierce and formidable advocate for bicycling and bicyclists. While I lived in the often confrontational and contentious world of lawyering, Molly lived in an altogether different world where cooperation, compromise, and flexibility were the most valuable assets. She was one of the driving forces behind Maine's "Three-Foot Law," passed in 2013, requiring cars to leave at least three feet of clearance when passing bicyclists. When Molly first became the Executive Director at *Bike with ME*, there were virtually no bicycle lanes in Maine. Twenty-two years later, there were hundreds, along with miles and miles of cycling trails. One of the trails just outside of Belfast, "Molly's Mile," was posthumously named for her.

Molly was also a firm believer in the increasingly quaint notion that with more rights come more responsibilities. She spent a great deal of her time teaching biking safety, protocols, and signaling at schools and community events throughout the mid-coast. She liked making the presentations and felt a personal responsibility to cyclists. As bicycling in Maine grew increasingly more popular, Molly's schedule became busier and busier, which thrilled her. She was usually able to surprise most of the people in her audience by telling them that it is illegal for a bicyclist to pass a stopped school bus. She was never shy about letting other riders know that they had to obey traffic laws, stop signs, traffic signals, and rights-of-way. She was especially vigilant about pointing out to other bicyclists that they were to ride *with* the traffic, not *into* the traffic. Molly had the gift for making those that she chided thankful that she had educated them, rather than annoyed that she had corrected them.

Molly and I were out riding together one Saturday morning when we saw a middle-aged man biking towards us, riding into oncoming traffic. As he approached, Molly waved her hand to flag him down. When he stopped, Molly started explaining the rule about biking with the traffic. At first, the man looked pretty annoyed, and seemed about ready to ride away, but Molly could be a charmer. By the time they were done talking, they were smiling and laughing like old pals. She gave him her business card, as she always did in these circumstances, and invited him to call her if he had any questions. Molly never went anywhere without her business cards.

A few days later, Molly got an envelope in the mail at work. It was from the man that we had encountered on Saturday. Enclosed was a $500 check to *Bike with ME*, along with a note of thanks. He was by no means the only donor who was introduced to *Bike with ME* in that fashion. Molly was gifted in that way.

We made a home and a life in Belfast, first living in a modest apartment before buying a house on Saddle Road with a sloping front lawn and a spectacular view of the bay. We bought a pair of red Adirondack chairs and set them out on the front yard. Even though we were both from away, as native Mainers like to say, we at least wanted to seem like true Mainers, which can't be accomplished without owning at least one pair of Adirondacks. During the summer and early fall, we would watch from those chairs as dozens of sloops, schooners, cutters, and catamarans sailed the bay.

Our house had a wraparound porch with three hanging swings – one two-seater and two single-seaters, which Molly very reluctantly agreed to let me install myself after she grew tired of me bugging her about it. We spent hundreds of hours sitting and reading, drinking coffee, talking, and listening to music on that porch. It was Molly's favorite thing about the house. Although Belfast changed in many ways while Molly and I lived there, in other ways, it didn't change much at all. It remained a small city – a town, really. Belfast proper was home to only 6,300 people when we arrived, and had grown to just 6,900 by the time Molly died. It could be that mid-coast Maine weather is simply not for the faint-of-heart. Or maybe, people just have no idea what they're missing.

Molly and I were never able to have children, although we both wanted to. There were two pregnancies which ended in miscarriages – one in 1998 at nine weeks and one in 2000 at eleven weeks. Molly's doctor advised us that there would be a substantial health risk attached to a third pregnancy, so we very reluctantly abandoned the idea of having a family beyond just the two of us. I think that Molly felt a good deal of guilt over not being able to bear a child, although there really wasn't any reason for guilt. So we continued making a life for just ourselves, even though it wasn't our first choice.

We tried to explore as much of the Maine coast as we could. We were particularly fond of the lighthouses, of which there are sixty-five in Maine, with our favorite being Owl's Head Light Station near Rockland, about twenty-five miles southwest of Belfast. Only Michigan has more lighthouses than Maine. Owl's Head is a rather short, stubby lighthouse, with the tower itself standing just thirty feet tall. However, the light is perched on a cliff eighty feet above sea level with breathtaking views of Rockland Harbor and Penobscot Bay. Molly and I visited Owl's Head as often as we could, particularly in the late fall and early winter, when we would have the place all to ourselves.

We would climb the fifty-three steps up to the lighthouse and stare out over the water and the islands, momentarily struck silent by the majesty and beauty. As we left, we always stopped at the grave marker of "Spot, the Lighthouse Dog." Spot belonged to a keeper by the name of Augustus Hamor in the 1930s. Spot loved to pull the rope of the fog bell to greet passing boats, particularly the mail boat captained by Spot's friend, Stuart Ames, whose engine noise Spot always recognized. Spot would ring the fog bell until the passing boats acknowledged his greeting by sounding their horns.

Like virtually all lighthouses, Owl's Head is said to be haunted. Not by just one spirit, but rather by two. The first is an old sea captain, believed to be one of the former keepers, who was first seen by the three-year-old daughter of a subsequent keeper. The young girl had an "imaginary friend," and one night she awakened her parents by coming to their room and declaring, "Fog's rolling in. Time to put the foghorn on!" Her parents were bewildered, because they had never spoken of fog and the foghorn to their daughter. Subsequent keepers have reported seeing the old captain and finding footprints in the snow leading up to, although never back from, the light tower. Later keepers have also found that the lighthouse brass had been polished, even though they themselves had not done it, and even though the lighthouse door was locked. The second spirit at Owl's Head, the "Little Lady," has been seen, but mostly heard, by subsequent keepers, and is best known for slamming cabinet doors and rattling silverware in the kitchen. *Coastal Living* magazine claims that Owl's Head is the most haunted lighthouse in Maine.

Fortunately, its spirits are benevolent, unlike those that haunt other lighthouses. I never personally picked up on any spirits at Owl's Head. If Molly did, she didn't say.

Seguin Island Lighthouse was another of our favorites, and it, too, is haunted. Molly and I only went there twice, since it required committing the better part of a day to the boat ride out to the island in the Gulf of Maine and to the lighthouse tour itself. Seguin Island Lighthouse, commissioned by George Washington and built is 1795, is the second oldest lighthouse in the state. Seguin Island's haunting is of a far, far more malevolent kind than Owl's Head's, and for good reason. During the 1800s, the Seguin Island Lighthouse keeper's wife became increasingly depressed from the isolation and monotony of life on the island. Thinking that he was being helpful, the keeper made arrangements for a piano to be delivered to the island, hoping that his wife would entertain herself by learning to play the piano and thereby overcome her depression. She picked out one single piece of music and practiced and played it over and over and over again, refusing to learn or to play any other piece. Finally, the keeper could take it no longer. He took an ax to the piano, and then to his wife, before taking his own life. Subsequent keepers and visitors to the island report hearing piano music coming from the lighthouse even though no piano remains there. A few visitors have reported seeing a ghostly man roaming the island wielding an ax.

Molly played a practical joke on me during our second visit to Seguin Island. She had downloaded some soft piano music onto her phone before our visit. When we got close to the lighthouse, she turned it on, with the phone in her pants pocket, very softly.

"Stop!" she said. "Do you hear that?"

"Hear what?" I answered.

"Listen," she replied, "A piano."

Between the wind and the waves, it was tough to hear, but I did make out the faint sound of a piano. "Holy shit," was all that I could say. We stood there, listening intently, before Molly broke into laughter. "Gotcha," she said proudly. Yes, she had.

Pemaquid Point Lighthouse, with some of the best rocks for clambering, was our second favorite after Owl's Head. So spectacular is Pemaquid Point Lighthouse that it was chosen to represent Maine on its state quarter in 2003. The lighthouse also just happens to be haunted by the ghost of a young woman, always soaking wet and wearing a red shawl, who sits by the fireplace sobbing and moaning. Perhaps she herself came ashore from a shipwreck, or maybe she lost a husband or child in one of the many shipwrecks near Pemaquid. For whatever reason, lighthouses are very appealing to ghosts and spirits.

At Pemaquid, there is a long, sloping ledge of rocks a couple of hundred yards long and jutting into the sea, which is great for scrabbling along. There is one particular formation of rock which rises about fifteen feet above the rest, an odd byproduct of erosion. Every time that we visited Pemaquid, Molly insisted on climbing it and having me take her picture while she stood atop the rock striking the same pose year after year. "Take my picture! Take my picture!" she commanded every time she scaled it. You can actually watch her grow older by looking at fifteen years' worth of Pemaquid rock-climbing pictures. She looked more beautiful with each passing year.

One September, on Maine Open Lighthouse Day, Molly and I drove south to Fort Williams Park in Cape Elizabeth to climb the tower of Portland Head Light, reported to be the most photographed lighthouse in the world, and for good reason. Constructed between 1787 and 1791 at the direction of George Washington, it is the oldest lighthouse in Maine. Portland Head

Light originally burned whale oil, then used Fresnel lenses for more than 100 years. Some of the lenses can still be seen in the lighthouse museum in the old keeper's house attached to the tower. They are works of art.

Maine Open Lighthouse Day, an annual event held every September, is the only day of the year on which visitors are allowed to climb the tower, first-come, first-served, so we started our trip down the coast before the sun rose. The view from the top of the tower was spectacular on the crisp, clear, late-summer day. We could see Mount Washington sixty-five miles away to the west in New Hampshire, above the Portland skyline, and the Atlantic Ocean stretched to the horizon.

After climbing Portland Head Light, we spent a good chunk of the day in the city, walking the Eastern Promenade on Munjoy Hill overlooking Casco Bay, sharing oysters at J's on the working waterfront, watching the kiters flying their kites at Bug Light, and drinking pumpkin beer at Shipyard Brewing. Molly and I didn't spend nearly as much time in Portland as we should have over our twenty-five years of living in Maine. That, I regret, because every visit was a treat to be savored.

Molly and I loved eating oysters. If there was a Buck-a-Shuck to be found anywhere near Belfast, we were sure to be there for a couple dozen Glidden Points, Pemaquids, Wawenauks, Moondancers, or Winter Points. We ultimately decided that oysters from the Damariscotta River were our favorites. Molly preferred lemon and cocktail sauce on hers. I went with just horseradish. She put lemon on just about everything, while I don't much care for it. Every fall, we would book an oyster farm tour, usually on the Damariscotta River, but sometimes elsewhere, and sample oysters right out of the water. On one of the tours, we learned how to shuck without losing a finger. Molly became a far better shucker than me, I must admit.

If the weather, the season, and the mood aligned, we would buy a couple dozen, shuck them at home, and sit on our porch swing slurping them down, chased by a Maine craft beer, of course.

I even convinced Molly to go with me to see the Glidden Midden in Damariscotta, just because. The Glidden Midden is a 2,000-year-old mound of shells, mostly from oysters, created by the Wabanaki people when they disposed of the shells at what was essentially the town dump. The Glidden Midden rises thirty feet above the west bank of the Damariscotta River and extends for 300 feet along the shore. I was pretty impressed by the Glidden Midden, Molly much less so.

Although neither Molly nor I were boaters, we loved being out on the water and found a reason to go out whenever we could. One summer day, we headed out on a tour to see the Atlantic puffins nesting on Matinicus Island, twenty-three miles out in Penobscot Bay. Hundreds of puffins, looking like miniature flying penguins, although they are unrelated, nest at Matinicus each summer after spending the rest of the year living at sea in the North Atlantic. We saw dozens of them, floating, flying, and fishing, along with razorbills, black guillemots, and gulls. They were many of the same species who also happened to make the island of Ailsa Craig in Scotland their summer home.

We grew to love just about everything about living in Belfast, even the weather. We were partial to sitting outside at Marshall Wharf Brewing Company's small-batch brewery on Belfast Bay and nursing a beer at sundown after work. Molly was especially fond of their *MyShahRona* New England IPA. We also liked Lake St. George Brewing with its loon logo, not technically in Belfast, but rather in Liberty, just down the road past the Belfast Curling Club and Lake St. George State Park. Not only is there a Liberty, Maine, but there are also towns with such great, aspirational names as Freedom, Friendship, Harmony, Hope, Strong, and Unity.

We shopped at the United Farmers' Market of Belfast, the largest farmers' market in the state, most Saturdays when Molly wasn't involved in some kind of biking event. A couple of times, we bought what were called "Ailsa Craig onions," rather large, sweet onions which can grow to weigh as much as five pounds. Ailsa Craig onions were first grown by a man named David Murray, who was the gardener for the Marquis of Ailsa, at Culzean Castle in South Ayrshire, Scotland, a bit of trivia which meant nothing to me at the time.

In the summer and early fall, Maine hosts dozens of cycling events, large and small. Some are competitive, some raise money for charity, some are group tours, and others are simply for the joy of biking together. Molly had a hand in almost every one of them, although the competitions were her least favorite. Had she wanted to, she would have done very well in the competitive races – she was that good – but her heart was in the comradery of riding together, not in the competitiveness of trying to win. Biking, to her, was a communal, spiritual, tribal thing; it wasn't at all about who could ride the fastest.

Molly's absolute favorite place in Belfast, except maybe for the Rail Trail, where she rode her mountain bike, was Left Bank Books, a small, independent bookstore full of grace, charm, and warmth, with an outstanding selection of books about Maine or written by Maine authors. Its walls are lined with autographed pictures and books from the many authors who visited the shop. It seemed as if Molly was at Left Bank Books weekly, if not more often, usually on Sunday mornings with a dark roast coffee from Downshift Coffee, a coffee shop which, purely coincidentally, shares its space with a bicycle shop. Molly also helped to organize a book club which met at Left Bank Books, with the owners suggesting which books the club members should read and discuss. If Molly were to construct a heaven, it would include books, bikes, and coffee. Space permitting, there would also be oysters and beer.

Molly wasn't always faithful to Left Bank Books. She was also very fond of Owl & Turtle Bookshop in Camden, eighteen miles to our south – a short bike ride for Molly and a pretty challenging one for me. A few times a year, usually during one of the shoulder seasons when there were fewer tourists around and there was far less traffic, we rode down to Camden for the day, with a good chunk of our time spent at Owl & Turtle. We explored other parts of Camden, as well. We sometimes biked or climbed Mount Battie in Camden Hills State Park, sitting on the rocks at the summit and watching as the eagles soared over the water, hunting and fishing. We strolled the harbor area – perhaps the most beautiful one in all of Maine – and the downtown shops, before beginning the bike ride home.

If Molly was feeling especially adventurous, we would ride down to the Rockland Breakwater south of Camden and walk the nearly mile-long granite breakwater to the lighthouse perched at the end. In windy weather, the walk was harrowing, with no handrails or protection from the wind and the waves crashing onto the breakwater. The breakwater was constructed in the 1890s, using 700,000 tons of granite, to protect Rockland Harbor and to provide a safe haven for small boats. On one particular day, we got caught in a little pop-up storm right after we reached the lighthouse. With winds gusting at twenty or thirty miles an hour and waves crashing onto the breakwater, we started the slow, slippery walk back toward shore, salt water spraying on our faces. By the time we reached land twenty-five minutes later, the weather had passed, but we were soaked and I had lost my favorite hat to the wind and sea. Sensing my profound loss, Molly promised to get me a new one, like a mother would promise a child.

In one way or another, we were involved, at least tangentially, in seemingly everything that went on in town, except for two things – politics and religion. Molly stayed away from politics because she had to work with politicians and bureaucrats of all leanings, and being saddled with any kind of political label would have made her job infinitely more difficult; I because I represented clients whose beliefs ranged from far right-wing to socialist, from fundamentalist to atheist, and business, after all, is business. So we kept our liberal, or progressive, political leanings to ourselves. We stayed away from organized religion because we both tilted heavily toward agnosticism and because we both believed that most of the troubles that humankind brings on itself seem to be caused, or at the very least enabled, by organized religion. We never joined a church in Belfast.

We were each recruited to sit on various boards of directors for local, apolitical nonprofits. I served terms on the Waldo County Chapter of Habitat for Humanity, Sebasticook Regional Land Trust, and the Belfast Bay Watershed Coalition. For reasons that I don't completely understand, boards love to have lawyers as members. And law firms love to boast about their civic engagement, when they're usually really just trying to make it rain. We both chose causes that we believed in rather than sitting on a board just for the sake of sitting on a board.

Molly was elected to the board of directors of the Waldo County Society for Animal Protection in 2006, after serving two terms on the board of the Belfast Free Library. When she was initially approached about joining the board of the Society for Animal Protection, the first thing she wanted to know was whether it was a "no-kill" shelter. Assured that it was, she signed on.

In 2009, Molly fell in love with one of the dogs in the shelter, a golden retriever mix who was thought to be about a year old, although no one knew for sure. Molly and I had both grown up with dogs, but had been hesitant about adopting one while trying to start a family and working long hours. With our hopes of having a child gone, we adopted him right away. His shelter name was Max, which wasn't too bad of a name, but Molly christened him "Bozo." Although Bozo was "our" dog, there was never any doubt about where his loyalties truly were. Bozo tailed Molly everywhere, often just sitting or lying and staring at her. They were bonded. If Molly was going to be in her office most of the day, and not up in Augusta or at some state legislator's office, Bozo would go to work with her and sleep on his dog bed under her desk, with Molly's feet resting on him, at least when he wasn't roaming the office looking to get petted. If she couldn't take him to work with her, he stayed home and moped until she came home.

The only real celebrity who lived in Belfast was Genie Francis, one of the stars of *General Hospital*, the most popular soap opera in the 1980s. Genie played Laura Webber Baldwin Spencer, who was raped by, and then ultimately married to, her rapist, Luke Spencer. The show received some serious blowback for that plot twist. Luke and Laura's wedding on November 16, 1981, was apparently the single most-watched episode in soap opera history, although neither Molly nor I had watched, since we were still just kids and couldn't have cared less about the soaps.

Genie opened a home furnishings store in 2006 in Belfast, called The Cherished Home, on Searsport Avenue. She and her husband, Jonathan Frakes, an actor most famous for his role as Commander Riker on *Star Trek: The Next Generation*, had a home in Belfast. Molly and Genie became friends after Molly bought a couple of things in the store. Maybe they became friends because Molly didn't even know who Genie was before meeting her and was singularly unimpressed by celebrity status. Molly didn't visit the store just to get a glimpse of "Laura" while she was shopping, as others often did. I think that Molly noticed a book Genie was reading and they struck up a conversation about it. Book lovers are like that. Soon thereafter, they began meeting at Left Banks Books on Sunday mornings for coffee and browsing.

Every year on our anniversary, or as close to it as our schedules and the weather permitted, Molly and I would take a sunset cruise on a schooner somewhere along the Maine coast. We sailed out of Portland, Boothbay Harbor, Camden, Rockland, Bar Harbor, and, of course, Belfast, over the years. If it was a BYOB sail, which most of them were, we would bring a bottle of champagne and toast to another year of marriage. On our twenty-fifth anniversary on August 27, 2020, we sailed from Belfast so that we wouldn't have to travel very far, given how weak Molly had become. By then, we both knew that we would only be alotted those twenty-five years together and no more. Molly wore a scarf over her head. I had volunteered to shave my head in a show of solidarity with her, but she gave me the look which I immediately recognized as meaning that I had better not so much as think about it. She punctuated the look by adding some gallows humor, "If you dare do that, I'll have to kill you. Then what would I do?"

I don't want to make it sound like everything was always perfect with us and that we didn't have our occasional moments. Sometimes, we disagreed about things. Sometimes, we argued like cats and dogs. Sometimes, we just needed to get away from each other for a few hours. Occasionally, I disappointed her. Far less frequently, she disappointed me. And yet, we made it work. Through all of our respective faults and flaws, we stayed loyal and committed to each other until the end. We were in love.

Chapter 4

Cuthbert Urquhart

The Royal Bank of Scotland was chartered in 1727 in Edinburgh. The charter for a new bank was granted largely because the British government suspected that the existing Bank of Scotland had Jacobite sympathies, clandestinely plotting to return the House of Stuart to the English throne. The occupant of the throne at the time, the House of Hanover, was less than thrilled at that prospect, and was more than happy to give the Bank of Scotland a little something to worry about. The upstart Royal Bank of Scotland spent the better part of the 1800s acquiring and merging with other banks, usually those in the midst of financial difficulty. By the time that the twentieth century rolled in, the Royal Bank of Scotland had more than one-hundred branches and 800 employees. One of the men who was most responsible for the prolific growth of the Royal Bank of Scotland was Bryson Urquhart.

Bryson Urquhart attended one of the great global universities, the University of Edinburgh, studying history and economics in the early 1850s. The University of Edinburgh at that time was at the epicenter of the Scottish Enlightenment and a new age of rationalism and intellectualism. Bryson was an exceptional student, with a particular, innate aptitude for understanding how numbers and math explained the workings of the world at least as well as, and oftentimes better, than words did. Upon his graduation, he immediately took a position with the Royal Bank of Scotland, where he would spend his entire career. Bryson became legendary in banking circles for an instinctive and uncanny ability to identify other banks which were in distress, or heading for distress, and gobbling them up into the ample, growing belly of the Royal Bank of Scotland.

Bryson's father had been one of the early officers at the Royal Bank of Scotland, setting the course for its phenomenal expansion and growth. The elder Urquhart had made certain that his son would be prepared to join the bank after his studies at the university by introducing him to the world of banking and the financial goings-on in Edinburgh. Bryson was a quick learner.

Bryson Urquhart's position and stature within the banking world meant that he was welcomed into Edinburgh society. Not the very upper crust, like the royals and the aristocrats, but rather the class comprised mostly of the industrialists, professors, notable artists, philosophers, doctors, judges, and solicitors. His presence was requested at many of the important weddings, parties, and shows. Entry into the best and most desirable social clubs was granted easily. It was at one of those parties that Bryson met Lottie Moore. After a brief, thoroughly proper courtship, they were married in 1857 at St. Giles Cathedral, also known as the High Kirk of Edinburgh.

Throughout Edinburgh, Bryson Urquhart was known and renowned as a sportsman. He was an excellent golfer and was a member of the Royal Musselburgh Golf Club, one of the oldest in the world, twice winning the cup as its champion golfer, a high honor in Scotland, which, in addition to being the home of curling, is the birthplace of golf. He was twice elected vice-chairman of the club. At the University of Edinburgh, Bryson had excelled at archery and rowing. In fact, he excelled at everything he did. It was during his time at university that Bryson was introduced to the sport of curling by some of his classmates. The Royal Caledonian Curling Club had recently been founded, and interest in the now 300-year-old sport was growing quickly throughout the country.

After his graduation and rapid rise to prominence in Edinburgh society, Bryson Urquhart became a member, and eventually was elected patron, of the Duddingston Curling Society. As the patron, Bryson assumed for one of his duties the securing of a suitable location for the construction of an artificial curling pond, so that the club would be less reliant on natural ponds and lochs, with their inconsistent ice frequency and quality. With his connections and stature at the bank, Bryson knew almost everything that was happening in Edinburgh, particularly relating to financial positions, and he was able to arrange for the club to lease, on extraordinarily favorable terms, a suitable site on the edge of the city. For his work as patron, the Duddingston Curling Society named its championship trophy after him.

Out of Bryson and Lottie's marriage, they produced four children, three girls and one boy, Cuthbert, who was born on January 29, 1860. Although his Christian name was Cuthbert, he was called "Cuddy" from the day he was born. Cuthbert Urquhart was baptized to some fanfare, much more so than for his sisters, at St. Giles Cathedral.

Cuddy grew up in Edinburgh, attending only the finest schools during his childhood. At the time, Edinburgh was known by two nicknames. The first was the "Athens of the North," because of similar architecture and because of its culture of intellectualism. The second, much more popular nickname, was "Auld Reekie," Scottish for "Old Smoky," which was given because of the cloud of black smoke which seemed to constantly be hovering over the city, darkening its sky and buildings.

Cuddy learned art, culture, and manners both at school and from Bryson and Lottie. He was an extremely able student, but

Cuddy had little interest in attending university, as his family simply assumed that he would. His father never doubted that Cuddy would follow him into a long and beneficial career at the Royal Bank, so he taught Cuddy about banking and finance and mathematics, just as his father had taught him. Cuddy, though, had no designs on university or on an office filled with stuffy air in the Royal Bank of Scotland. Cuddy's love was always for the sea, ever since the first time that his father took him sailing on the firth. It was the salt air that Cuddy longed to breathe. He seemed to have the "salt blood" which drew him toward the sea. By the time that he was fifteen years old, Cuddy was one of the most accomplished sailors in Edinburgh. Cuddy had spent two full years as a teenager building his own sailboat in the barn at his home. Bryson secured the finest mahogany and brass for Cuddy. Cuddy christened his sailboat the *Lottie*.

To his parents' profound disappointment, most particularly Bryson's, upon turning eighteen years old, Cuddy applied to the Northern Lighthouse Board to become an apprentice lighthouse keeper. Since Bryson knew all of the Commissioners, he could have easily exerted his considerable influence to block Cuddy's application had he chosen to, but he did not. He loved his only son. Cuddy's lighthouse aspirations were a youthful and fleeting fancy, Bryson supposed, and he was willing to indulge him.

Cuddy's application was quickly approved by the Commissioners, but not before they first conferred with Bryson Urquhart. Like all apprentice keepers, Cuddy was assigned to many lighthouses over the next few years, at first for two-week turns and then for four-week turns. The rotation was specifically designed so that apprentices could learn from a variety of experienced keepers and could also learn about the different routines and equipment at the scores of lighthouses around Scotland. Cuddy learned quickly and learned well. It was of immense help that Cuddy intuitively understood precisely how things worked. It seemed that he could reverse engineer almost anything and could fix almost anything, as well. Because keepers were constantly called on to make repairs during the course of their careers, a keeper who could successfully keep all of a lighthouse's infrastructure in working order was invaluable to the Commissioners. Cuddy's performance at each light where he trained was exemplary, earning praise from even the most persnickety of principal keepers, and the Commissioners took due note of Cuddy's progress.

Most of Scotland's lighthouses, Cuddy quickly discovered, had very similar, yet subtly different, routines. Watches and duties at most lights were broken down into four-hour shifts, each with its own particular set of duties and responsibilities. The 6:00 p.m. – 10:00 p.m. watch, for example, was usually responsible for lighting the light and for staying in the lantern room until the watch was over, winding the clockworks, trimming the wick, and replenishing the oil. The 10:00 p.m. – 2:00 a.m. watch, in addition to clockworks responsibilities, was tasked with verifying that the other observable lighthouses were illuminated at midnight, making weather checks, and ensuring that the wick was properly trimmed. The 2:00 a.m. – 6:00 a.m. watch was universally considered to be the worst, since there was nothing much to do except to desperately try to stay awake and attend to the clockworks, although sometimes the wick would need further trimming as well. The 6:00 a.m. – 10:00 a.m. watch was tasked with extinguishing the light after sunrise and pulling down the blinds in the lantern room. Each watch in snowy or icy weather required the keeper on watch to go outside of the lantern room to remove the snow or ice from the enormous windows. The nighttime watches provided a lot of time for a man to think on things, both real and imagined.

Not all watches were during the nighttime hours, though. There was also plenty of work which needed to be done during the day, which meant that a wickie very, very rarely had an eight-hour sleep. The daytime watches were responsible for preparing the meals, cleaning the lens and windows in the lantern room, polishing the brass, painting the tower when needed, tending to the vegetable garden, making weather checks, cleaning the common areas of the tower and quarters, and, very importantly, making sure that the privy was limed. The watches, each with their own specific and unique duties and responsibilities, were known as "the routine." The other thing about "the routine" at any given lighthouse is that it was always subject to change or modification at the will, or even merely the whim, of the Principal Lighthouse Keeper. The Commissioners made it absolutely clear that assistant keepers and apprentice keepers were to obey all orders from the Principal Lighthouse Keeper, without question, complaint, or hesitation. Most Principals did not abuse this power, but all keepers knew that it was there and that disobedience would likely have serious and unpleasant consequences.

Each lighthouse where Cuddy apprenticed adhered to the same general routine, although each had its particular variations. The routines could vary depending on the particular preferences of the Principal Lighthouse Keeper or, perhaps more importantly, on the relative cooking skills of each of the keepers. No one wanted to serve at a light where the other keepers were terrible cooks, and serving a stint with an excellent cook was to be cherished. What never varied at any lighthouse were the strict requirements of the Northern Lighthouse Board – timely weather checks, midnight checks on the other lighthouses, entering everything into the lighthouse logs, and an unwavering commitment to "keeping a good light."

During the five years that Cuddy was an apprentice, he served at ten different lights – Auskerry Lighthouse, Barra Head Lighthouse, Butt of Lewis Lighthouse, Cloch Lighthouse, Dubh Artach Lighthouse, Eilean Glas Lighthouse, Girdle Ness Lighthouse, Kinnaird Head Lighthouse, Muckle Flugga Lighthouse, and Pladda Lighthouse. The detailed reports on his progress submitted by the Principal Lighthouse Keeper at each of them were quite favorable, sometimes glowing, even. Once he received his license from the Northern Lighthouse Board, Cuddy was assigned as an assistant keeper at two lights – Skerryvore Lighthouse for a total of eleven months and Turnberry Lighthouse for nine. Cuddy was well-trained, qualified, and more than ready to become a full-fledged keeper.

On January 18, 1886, just before his twenty-sixth birthday, Cuddy Urquhart received his first assignment as a Principal Lighthouse Keeper at the Isle of May Lighthouse in the Firth of Forth, five miles east of the Scottish mainland. Bryson Urquhart by now had sadly come to accept that his son would never be joining him at the Royal Bank. The Isle of May Lighthouse was a Stevenson-built lighthouse, with a Gothic tower atop a building resembling a castle. Cuddy had two assistant keepers under his charge, and he passed on the routines he himself had begun learning eight years earlier. On the day that Cuddy received notification of his first assignment as Principal Lighthouse Keeper, the winter weather was frigid and outdoor curling matches were ongoing around Scotland. Bryson Urquhart himself was curling in Aboyne on that day, leading the Duddingston Curling Society rink.

The Northern Lighthouse Commissioners were notably impressed with Cuddy's performance during his two years at the Isle of May Lighthouse, and after six weeks of leave when Cuddy returned to Edinburgh to see family and friends, he received his orders from the Commissioners to report to the island of Ailsa Craig for his second assignment as a Principal Lighthouse Keeper.

On October 1, 1888, Cuddy rode the tender the ten miles across the Firth of Clyde from Girvan to Ailsa Craig. He was greeted at the pier by Malcolm Campbell, the Principal Lighthouse Keeper whom Cuddy was replacing. In the distance, Cuddy saw the assistant and the apprentice keepers painting the lighthouse tower white under orders from the Commissioners, while it was still warm enough and dry enough for painting, before winter arrived.

The tender would leave for the return trip to Girvan in an hour, delivering Malcolm Campbell from his turn as the Principal Lighthouse Keeper on Ailsa Craig. Malcolm and Cuddy used the time to acquaint Cuddy with the facilities, foghorns, quarters, and routine on Ailsa Craig. There was no time to visit the castle, chapels, caves, or quarries. That would have to wait, although Cuddy looked forward to exploring the island. The thousands upon thousands of birds needed no introduction. The brown rats had not yet asserted their dominance, but they would soon enough.

After being introduced to both the assistant and the apprentice, Cuddy escorted the older keeper to the pier, where they shook hands and said warm goodbyes. Even though they had just met, there was a silent, unspoken kinship among those who kept the lights. Cuddy walked back up the hill to the lighthouse, where he would eat his first meal and spend his first night on "the crag."

Cuddy's first months on Ailsa Craig were busy, but without serious incident. The quarrymen had left for the season soon after he arrived. Cuddy got along well with the series of assistants and apprentices that the Commissioners assigned to Ailsa Craig. They respected Cuddy, and Cuddy, in turn, treated them with respect. The Commissioners knew that Cuddy would train them well and treat them fairly. The discipline and bearing that he had learned from his mother and father, as well as during his schooling, served him well in his young career, even if it was not the one his father had wished for him.

When he was not on watch, Cuddy spent much of his time alone, reading. The Commissioners, when they sent food and supplies to the various lighthouses, also sent books and newspapers. Cuddy requested particular books, largely recommended by his father, which the Commissioners took special care to include in their deliveries. While most keepers who enjoyed reading favored fiction and books of poetry, Cuddy studied the great economists and philosophers. His father, even though resigned to the fact that Cuddy would make his career as a lighthouse keeper rather than as a banker, had carefully curated a list of books which he nonetheless thought Cuddy should study, including *The Wealth of Nations*, by Adam Smith; *Principles of Political Economy*, by John Stuart Mill; and *Principles of Economics*, by Carl Menger, all of which Bryson himself had read and studied at university. Cuddy had enormous respect for his father, and very much wanted to please him, so he read all of Bryson's suggested texts. Cuddy learned well, and whenever he had the chance to visit with his parents, he would discuss and debate economic theories with his father.

The three keepers on Ailsa Craig made it through the long winter, with the help of periodic relief and leave back on the mainland. With the days growing longer and the nights shorter, and with the quarrymen returning, the Commissioners concluded that by April 15th, only two keepers were necessary, and that by June 1st, only one. On May 31, 1889, Cuddy escorted his assistant to the pier, where the assistant left the island aboard the tender. Cuddy returned to the tower alone for a summer where he would be solely responsible for keeping the light on Ailsa Craig.

Chapter 5

Molly's Tree

In the days after Molly died, I was often visited by friends and even by mere acquaintances, many times unannounced, who usually brought food and who wanted to talk, mostly about Molly's death. I was not at all interested in talking to them about that, and it would certainly not be a source of comfort for me, as many of them seemed to think. Other than those uncomfortable visits, I spent almost all of my time alone. After a few weeks, though, the frequency of the visits tailed off dramatically, and I was largely left to make a life on my own.

Despite our twenty-five years of marriage and thirty-two years of friendship, I actually knew surprisingly little about Molly's family history. I knew that she had some Scottish heritage somewhere along the line, but not very much else. In life, she preferred to look forward, not backward, and we never really talked much about our families' histories. It wasn't because there were any deep, dark secrets that needed to be kept hidden away, at least that I knew of, but just because we always tried to focus on the life ahead, not the one behind. After she was gone, I wanted desperately to find a way to keep her memory fresh and alive, and maybe learning about her family would help.

It was winter. Most of the snowbirds had long-since fled Maine for anywhere that was warmer, and Belfast was much darker and quieter. I no longer had work to keep my mind occupied, Molly and

Bozo were both gone, and I never had any real hobbies to keep me busy. It was just me – lonely, bored, and living within the confines of my own mind. Our house suddenly seemed much larger and colder with only me inhabiting it. I wasn't going mad, I don't believe, but I was drifting farther away from anything that was concrete, centering, and familiar. Or maybe I *was* going mad. One way or the other, there was certainly a grayness and lack of meaning to my life. I felt totally abandoned and utterly alone.

I was an only child and both of my parents, as well as both of Molly's parents, had passed away within a span of just over nine years. Between 2009 and 2019, Molly and I planned four funerals and wrote four obituaries. It was yet another one of those quirky little things that Molly and I had in common, each losing both parents while we were in our forties, both of us being born on January 22nd, and each being an only child. I didn't have any really close friends in Belfast, despite having lived there for more than two decades. I just never took the time nor made the effort to cultivate and nourish any deep friendships. Those friends that I did have were all still working and were heavily involved with their own families. I always preferred living out my life with Molly, anyway. She was all that I needed.

One of the chores which I needed to do after Molly died was to go through her things and decide what I would do with them – clothes, shoes, jewelry, lots of books, and various boxes filled with picture albums, loose photographs, report cards, school awards, yearbooks, newspaper clippings, and the like. Typical "family memories" boxes. I set about going through Molly's things, which was difficult and sad. It felt like making her vanish in slow-motion. Most of her things, like the clothes and the books, could be donated to various charities.

Although Molly looked great in just about anything, she wasn't really a clotheshorse, and clearing out her closet was not an overwhelming chore, even though nearly every piece of clothing triggered a specific memory or two about where she had gotten it or when she had worn it. There were lots of tee shirts from the various cycling events which she had been involved in and from the lighthouses and breweries which we had visited. Many of the clothes were presents which I had given to her as birthday, anniversary, or Christmas gifts, like the cream-colored First Maine Flag hoodie which I had gotten for her on her fortieth birthday and the alpaca cardigan sweater which I bought for her on one of our bike rides down to Camden. Those things were the hardest for me to let go.

I took what jewelry she had, except for her wedding ring, engagement ring, and the silver cross necklace which she wore nearly every day, to *Bike with ME*. I simply couldn't let those three pieces go. I told Julie to let the staff take whatever they wanted for themselves and to sell the rest to raise a little bit of money. Over the ensuing years, I would sometimes run into someone from *Bike with ME* who was wearing a piece of Molly's jewelry.

I saved the boxes for last. As far as I knew, they hadn't been opened in years, which the musty smell seemed to confirm. I think that Molly had brought them over from her parents' house after her family home had been sold.

In late January of 2021, nearly two months after Molly died, I finally got around to the boxes. I wouldn't be going anywhere for a few days – not that I had anywhere in particular *to* go. It was the photographs that captured my attention. There were hundreds of them, mostly in black and white and mostly old and faded. Maybe I had seen some of them before, but I couldn't be certain. Some were in albums, some were in envelopes, and some were just scattered loose. Most of them had no name or identification on the back,

but some were dated, such as "Christmas 1976" or simply "1949."
Who were all of these people? Why weren't they identified? Why did
I suddenly feel so totally and inexplicably consumed with finding
out? It would be some small way of keeping her alive, I supposed,
learning things about her in death that I didn't know about her in
life. It was an odd, inexplicable feeling, disorienting in a way, this
sudden compulsion to discover who all of these strangers were and
what their relationship to Molly might be. At times, I imagined
that perhaps Molly was directing me. She did say that she would be
around to watch over me.

Meticulously, I started to remove the old photos from their
albums, trying my best to keep from damaging them in the process.
Decades of being bound in the musty, unopened albums had caused
many of them to meld onto their page. It took me hours to remove
the pictures from the albums and to remove the paper which
adhered to the pictures' backing, so that I could read whatever date
or name might be written there, if there even was one.

I cleared everything from our – my – dining room table, putting
some things on chairs and some on the sideboard. I naively thought
that I would only need the table for a day or two. I had no intention
of spending hour-after-hour, day-after-day, and week-after-week, on
this relatively simple little project. I never imagined at the time that
most of the pictures would still be lying on the table a year later.

I took what I now knew to be 213 pictures and divided them
into two groups – those with dates on them and those without. I
laid out the pictures that had dates on them in chronological order,
with the earliest having a date of 1886 and the latest a date of 1983.
Some of the people I recognized immediately, like Molly's mother,
Gail (*nee* Forsythe) Watson, and her father, Bruce Watson. I wrote
their names on the back. Had they been alive, they surely would have
helped me in this little project by identifying at least some of the

other people. Bruce passed away in 2011 at the age of seventy-one and Gail passed away in October of 2019 at the age of seventy-nine, just five months before Molly was diagnosed with brain cancer and thirteen months before she died. If there is, perchance, a kindness or benevolence to the Universe, and not merely complete randomness and ambivalence, at least it intervened so that Bruce and Gail did not have to watch their only child die.

When I had finished arranging the seventy-seven pictures which already had dates on them, I set about trying to make some order and sense out of the remaining undated ones, which turned out to be a much more challenging task than I would have thought. A few of the pictures were easy to sort, obviously taken on the same day or in the same place as a dated one, and I set them down with their appropriate counterparts. Others, I simply had no context for, and spread them out in the "unknown" section, which housed the majority of the pictures.

At this stage of the project, I wasn't even studying the pictures themselves all that closely, since I was so focused on carefully removing them from their albums and ordering them by date. One particular picture, obviously very old, faded, and crinkled, did catch my attention, though, and I froze, dumbfounded. I suddenly felt very cold, like when first stepping outside in the winter. It was a black-and-white picture, undated and with no name on it, of a young woman, perhaps twenty years old. She was slim and, appearing from the picture, very happy and quite beautiful. What stunned and unnerved me was that she looked almost exactly like Molly, like a twin sister, albeit from a long, long-ago time. It obviously was not Molly, given the age of the picture and the young woman's fashion, but it could have been her. I couldn't tell for certain whether the dress that she wore was a wedding dress, but it seemed like it might be. I quickly rifled through the rest of the photographs, but there were no more pictures of her, whoever she may have been. Somehow, I was going to find out.

Until the loneliness and monotony of life after Molly, and the task of going through her things, I had never had even the slightest passing interest in family trees and genealogy. And I still didn't have any real interest in my own. But after seeing that picture, that young woman obviously connected in some as yet unknown way to Molly, I became consumed with finding out who she was, and in some larger way, perhaps, more about who Molly was. Seeing that picture left me inexplicably, yet unmistakably, shaken.

With all of the pictures arranged by year, or in the large "unknown" pile, I took a stack of index cards and began writing years on them, from 1983 backwards to 1886, and placed them in chronological rows with the dated pictures beneath the appropriate date. I had to use some other tables and chairs to accommodate nearly a century's worth of photographs. With the index cards lined up and the dated pictures in their appropriate years, I set about tackling the 136 undated pictures. I looked for clues, like automobiles or military uniforms, which might help me to estimate the date. Some pictures appeared to be of the same person, at a younger or older age. Those I placed at what I guessed might be the closest date. I happened to glance at a clock. It was 1:40 a.m.

I looked out the dining room window, which I realized that I hadn't done for hours. There were at least seven inches of snow on the ground, with more still coming down. I didn't even know that it had been snowing. I retired to the bed that Molly and I had shared. Sleep came only after my brain, racing with thoughts of pictures of people that I didn't even know, in particular that mysterious woman, could no longer stand it. My sleep was deep, but brief. I awoke at 5:50 a.m., nearly an hour before the sun would rise. I immediately, but wholly unintentionally, returned to thoughts of the pictures and index cards awaiting me in the dining room. I knew that it was pointless to try to go back to sleep.

I made a larger-than-normal pot of coffee and by six-thirty I found myself once again standing bent over the dining room table and the century's worth of black-and-white photographs. Other than Molly's parents, I didn't recognize most of these people. I knew Molly's maternal grandparents – Abigail (*nee* Stewart) Forsythe and Charles Forsythe. Abigail had died in 1992 at the age of seventy-five, a widow for nearly fifty years, after Charles was killed in World War II while serving on the *USS Liscome Bay*, an escort carrier in the Pacific. On November 24, 1943, the *Liscome Bay* was torpedoed by a Japanese submarine, killing 644 of the 916 crewmen, including Charles Forsythe. I assumed that the two pictures of a young serviceman in my stack of "unknowns" were of Charles, although I was far from certain. One of the few stories that I *had* heard about Molly's family was that her grandfather had been killed during World War II. I placed the two pictures of the young serviceman, proud and handsome in his uniform, under the "1942" index card, which seemed like a reasonable estimate.

I also knew that Molly's paternal grandparents were Evelyn (*nee* Duncan) Watson and Robert Watson, who died in 1989 and 1988, respectively, while Molly and I were still dating. I had met them a few times at family events, but couldn't quite remember exactly what they looked like. Nevertheless, I found what I was fairly sure were pictures of them in my stack of unknowns. I started to make a rudimentary, hand-written family tree of Molly's genealogy, so that I could keep track of who was who, although at this point it contained little more than Molly, with her dates of birth and death; her parents, Gail and Bruce Watson; and two sets of grandparents – Abigail and Charles Forsythe, and Evelyn and Robert Watson.

Increasingly obsessed and consumed with identifying the people in the old photos, it wasn't until two o'clock in the afternoon that I finally realized that I hadn't eaten, nor had I plowed the snow from the sidewalk and driveway. My back was aching from standing bent over at the dining room table for nearly seven straight hours. I reluctantly abandoned my project, went into the kitchen and fried a couple of eggs, made toast, and had a quick lunch before starting up the snowblower and clearing the nine inches of snow. I cleared off the car, too, just in case of the unlikely event that I found myself with somewhere to go. By the time that I came back inside, the sunlight was all but gone. I immediately returned to the dining room table and the photographs of strangers.

I was at a loss. I still couldn't date or identify most of the people in my pile of old photographs, much less know anything about them. At this point, I knew that Charles Forsythe was Molly's maternal grandfather, but I had no specific idea yet about the story of the ill-fated *USS Liscome Bay,* which I would later come to learn about. I had to find out who all of these people were and what their stories were. Above all else, I needed to know who the beautiful young woman who looked like Molly's twin sister was. I didn't just need to know – I became completely, perhaps even irrationally, obsessed with knowing. After all, what difference could it possibly make even if I *were* to find out who she was?

I spent hours on my computer searching for Gail Watson, Bruce Watson, Evelyn Watson, Robert Watson, Abigail Forsythe, and Charles Forsythe. I found absolutely nothing useful aside from the obituaries for Bruce and Gail, which I had helped Molly write, and a newspaper story abou the *Liscome Bay*. I stood staring down at the table which was completely covered with pictures. I had been up for eighteen hours and had spent all but three of them standing over the dining room table. I was crossing a line, although I didn't realize it, between the natural curiosity of wanting to learn more about Molly and the growing sense that I had no real choice but to find out who the young woman in the picture was. It was time for bed and another fitful attempt at sleep.

The next morning, I did something that I could never have imagined myself doing a week, or even a day, before. I registered at one of the online genealogy sites, not having the slightest idea what to expect or what, if anything, I might possibly discover. I had seen the ads with tearful stories about people finding their links to heroes, royalty, and assorted other relatives, but those were just ads, and I was skeptical, to say the least. My expectations were quite low. Just to see how it all worked, and even *if* it worked, I entered my own name, date of birth, place of birth, and parents' names. In a matter of seconds, I was swamped with "clues" about where I had lived, where my parents had lived, when they were born and died, and who *their* parents, grandparents, and siblings were.

I found that the genealogical websites have literally billions of documents in their databases for hundreds of millions of people. I had to grudgingly admit that it was really quite amazing. Simply by entering a name and a little bit of information, like a birth date or place, the sites will suggest source documents to examine – most relevant, some not. The accuracy, though, is quite remarkable. Handwritten census records with addresses, the names and ages of household members, military service records, baptisms, death certificates, marriage licenses – they were all in there. Each document that I confirmed as relevant seemed to lead to yet another and another and another. All the while, the site was creating its own version of a family tree. It was eerie. The site knew more about my family than I did.

I looked at the source documents – census records, marriage certificates, baptismal records, cemetery records, draft cards, obituaries – and added the ones which I knew to be accurate to my own tree. It was astonishing. For some people, like my father and two of my grandparents, there were even pictures. Where the pictures came from, or how they got into the database, I had no idea. I spent the entire day looking at records for my own parents, grandparents, and great-grandparents, which the database seemed to locate with ease. At times, I forgot why I was even doing all of this. Every time I accepted a "clue," it seemed like two or three more would pop up. I had actually forgotten that it was *Super Bowl* Sunday until it was 9:00 p.m. and the game was more than half over. I didn't really mind missing the halftime show with The Weeknd, but I wished that I hadn't missed the first half of the game. With tired, bloodshot eyes and a racing mind, I sat down to watch what was left of it. I missed the final seven minutes, having passed out as much as having fallen asleep.

Now convinced that the genealogy site could actually locate and access accurate information for my own family's tree, the next morning I returned to my original purpose in undertaking all of this and entered Molly's name, date and place of birth, and date of death. Much like when I had entered my own name, dozens of clues popped up for Molly. I found the birth certificate for Molly June Watson from Frisbie Memorial Hospital in Rochester, New Hampshire, identifying her parents as Gail and Bruce Watson from Milton Mills, and listing her time of birth as 3:12 p.m. on January 22, 1972. I was directed to another clue which turned out to be our Maine marriage certificate. The database didn't seem to know that Molly had died, however.

I began populating the website's family tree for Molly with the various people, dates, and source materials which I was finding. I was determined to conduct all of this research in a very meticulous and systematic way, because I wanted to learn everything that I could about Molly and her family, find out who all of these strangers in the old photographs were, see what stories they might tell, not overlook any details, and ultimately discover who the lookalike young woman in Molly's family might be. I wasn't going to be careless or rushed.

Once I had exhausted every clue about Molly herself and had entered it into her tree, I set about creating the record and links for her parents. One-by-one, I began looking at the clues for her father, Bruce Watson. I knew his birth date – May 4, 1940 – and knew that he had two older brothers, Lee and Henry, both of whom had predeceased him. I then did the same for Molly's mother, Gail.

Over the ensuing days, I continued to delve deeper and deeper into Molly's family history, gradually working my way back through time and generations. I did little else other than stare at the computer screen, click on links, and make copious notes. I found records, to varying degrees, for all eight of her great-grandparents, at least enough to learn their names and dates of birth and death, where they had lived, and who their siblings were. For each, I entered all of the information that I could find and that I could verify into their individual records. I eventually learned that it was one particular set of great-grandparents, Brian Duncan and Emma Duncan, who had left Scotland in search of the American Dream in 1910. At last I had discovered Molly's Scottish heritage. I had traveled back more than a century, identifying four grandparents, eight great-grandparents, and all of their respective siblings, but as far as I knew, I hadn't yet found out who the mystery woman was. I was beginning to think that perhaps I would never know.

Now that I had traced one set of great-grandparents back to Scotland, I had to upgrade my genealogy website membership to access international records. I didn't remember being informed of this when I first signed up with the service a couple of weeks earlier. Nonetheless, I signed up immediately and paid the extra fee. I could now access birth, death, baptismal, census, and marriage records from around the world, although I would most likely only need those from Great Britain. I decided, at least for now, to focus my attention on Brian and Emma Duncan and Molly's Scottish blood.

I continued to enter everything that I was learning into Molly's on-line family tree, as well as into my own handwritten notes. By this time, the notes went on for pages, encompassing Molly, her two parents, four grandparents, eight great-grandparents, as well as each of their respective siblings and children. There were lines and arrows and sticky notes everywhere. It took days. I was doing nothing other than sleeping, reading about Molly's ancestors, organizing pictures, and, when absolutely necessary, shoveling snow and eating. Every single person generated their own set of clues and required that I pour over dozens of source documents, many handwritten and barely decipherable. At times, I could hardly think coherently, trying to remember who was related to who and in what way. At other times, I couldn't even remember why I was doing all of this. It seemed like I was being propelled not by any kind of higher-order thinking, but by a kind of primitive, instinctive drive. The further back I went, the more people I had to learn about and think about, and the more tangled and complicated it was all becoming.

Having researched as far back as eight great-grandparents, I now had to locate and learn about sixteen great-great-grandparents, the very definition of things becoming exponentially more complicated. The clues kept coming and coming, relentlessly, and I felt myself sinking deeper and deeper into the genealogical abyss. But I simply could not stop. It was as if I were watching myself from a distance. All the while, staring up at me, unblinking, from the dining room table was that picture. It felt like I had to be getting closer.

On a Wednesday, during yet another snowstorm, this one a fierce Nor'easter, I was working on clues for one of Molly's maternal great-great-grandmothers – Emma Duncan's mother – Sally Gilday, from Glasgow. The clues led me, circuitously, to Sally Gilday's siblings – two brothers, one sister who had died as an infant, and another sister, Darcie Gilday, born in Scotland in 1866. I could not possibly have foreseen what was about to happen. In fact, I had seriously considered simply giving up on all of this. I clicked on the name Darcie Gilday and came face-to-face with the young woman I had dedicated this portion of my life to finding. Darcie Gilday was looking right at me. It had to have been one of the last pictures ever taken of her.

Although the digitized picture was cracked and faded, there was no doubt that it was the same person as the one in my picture. She was wearing the same dress and had the same effervescent smile. The similarity to Molly was again uncanny. I was shocked that I had actually found her, and perhaps even more shocked when I learned that she had died shortly after the picture was taken. I sat staring at her for a long time. She seemed to return my stare.

Darcie Gilday, I learned, was born on February 26, 1866, to Molly's maternal great-great-great-grandparents, Beatrice Gilday and Magnus Gilday, in Glasgow. Darcie was baptized into the Roman Catholic Church at St. Andrew's Cathedral. She lived with her parents on River Street, according to the 1871 and 1881 handwritten Scottish census records. Her marriage license indicated that she was married to Mr. Murdock Ross, also at St. Andrew's Cathedral, on July 16, 1887. The site directed me to a picture of her gravestone at the Glasgow Necropolis, carved with her date of birth and her date of death, August 7, 1889. Darcie's gravestone was next to the gravestones of her parents. I did the quick math in my head. Yes, she was only twenty-three years old when she died. What I still did not know was how or why she had died at only twenty-three.

A plague, perhaps, or an accident, or maybe she had died during childbirth. I would learn the answer soon enough.

One of the clues about Darcie Gilday Ross directed me to the online archives of *The Scotsman*, a 200-year-old newspaper in Edinburgh, which, naturally, required a separate subscription to access. I paid the fee and immediately searched for any mention of Darcie Gilday Ross. To my surprise, there were dozens of stories which mentioned her, all from the late 1880s and early 1890s, many from the front page of the newspaper. I read them all, over and over again, with fascination, sadness, and a developing fury.

Chapter 6

Belfast Curling Club

I had driven or biked past the Belfast Curling Club on Route 3 hundreds, if not thousands of times during my years spent living in town. The building is hard to miss, standing alone with its depiction of curling scenes painted on the outdoor wall facing the road, and with its name and logo on the sign. To visitors, it might be a bit of a curiosity, but I hardly even noticed it after a while. I had been inside on a few occasions, but had never actually tried curling.

The Belfast Curling Club is the only curling club in the entire state of Maine with its own curling facility and its own dedicated curling ice. There is another club, in Portland, the Pine Tree Curling Club, but it curls, unfortunately, at a hockey rink, somewhat condescendingly referred to within the curling community as "arena curling." Ridges, ruts, gouges, imperfect pebble, and slanted ice are all hallmarks of arena curling, largely caused by hockey players, figure skaters, and Zambonis. There are tournaments, better known as bonspiels, which exclusively cater to the poor unfortunates who are consigned to curling at arena curling clubs. Someday soon, Pine Tree will join Belfast with its own dedicated curling facility.

The club in Belfast, though, owns its own building with three sheets of curling ice, locker rooms, a kitchen, a warm room with a bar, and a banquet room. The Belfast Curling Club first opened as a two-sheet curling club in February 1959, on a piece of land which curlers had previously flooded in the winter to play the outdoor version of the game.

The Belfast Curling Club was founded by Dr. Norman Cobb and some of his Canadian curling buddies from the St. Stephen Curling Club in New Brunswick, who, along with a crew of volunteer carpenters, masons, plumbers, and electricians, built a two-sheet curling club on the donated land outside of downtown Belfast, the same parcel of land that they had been using for outdoor curling. Before the club was built, curlers from Belfast often traveled all the way to St. Stephen just so that they could curl indoors. After the Belfast facility was built, it was the closest United States curling club to the Canadian Maritimes and hosted many curling events attended by players from the Maritime Provinces of New Brunswick, Nova Scotia, and Prince Edward Island. The St. Stephen Curling Club is still operating today, one of 1,500 curling clubs in Canada, compared to the mere 200 or so sprinkled around the United States, mostly, but by no means any longer exclusively, in the colder regions. No self-respecting town of any size in Canada would dare to be without its own curling club.

Only three years after the Belfast Curling Club opened its two-sheeter, the members decided that what they really needed was a larger facility, so in 1962 they razed the three-year-old building to make way for a three-sheet club. A dining room was added in 1977. Belfast Curling Club now boasts some of the finest curling ice in New England, and to this day remains the only dedicated curling facility in Maine.

One of the more quirky and charming things about the Belfast Curling Club is found in the warm room, which is where curlers gather to have a drink, eat, and watch matches being played on the ice below. Most clubs have chairs set up so that people can watch. Belfast, however, has repurposed some old church pews for people to sit on and watch. Each curling club has its own particular idiosyncrasies, and that is one of Belfast's.

I knew a few people from the Belfast area who were members of the club and who were quite serious about their curling. I had declined a lot of invitations over the years to try the sport, which seemed to me, quite frankly, like a fairly stupid game. One of the regular, but by no means hard-core members, a friend named Rich Scamman, called me one day in March of 2021 and asked if I would like to be a substitute on his team the next night. Rich had asked me to try curling a few times, but I had always passed. I'm not sure why, exactly, but this time I said yes. I hadn't really done anything for two months other than obsess over my research into Molly's genealogy and reflect on what had happened to young Darcie Ross in Scotland 130 years earlier. It felt like both my mind and body had atrophied. A couple of hours on the ice might do me good.

Although Molly and I had lived in Belfast for over twenty-five years, neither of us had even once gone curling. I had been inside the club for meetings and banquets and parties, but I had never actually played. How hard could it be, I thought? I was in better shape than Rich from my years of trying to keep up with Molly while cycling, and Rich could apparently manage to curl with no problems. I was also still self-aware enough to know that I really needed to get out and do something that didn't involve studying old pictures and drawing family trees. So I met Rich and his two teammates at seven-thirty the next night for my introduction to playing *The Roarin' Game*.

Just as I had suspected, the acts of sliding the stone down the ice and of sweeping in front of it weren't that hard, physically. If I could keep up with Molly on our bike rides down to Camden and up Mount Battie, I could certainly slide a stone down some ice. Between sliding the stone and sweeping, though, serious sweeping was the one that left me a little short of breath.

Playing the game well, I quickly discovered, is a different matter altogether than simply playing it. I learned the basics of stepping into the hack, which is like a starting block in track, only embedded into the ice, and pushing out to deliver the stone over the course of maybe a two or three minute tutorial from my teammates before our game started. Rich showed me how to approach the hack. Being right-handed, and right-footed for that matter, I first put my right foot onto the hack and then placed my left foot on the Teflon slider. Doing those two things in the wrong order would likely leave me on my ass, Rich said, and so I constantly reminded myself, "Hack first." Rich then showed me how to draw my left foot back, then forward, while gripping the stone's handle and driving forward with my right leg to slide down the ice and deliver the stone, all the while keeping my left foot firmly atop the Teflon slider. After a couple of quick practice shots, neither of which traveled even halfway down the ice, it was time to start the game.

I would come to learn the etiquette, and there was a fair amount of it to learn, and what the skip's hand signals and verbal directions meant during the course of the game. The skip, in essence, is the team captain and directs the other members of the team as to what kind of shot should be attempted. I had to learn what "hack weight," "draw weight," "take out weight," "inturn," "outturn," "guard," and "freeze" each meant. I started to understand, if not execute. Over the course of eight ends, throwing two stones in each end, I think that I successfully landed precisely two stones in the house, which is basically a twelve-foot in diameter bulls-eye. I did make it through the game without falling on the ice, though, which I viewed as a small measure of success. We lost, something like 13-4, if I remember, but Rich and his buddies didn't seem to much care, complimented me on my play, and we all grabbed a beer in the warm room afterwards, courtesy of our victorious opponents, a tradition which I was told is called "broomstacking" or "stacking the brooms."

We had a good laugh over the players who yell at their stones as they rumble down the ice. Rich told me the story of James Millar of the old Duddingston Curling Society in Scotland, who would legendarily "squat on his belly on the middle of the rink after the stone went off, and kick, roar, sputter, and gesticulate after it, to the infinite amusement of the onlookers." Belfast didn't have any James Millars, but it did have a few folks who talked to the stones, like golfers admonishing errant shots. "Curl, you bastard!" was a common reproach.

Much to my surprise, I quickly came to love everything about curling. I played a few more games in March as a substitute, before the club closed for the warm months when it becomes too expensive for smaller clubs like Belfast to maintain good ice. Everyone in Maine wants to be outside then, anyway. The club reopened in the fall with a new member.

Curling actually gave me something to do and a reason to get out of the house and be with people. The past four months since Molly's death had taken a silent, but unmistakable toll on me. I felt like I had aged quickly, and I knew that I was depressed, even if not clinically so. I was sometimes shocked by what I saw reflected in the mirror. Still researching every day, I remained obsessed with Molly's family tree and with Darcie Ross, but curling was quickly becoming a second obsession. I didn't abandon my research into Molly's family history, but I did stop doing it virtually all day, every day. I had, after all, finally discovered who the young woman in that picture was.

Over the summer, I bought curling shoes and my own curling broom and read everything that I could about the game and its history. I ordered six books about curling with the help of Left Bank

Books, rather than from some faceless online behemoth. I hadn't been to Left Bank Books since Molly had died and the owners, who had attended Molly's memorial service, seemed happy to see me. I studied the books about curling technique, strategy, and history. I found the books about the sport's history particularly fascinating. For good measure, after reading those six, I drove down to Owl & Turtle Bookshop in Camden and ordered three more.

———————◦———————

From my reading, I learned that the modern sport of curling traces its history back more than 500 years to the frozen rivers, lochs, and ponds of Scotland, although it was a very, very different game back then. Writer Sir Walter Scott and poet Robert Burns both referred to curling as "the manly Scottish exercise."

Early on in its history, and for hundreds of years thereafter, curling was played with stones of widely varying shapes and sizes, picked up from fields or rivers. Some curlers eventually began to cut holes for the thumb and fingers into their stones, akin to modern bowling balls. For centuries, curling was played exclusively outdoors, where sweeping snow away with brooms was often necessary.

Curiously, Protestant ministers played a pivotal role in the early history of curling, and their approval and blessing certainly contributed to its growth and acceptance. Many curling clubs appointed chaplains and many more counted clergy among their members and officers. Some clergy actively promoted the sport, pointing to the sportsmanship and fellowship which curlers displayed toward their opponents, as well as to its healthful benefits. In the late 1700s, Reverend John Shephard, Minister of Muirkirk, for example, wrote about his parishioners:

Their chief amusement in winter is curling, or playing stones on smooth ice. They eagerly vie with one another who shall come nearest the mark, and one part of the parish against another, one description of men against another, one trade or occupation against another, and often one whole parish against another, earnestly contend for the palm, which is generally all the prize, except that perhaps the victors claim from the vanquished the dinner and bowl of toddy, which, to do them justice, both commonly take together with great cordiality, and generally without any grudge at the fortune of the day, wisely reflecting, no doubt, that defeat as well as victory is the fate of war. Those accustomed to this amusement, or that have acquired dexterity in the game, are extremely fond of it. The amusement itself is healthful; it is innocent; it does nobody harm; let them enjoy it.

Reverend Shephard may not have approved of what transpired in Dalpeddar in 1826 regarding "the manly Scottish exercise," however:

On Tuesday last, 28 blooming damsels met on Dalpeddar Loch in the parish of Sanquhar, to play a friendly bonspiel. They formed themselves into two rinks, and although wading up to the ankles in water, seemed to enter into the spirit of the game, and to contest it with as much intense anxiety as if the question that the losing party should all die old maids had depended upon the issue. At the conclusion of the game neither party became victors, the number of shots having been equal. Many individuals of the other sex were attracted to the scene of action; and as the ladies, like true curlers, had resolved to adjourn to the toll-house, where a het pint had been ordered, they kindly invited the gentlemen to accompany them. It soon became a matter of doubt if this was of sufficient potency to counteract the bad effects resulting from wet feet, and as tea could not be expected to prove more efficacious, our heroines resorted to whisky toddy, and through its inspiration . . . a dance was proposed, to put all matters into proper sorts, and the ball was kept up with great vigour until far into the wee hours o' the morning. It may be true that there is no good reason why females should not have their hours of recreation as well as men, but it seems advisable that those recreations which they do engage in should be of a character befitting their sex. Ice playing is certainly not a game of this description – it has nothing feminine pertaining to it either in theory or practice. If, therefore, prudence and propriety are to be consulted, the fair maidens of the lower end of Sanquhar parish will not again resort to the same expedient for obtaining a day's relaxation and enjoyment.

Even in 1820s Scotland, apparently, girls just wanted to have fun. Had she lived back there and then, I'm quite certain that Molly would have joined the "blooming damsels" on the ice and at the dance.

In the mid-1800s, the "maidens" of Copenoch played a bonspiel against the "maidens" of Waterside. On a warm day, with the women "fetlock-deep in water," the match was played, with "the curling broom being handled as dextrously as the domestic one," according to John Kerr's 1890 book, *History of Curling: Scotland's Ain Game*.

Despite its increasing popularity and blessing by many clergy, curling had its critics. Some criticized it as "an encouragement to idleness, a temptation to profane swearing, an incitement to quarrelling, and an inducement to dissipation." The Peebles Curling Club, in its 1821 preamble to its rules and regulations, found it necessary to defend the game as "an enemy to every spirit of sensual indulgence, debarring those who engage in it for the time being from tippling in taverns, lounging lazily and effeminately at a fireside, or devoting themselves to worse employments . . ."

To understand modern curling, it is important to understand what the World Curling Federation calls "The Spirit of Curling" in its *Rules of Curling*:

> *Curling is a game of skill and of tradition. A shot well executed is a delight to see and it is also a fine thing to observe the time-honoured traditions of curling being applied in the true spirit of the game. Curlers play to win, but never to humble their opponents. A true curler never attempts to distract opponents, nor to prevent them from playing their best, and would prefer to lose rather than to win unfairly.*

> *Curlers never knowingly break a rule of the game, nor disrespect any of its traditions. Should they become*

aware that this has been done inadvertently, they will be the first to divulge the breach.

While the main object of the game of curling is to determine the relative skill of the players, the spirit of curling demands good sportsmanship, kindly feeling, and honourable conduct.

As far back as the 1700s, curling was viewed as a "gentlemen's game." Almost all of the early references to curling matches make note of the "kindly feeling" and congeniality demonstrated both during and after matches. Most of the early Scottish curling clubs and societies also codified strict rules against swearing and gambling. In 1783, for example, the Coupar-Angus Club had the following rule: "That if any brother in the course of play, or at society meetings, shall be guilty of swearing or giving bad names to any member, he shall pay two pence for the first offence, and be at the mercy of the court for repeated acts of said crimes." The mere fact that such conduct was considered to be a "crime" reveals the seriousness with which such acts were taken. Of course, enforcing rules such as those was a different matter altogether. The Coupar-Angus Club once attempted to enforce its no-swearing rule against one of its members, Jonathan Crockett, as reflected in the club's minutes:

At a meeting of the Curling Society held here this day . . . it was reported by some of the members that [Jonathan] Crockett . . . was this day on the ice curling and had been guilty of swearing several times . . . and therefore he should be called to court and make payment of the usual fines. [A]fter being several times sent for to appear for the above crimes . . . and never appearing, a party of the members was accordingly sent to bring him, and after having gone to his house and asked him to come, he presented a gun to them and swore that he would shoot the first person who should attempt to lay hands on him . . .

Hopefully, it was not necessary for the Peebles Curling Club in Scotland to adopt the following regulation when it was first established in 1821, but they adopted it anyway: "When a member falls and is hurt, the rest shall not laugh, but render him every assistance to enable him to regain his former erect position." Such is the true spirit of curling.

———— ◆ ————

By the time that the Belfast Curling Club re-opened in the fall, having read nine books about the sport and its history over the summer, I may have known more about curling, at least in the academic sense, than anyone else there. I practiced on my own when I could and joined several of the different leagues – the over-fifty league, men's league, mixed league, it didn't matter. Despite all of my reading and practicing, though, I was still one of the worst players in the club. There is simply no substitute for experience, and many of the members had been playing the game since they were kids. Sitting around having a beer after the games, though, I found myself regaling people with unending stories about the island of Ailsa Craig and the long history of *The Roarin' Game.*

Shortly after I joined the club, the United States Women's Curling Association Scot Tour made a stop in Belfast. There were more than forty Scottish women on the tour playing matches against other women's teams from around New England. I spent the entire day at the club, taking in the pipers, fiddlers, drums, flags, and, of course, the curling. I found that I could hold my own in most curling discussions with the Scots, although it was mostly just book-knowledge. They were delightful, especially those who spoke with a Scottish brogue, which was almost all of them. They seemed to be thoroughly enjoying curling in the States.

Between games, I struck up a conversation with Fiona Troup from the Lochmaben Curling Club in Lockerbie, a club which was founded in 1823, she told me. We chatted briefly about what Lockerbie is most known for and then about the stops that the tour was making, but we soon moved on to talking about what Fiona loved the most about curling – playing outdoors with her club once a year. She told me that shortly after she returned home, her club's outdoor matches would be played on a pond on the property of one of Lochmaben's members, John Frost willing. It took me a moment to discern what John Frost referred to, but I finally realized that it referred to the winter weather. The outdoor curling party was an all-day event with many people from the town circling the pond and watching the games, cheering on their curling friends. There would be plenty of food and drink to keep the players and spectators warm. If she had to choose, Fiona said, she just might prefer playing the outdoor game.

The only real downside to the entire day of watching the Scot Tour was the fact that someone went to the trouble of preparing a large quantity of haggis for the banquet in the evening, which everyone was expected to sample and enjoy. I sampled it, but only because it would have been rude not to. The mere thought of haggis is rather repulsive, being a pudding-like mixture of a sheep's "pluck," consisting of the animal's heart, liver, and lungs, combined with onion, suet, oatmeal, and spices. For good measure, it is boiled in the sheep's stomach. It wasn't until after-the-fact that I learned that what we were served wasn't *true* haggis. It was lacking the sheep's lungs, which are illegal to use in food in the States. The cook must have gotten creative and used brains or tongue, instead. When I later traveled to Scotland, I passed on the haggis.

Curling quite literally changed my life, and others' lives as well. It led me on a journey that I could never have imagined. A journey into both the past and the future. It tested my will, my resolve, my character, my morality, and perhaps even my sanity. Once I had thrown that first stone, there was no going back. Curling, it turned out, would lead me to my destiny.

<hr />

All of this reading and studying and practice, of course, didn't make me anything close to a keen and dedicated curler. No matter how much of the origins and history of the game I learned, it wasn't nearly enough to make me anything other than a wannabe. Even curling in several leagues at the Belfast Curling Club and watching the women's Scot Tour wouldn't get me where I needed to be. No, in order to truly understand the spirit of the game and become a serious curler, I would have to start attending bonspiels – curling tournaments with curlers from other clubs. I crossed that line by attending the Pumpkinspiel in New Hampshire.

Chapter 7

The Pumpkinspiel

It was at the Pumpkinspiel in Nashua, New Hampshire, that I first met Skye Brodie, in November 2021, a little less than a year after Molly had died. Skye was from the Heather Curling Club in St. Andrews by-the-Sea, New Brunswick, Canada, a nearly century-old club founded in 1922. The club was hard at work planning for its 100-year anniversary celebration, Skye told me. The Pumpkinspiel was, of course, the first bonspiel that I ever attended, and it attracted twenty-four teams from curling clubs across New England and Canada over the weekend of November 12th to 14th. Bonspiel teams – also called "rinks" – compete against each other, usually over the course of a weekend, and usually for nothing more than the sheer glory and joy of winning a bonspiel, sometimes referred to as playing "for the palm." There are a few teams that treat bonspiels much more seriously than others, but most come for nothing more than the fun of being with curlers from other clubs and competing against them. There are men-only bonspiels, women-only bonspiels, mixed bonspiels, junior bonspiels, senior bonspiels, college bonspiels, arena club bonspiels, wheelchair bonspiels, and "under five" bonspiels for players with fewer than five years of curling experience. I probably should have chosen an "under five" bonspiel for my first, given how we fared over the weekend.

Teams participating in bonspiels traditionally give themselves names, usually a play on words for some curling term, like "Sweeping Beauties," "Besom Buddies," or "Baby Broomers." Bonspiels themselves are also traditionally themed and given names to match the season or locale, and curling is about nothing if not tradition. Hence, the autumn "Pumpkinspiel" in Nashua which I was attending. There are bonspiels with names like the "Hotter than Hell" bonspiel held in Arizona during the summer, the "Steers 'n' Beers" bonspiel held in Texas, and the "Grits and Granite" bonspiel in North Carolina.

Skye Brodie played for a team called the "Nae-Sayers," and they wore matching kilts, hose, belts, and tams when they played. The Nae-Sayers, comprised of two men and two women, spent fifteen or sixteen weekends during each curling season attending bonspiels across the Canadian Maritimes, Quebec Province, and New England, and each player on the team was very good. At the Pumpkinspiel, my team's second draw, on Saturday morning, was against the Nae-Sayers, who had years, if not decades, of curling experience. Plus, they were from Canada, where people grow up with curling. Not only that, but each of the Nae-Sayers traced their ancestry to Scotland, where the sport was born, giving them yet another seeming advantage. They wore their Scottish outfits with pride as an homage to their individual and collective ancestries. On the other hand, no one on the team that I, along with my friend Rich Scamman played for, the "Stoneheads," had been curling for longer than three years, and I for just a few months. The match was not fated to end well for us, and it didn't. As one might expect, we were outclassed by the much better team and lost 14-3, shaking hands and saying, "Good Curling" after just the sixth end in concession. In our first draw on Friday night, we had fared only slightly better, losing by a score of 11-4 to another team of experienced Canadian curlers.

Despite being outscored by a combined 25-7 in our first two draws, we were having fun at the Pumpkinspiel and losing was made significantly more palatable by the tradition of the winning team buying drinks for the losers, with all eight players sitting around a table chatting and reveling in the pure joy of playing games for no other reason than because we could. Neither I, nor my teammates, ever turned down free beer, and we were becoming used to being the beneficiaries, both at our own club and now at a bonspiel, so we raised a glass with the Nae-Sayers and talked curling. The Nae-Sayers, of course, insisted on a traditional Scottish Gaelic toast of "slàinte," or "good health," and taught their opponents to respond with, "do dheagh shlàinte," or "to your good health."

I happened to be sitting next to Skye after our loss to the Nae-Sayers, so she was the one who treated me to a coffee stout from Smuttynose, a New Hampshire brewery. Naturally, we talked about curling. We also talked about one of the other Canadian teams at the bonspiel which was legendary for one thing not directly related to curling. This particular team is best-known for having come to the Little International Bonspiel in Belfast each year for the past decade. Every year, this team stays at the same hotel in the same room, not necessarily because that particular hotel is so wonderful or that particular room is so special, but rumor has it that it does hold a secret treasure.

The hotel room has a drop ceiling with suspended acoustical tiles. Rather than shuttle their libations back and forth across the border every year, the team simply stores their liquor up in the ceiling until the next year, figuring what are the odds that anyone is going to go up there and nose around? And so, they make their hotel reservations early each year, as soon as the Little International is scheduled, along with their peculiar request to stay in the same hotel room year after year after year.

As we were talking, I asked Skye about the kilts and tams, and she told me that all of the members of the Nae-Sayers traced their ancestry back to Scotland. I asked what part of Scotland her family came from and she told me that they were mostly from Edinburgh and that she was third-generation Canadian. She told me that she had managed to trace her ancestry and clan back to the early 1600s, but that beyond that it was very difficult to get much really accurate and verifiable information. And no, she joked, she had not discovered any royals or heroes in her background, just a bunch of hard-working Scots. Unlocking four hundred years worth of family history is pretty impressive in itself, though. Many Scots, she told me, like those in her family, emigrated to the Canadian Maritimes in the 17th, 18th, and 19th centuries, bringing curling with them to Canada.

Skye obviously loved talking about her family history and about curling, and I guess that I made for a good audience. Because I had done so much reading about curling and its history, I was able to follow most of what she was telling me about curling's roots in Scotland. I'm pretty sure that she was at least a little bit impressed and intrigued that an American could hold up fairly well in a discussion of curling history. For my part, I was really, really enjoying having an adult conversation that didn't involve someone taking pity on a poor widower.

Skye told me about one of her relatives in particular who, many generations ago, had been named the patron of a curling club in Edinburgh, the Duddingston Curling Society. This gentleman, apparently quite well-respected and connected in Edinburgh, secured a parcel of land on which the club successfully constructed its first artificial curling pond, which it curled on for years. The club championship trophy which is awarded each year is named in his honor. Skye carried around with her a little scrapbook with a few old newspaper clippings that she had found which mentioned her relatives and curling in Edinburgh. She showed me one about the winner of the Duddingston curling championship trophy. I told Skye that some of my wife's relatives were also Scottish, although from around Glasgow rather than Edinburgh.

I mentioned to Skye that I had been working on my wife's ancestry as kind of a wintertime lark, something to occupy my time, not revealing the true extent of my interest and obsession, but also mentioning that I hadn't found a format for creating the family tree that I really liked and that I could visually follow, especially when it came to indirect relatives like great-aunts and uncles. I explained to her that I am a visual learner, and she confessed to being the same. Skye said that she had the same problem when she started, and that she had spent months trying to find a family tree format that could accommodate everyone in a way that she understood. Finally, she gave up and developed her own elaborate, color-coded chart, which, she claimed, only partly in jest, was truly a work of art. I liked her sense of humor about herself.

Skye explained that she had tried any number of online templates and spreadsheets, but that her best results came from an old-fashioned, hand-drawn family tree. For anyone in her tree – paternal great-great-great-grandmother, great-uncle, maternal great-cousin twice removed – she captured their date and place of birth, date and place of death, immigration status, picture (if she could find one), and maiden and married names for the women, all in one place and all in color-coded splendor. Once she had given up on trying to use any of the computer programs or apps, she was far happier developing her hand-drawn tree. I enjoyed just listening to her talk and felt completely at ease sitting next to her in the warm room, chatting. For the most part, we ignored everyone else at the table, which was fine by me, although we occasionally joined in the rest of the conversation.

I told Skye that I really wasn't that far along yet, which was a bit of a fib, and that I was still trying to just get some basic information together for a few generations to see if anything interesting turned up. I intentionally hadn't told her about Molly's death, just not wanting to turn that into the main topic of conversation and not wanting everyone around the table suddenly falling silent and taking pity on me. So I just didn't bring it up. Fortunately, none of my teammates who were sitting with us mentioned it, either. I suspect that everyone, or at least Skye, took notice that I was wearing a wedding ring. I was enjoying being out at the Pumpkinspiel, and revisiting Molly's death at a table full of strangers was only going to dampen my mood considerably.

I asked Skye if I could see her work of art and maybe use it as my own template. It was on a two-by-three-foot sheet of laminated paper, she told me, but she said that she could have a copy made and would bring it to the next bonspiel that we might both be attending, if I wasn't in any particular hurry to see it. I told her that I wasn't in any rush, which was another small lie, and that our only curling plans so far were for the end-of-season Broomspiel at the Broomstones Curling Club in Massachusetts, in March. Skye told me that Broomstones was the Nae-Sayers' favorite U.S. curling club and that they never missed the Broomspiel, especially now that they had reached the championship game in three of the last four years. She told me that they had lost to a local Broomstones team in heartbreaking fashion in the final end each time. Skye half-jokingly told me that the Nae-Sayers fully intended to win the spring Broomspiel. Maybe less than half-jokingly.

I sat next to Skye at dinner on Saturday night at the Pumpkinspiel and we talked some more about curling and family trees and her several visits to Scotland. The conversation was easy and fun. I mentioned that I had never really been given any proper instruction on how to actually deliver a curling stone, just a few tips from my teammates, who weren't necessarily experienced or accomplished curlers themselves, and who certainly weren't qualified to be instructors.

Skye noticed that there was an empty sheet of ice and told me to come with her so that she could give me some proper instruction. "If you're serious about curling, you might as well do it right," she said. And with that, Skye Brodie gave me my first real curling lesson. She instructed me on my balance, posture, head position, and grip. She showed me how to get into the "lunge" position, with my slider foot under my chest so that I was perfectly balanced. She even had me deliver some stones with my eyes closed, so that I could feel what it was like to be balanced during the delivery, which she called "Zen curling." She kept reminding me, "Above all else, don't push the stone. Trust your leg drive to propel it. Think of it as oozing out of the hack, not thrusting out."

When she was finally satisfied that I seemed to grasp what I was supposed to be doing, my lesson ended. "If you do everything exactly like I showed you, and if you practice, practice, practice," she smiled, "You might actually be OK at this."

We played our final draw in Nashua on Sunday morning, losing again by a lopsided score. I decided against staying to watch the championship game, in which the Nae-Sayers were once again playing, although Rich surprisingly decided to stay and watch. Four hours after leaving Nashua, I was back home in Belfast, alone and tired from a weekend of curling and being treated to beer. On the ride home, I allowed myself to think a little bit about Skye Brodie. As far as I knew, she was just another typical Canadian obsessed with curling. As far as she knew, I was a happily married man just getting away for a curling weekend with the boys. We had known each other for barely twenty-four hours, and yet there was already a secret between us.

I really enjoyed talking to Skye. It had been almost a year since Molly's passing, and it felt good to have a real conversation with someone that didn't include them saying how sorry they were for my loss. She was warm and charming, without aggressively trying to be nice. She took her curling and her heritage very seriously, but herself less so. She had been divorced for years, I learned, had never remarried, but seemed neither bitter about it nor particularly interested in talking about it. It didn't hurt that she looked really nice in her kilt. I enjoyed her company and looked forward to seeing her in a few months at the Broomspiel, which, in ways that I could never have imagined, would change both of our lives forever.

At the club the next week, Rich told me that the Nae-Sayers had won the Pumpkinspiel championship on Sunday, not that I had asked. He told me that he had stayed until Sunday afternoon watching the championship game and the crowning of the Nae-Sayers as champions. I thought that it was a little bit odd that Rich had decided to stay and watch, but didn't really think too much of it. I surmised that he, like me, wasn't particularly excited about coming back to an empty house in Belfast and a rapidly-approaching winter, so he had probably been in no real rush to leave.

Chapter 8

The Volcano

There is a rock, a sea-girt rock,
That's known the world wide
As the beacon of the mariner
That's steering for the Clyde.
For Ailsa Rock is anchored sure;
It guides the pilot true,
Although his bark like seagull rides
On ocean-mountains blue.
Our sailor lads on foreign seas
For months or years may roam,
But here they hitch their breeches high,
And shout three cheers for home.
And emigrants in going forth
To seek the golden ore,
At Ailsa breathe a parting prayer
For dear friends left on shore.
And Pat, whose eyes are dim with tears
For Molly left alone
Exclaims, "Bedad, I'm half seas o'er,
There's Brian Boru's big stone;"
Bad luck to the gosoon spalpeen
Or Saxon idle drone,
Who would make filthy lucre

Out of Brian's blessed stone.
Irish Folk Song

My fascination – some might say monomania – with curling led me to study its centuries of history and its roots in 1500s Scotland. It also led me to learn about the tiny Scottish island of Ailsa Craig, for the story of curling is incomplete without the story of Ailsa Craig, and the story of Ailsa Craig is incomplete without the story of curling. The first time that I heard of Ailsa Craig and saw its picture, I felt connected to it. There was a recognition, a remembrance, an intuitive understanding of its importance. Yet, in spite of all that I learned about Ailsa Craig, I knew that there was something more that I needed to discover. Much more.

<hr/>

Three hundred million years ago, there was a single supercontinent known as Pangea. Pangea stretched from the north pole to the south pole and was formed by the collision of all of the large landmasses on earth over the course of tens of millions of years. Virtually all of the land on earth, covering one-third of its surface, was once a part of Pangea, which itself was surrounded by a single ocean called Pantalassa.

The supercontinent of Pangea's existence was first postulated 400 years ago, shortly after the coasts of Africa and South America were charted by Europeans. The close fit between the west coast of Africa and the east coast of South America was noted almost immediately – schoolchildren today notice it – but it was mainly not much more than a curiosity at first. Shortly thereafter, however, scientists began discovering and identifying similar and identical fossils in what were unconnected places, including the herbivorous lizard Lystrosaurus, which has been found in Antarctica, China, India, Mongolia, and South Africa. The fossils of the freshwater reptile, Menosaurus, have been found only in Brazil and western Africa, which were once connected as part of Pangea. More sophisticated proof of Pangea's existence evolved over the years as scientists studied the magnetic orientation of rocks found around the globe. Magnetic studies have connected the Palisades cliffs along the Hudson River to northwestern Africa. It soon became widely accepted that the continents which we know today had all once been joined together as Pangea.

When Pangea itself was initially formed by the collision of earlier continents, one of the results was the Appalachian Mountains, now most prominent in the eastern United States. At one time, the Appalachians were roughly the height of the present-day Himalayan Mountains, but erosion has diminished their stature, if not their magnificence. Rather amazingly, the Appalachians in North America, the Atlas Mountains in northwestern Africa, and the Scottish Highlands were once part of the same mountain range – the Central Pangean Mountains, which ran down the center of Pangea. They were born as a result of the collision of the pre-Pangean supercontinents of Laurussia and Gonwanda 300-350 million years ago.

Even before Pangea, which was a geological baby at only 300 million years old, there are believed to have been several other supercontinents – Pannotia, Rodinia, and Ur among them. The continents would collide and break apart, collide and break apart, collide and break apart, over the course of billions of years. But the story of Ailsa Craig begins with Pangea.

Pangea spent roughly 100 million years as a single supercontinent, but eventually began to break apart 200 million years ago. The first break came when what are now Africa, South America, Antarctica,

India, and Australia broke away from Eurasia and what is now North America, eventually creating the mid-Atlantic Ocean. They initially broke free together as a single landmass, but 50 million years later, India broke free from Antarctica and Africa broke free from South America. It wasn't until recently, geologically speaking, that North America and Europe broke apart.

After the existence of the supercontinent of Pangea became widely accepted as scientific fact, over the course of the 18th, 19th, and 20th centuries scientists tried to ascertain exactly how Pangea had been formed and how it had broken apart. The most widely debated theory was that of "continental drift," the idea that the continents somehow simply floated, or drifted, apart. In 1912, German meteorologist, geophysicist, and geologist Alfred Lothar Wegener attempted to prove continental drift as the explanation for Pangea's origin and demise. While Wegener's evidence that Pangea had once existed was almost universally praised and accepted, his theory that the continents simply drifted together and then apart was not, mainly because he was unable to offer satisfactory proof about the mechanism which caused the enormous landmasses to move.

In order to understand how continents continually move around the earth, it is necessary to understand a little bit about "plate tectonics," which only came to have wide scientific acceptance over the past 60 years. Plate tectonics, in its simplest terms, posits that the lithosphere, which is comprised of the earth's crust and the upper portion of its mantle, is generally about 50 miles deep. Beneath the lithosphere is the asthenosphere, where temperatures of nearly 2,400 degrees Fahrenheit cause the rigid lithosphere rock to melt. The lithosphere is rigid and cooler, while the asthenosphere is molten and hotter. Within the rigid lithosphere reside the tectonic plates – enormous sheets of solid rock which lie beneath all of the oceans and land on earth and which sit atop the molten and highly volatile asthenosphere.

It is now widely agreed that there are seven "major" tectonic plates – the Pacific Plate (39,884,000 square miles), the North American Plate (29,300,000 square miles), the Eurasian Plate (26,200,000 square miles), the African Plate (23,700,000 square miles), the Antarctic Plate (23,500,000 square miles), the Indo-Australian Plate (22,700,000 square miles), and the South American Plate (16,800,000 square miles). In addition to the seven major plates, there are dozens of much smaller minor and micro plates.

Forces below the tectonic plates cause them to be in nearly constant motion, although extremely slow motion. As a general rule, tectonic plates move at about the same rate that fingernails grow. The Pacific Plate is the largest and fastest, moving at a blistering 3-4 inches a year to the northwest, while the Australian Plate moves about 3 inches a year to the north. The other plates move at slower paces and in varying directions. Some are even rotating. As the plates constantly jostle for global position, they crash into each other, dive beneath each other, and pull apart from each other. As they do, they create such wonders as the Himalayan Mountains, where the Indian Plate and the Eurasian Plate collided; the Mid-Ocean Ridge, a 40,000-mile-long mountain range lying beneath the Atlantic, Pacific, and Indian Oceans; the 3,000-mile-long Rocky Mountains; the San Andreas Fault in California; the Andes Mountains in South America; and the Mariana Trench in the Pacific Ocean. Most of the earthquakes and volcanoes that we experience today are caused by the movement of the tectonic plates.

All of this movement and rotation means that, in another 250 million years or so, there will be another supercontinent made up of all of today's landmasses, although humans won't be around to see it. It also means that during an average person's lifespan, Scotland will move six feet farther away from Maine.

Around sixty million years ago, long after South America, Africa, Antarctica, Australia, and India had broken free from Pangea, a series of massive volcanoes erupted and sounded the final death knell for what was left of Pangea. The eruptions separated the North American Plate from the Eurasian Plate and North America from Europe. The northern Atlantic Ocean began to fill in, as did the Norwegian Sea. One of the many volcanoes created the tiny island of Ailsa Craig in the Firth of Clyde off of the Scottish mainland.

Ailsa Craig was much, much larger once. Today, all that remains is the volcanic plug, created when the liquid magma cooled and hardened within the volcanic vent. Through thousands, and even millions of years, Ailsa Craig became what it is today – what is known as a "crag and tail" island made up of mostly extremely dense microgranite. Over the millennia, most of Ailsa Craig has eroded away from wind, rain, freezing, and thawing, but most of all, from glaciers.

In the various ice ages which the earth has gone through, glaciers have repeatedly advanced during glacial periods and retreated during interglacial ones. As recently as the glacial period of 20,000 years ago, all of Scotland and all of Maine were covered by sheets of glacial ice which were, in some places, more than a mile thick. Even the rocks which Molly and I sat upon atop Cadillac Mountain were once buried deep beneath the glaciers.

As glaciers advance, they carve out the landscape. One way in which they shape the landscape is through a process known as "plucking," which is exactly what it sounds like. The flowing glacier, with its water, ice, incredible weight, and motion, cracks and breaks away weaker rock sitting atop the more solid bedrock in its path. As the glacier moves forward, it either incorporates the plucked rock into itself, pushes the rock forward like a bulldozer, or grinds the rock beneath it into clay or sand.

As glaciers from various ice ages have passed over and around Ailsa Craig, they have eroded all but the hardest of rock, leaving the volcanic plug and the "crag and tail" shape. As the approaching glaciers reached Ailsa Craig from the north, they began to erode it, finally down to the plug, which was hard enough and impermeable enough to water and ice penetration so as to resist the glacial plucking. As the glaciers reached the mass of hardened plug rock, they were unable to penetrate and break it, so they did the next best thing – they simply went over and around the plug. The steep side of the island, where the glaciers first made contact and were met by the plug, is the crag. It is the steeper northern side of Ailsa Craig, with almost vertical cliffs. Over the years, as the glaciers advanced over Ailsa Craig, they left behind some of the rock which they had removed from the plug as they passed. They deposited some of this softer, broken rock and sand on the leeward side of the crag, creating a more gently-sloped shape, called the "tail." After more than 50 million years of erosion and glaciation, Ailsa Craig now rises to just 1,120 feet, a little bit shorter than the Rock of Gibraltar; covers only 240 acres; and has a circumference of barely two miles. While we understand scientifically that Ailsa Craig was created by a volcano, one legend traces its creation to the Prince of Darkness, another to witches, and yet another to a rock tossed into the sea by a giant.

Even though there are hundreds of volcanic islands and plugs around the globe, Ailsa Craig is home to something that doesn't exist anywhere else in the entire world – blue hone granite. Blue hone granite is an extremely dense, alkali-rich microgranite, which was formed when the liquid magma quickly cooled and hardened within the vent. Exactly why blue hone granite is found nowhere else on earth is a mystery in itself, but the fact remains that its only known home is Ailsa Craig. Due to its tight molecular structure and low quartz content, blue hone granite is uniquely, and almost completely, impervious to water intrusion, which would cause the stone to crack and crumble as water penetrates, freezes, and thaws. That imperviousness is the major reason why Ailsa Craig's blue hone granite managed to survive the glaciers. A second kind of Ailsa Craig granite – common green – is almost identical to blue hone, except for clusters of greenish minerals, hence the name. Blue hone granite is found on the northern side of Ailsa Craig, common green on the southern side. It is the blue hone granite which holds the key to making the best curling stones in the world.

Ailsa Craig today is completely uninhabited, except for the hundreds of thousands of birds which nest and breed there, as well as some seals who fish and breed in the firth. The marauding brown rats, once the dominant species on the island, are all gone. The entire island is now protected as a wildlife preserve by the Royal Society for the Protection of Birds. A now-automated lighthouse, along with the remnants of a castle, one or two chapels, quarrymen's quarters, abandoned fog signals, and two small railways still remain on the island, remnants of a different time and way of life. Looking to the south on a clear day, one can see the Isle of Man, and to the southwest, Northern Ireland.

You may not realize it, but you have probably seen Ailsa Craig before. When the Open Championship, once known as the British Open, is played at the Royal Troon Golf Club on Scotland's western shore, the television cameras frequently focus across the Firth of Clyde, past the Isle of Arran, and onto Ailsa Craig, which rises dramatically from the sea. Before the last of the lighthouse keepers left in 1989, having been rendered obsolete by technology, the Open Championship was sometimes played at Troon. The lighthouse keepers stood outside on the gallery and waved toward Troon whenever the cameras panned to Ailsa Craig.

Nearly every corner of Ailsa Craig has acquired a name. Reverend Roderick Lawson, in his 1888 book, *Ailsa Craig: Its History and Natural History*, mapped the island and its place names. Swine Cave, Eagles' Seat, Boating Stone, Sliddery, Ashydoo Craigs, Balvar, Hingin' Stane, Dory's Yett, the Loutin' Stane, Water Cave, Stranny Point, MacNall's Cave, Little Ailsa, Rotten Nick, East Trammins, Craigna'an, Clashwaun, Barry Loch, Castle Comb, Loups' Well, and Nettley Howe remain familiar identifiers on the island to this day.

It wasn't until nearly four months after Molly died that I first tried curling. I was hooked from the moment that I threw a stone. I had to know absolutely everything about the game, its history, the equipment, and the strategy involved in playing well. In studying the history, I learned all of the above, and much, much more.

For whatever reason, I remained drawn to Ailsa Craig – its volcanic formation, its lighthouse, the castle, the chapels, the quarries, the rats, and the birds. I devoured whatever I could find about them. I read Reverend Lawson's 1888 book and studied his maps of the island. What I could never have imagined was that one day I would actually find my way there.

Chapter 9

The Rats and the Birds

M y newfound fixation with curling, and with Ailsa Craig in particular, led me to the story of the brown rats and their century of domination over animal life on the small island. In the 1860s, there were upwards of 250,000 pairs of puffins nesting and breeding on Ailsa Craig. *Half a million birds* on one small island, and that only counts the puffins, not the gannets, guillemots, and dozens of other species. An ornithologist once claimed that if the puffins were disturbed, they caused "a bewildering darkness" in the sky, furiously flapping their undersized wings. Passing ships would sometimes fire a gun to startle the birds so that they would all alight from the island, blacken the sky, and provide amusement and wonder for the passengers and crew. By 1935, though, each and every single puffin was gone, not to return for nearly seventy years. The birds were simply no match for the rats.

The first reported rat on Ailsa Craig was a brown rat, also known as a sewer rat, wharf rat, or Norway rat, sighted in 1889 by the new lighthouse keeper, Cuddy Urquhart. Reportedly, it was killed by Cuddy's dog. How rats arrived on the island is still the subject of some speculation and disagreement. The most popular theory is that they swam ashore from a shipwreck that same year, brown rats being excellent swimmers, but others claim that they had arrived five years earlier following the wreck of the *Austria* in 1884. Yet others claim that they arrived as stowaways on coal and supply boats making deliveries to the island's lighthouse keepers and quarrymen. However and whenever they first got there, they flourished. With no predators, save for the keepers' dogs, which could not keep up with the reproductive prowess of the fecund rats, and an unending food source in the eggs and chicks of hundreds of thousands of birds, the rats multiplied at an astonishing rate. Keepers reported that at night, from the gallery outside of the lantern room, they could look down upon a virtual sea of brown rats scurrying about their business, their eyes glowing red from the reflected light.

Brown rats breed at an exceptionally fast rate, aided by the fact that they are notoriously promiscuous. With a gestation period of only three weeks, and with the young reaching sexual maturity just five weeks after birth, under ideal conditions, a single pair of rats can produce a line of descendants numbering more than 10,000 in a single year. And for the rats, the conditions on Ailsa Craig were very nearly ideal.

Brown rats, through no real fault of their own, are pretty nasty creatures. They can grow to be quite large, weighing in at a pound or more and growing to be as long as twenty inches from nose to tail. They can and do eat almost anything, including insects, fish, and mice, although grains and seeds typically form the bulk of their diet. One researcher concluded, apparently after exhaustive study, that their favorite foods are scrambled eggs, macaroni and cheese, raw carrots, and cooked corn. Among their least favorites are beets, peaches, and celery. If brown rats are particularly hungry or can't find their favorite foods, they will eat soap, paper, and beeswax. Brown rats will sometimes even hunt together as a pack and prey on poultry and young animals as large as baby sheep.

Besides the eggs and chicks of the nesting birds, rats found ample food on Ailsa Craig in the carcasses of young gannets which had fallen from their nests and older gannets killed while fighting.

Rabbits were also found to be an excellent food source, and the rabbits could reproduce nearly as quickly as the rats. It was almost like being raised in a lab for the rats, with a constant and reliable source of food and virtually no natural enemies.

The outnumbered lighthouse keepers and their dogs tried desperately to keep up with the rats. On December 11, 1889, forty-eight rats were killed on the island in a single day. In the last three months of 1890, the lighthouse keepers recorded killing more than 900 rats, with the dog killing a hundred more. In November 1890, the keeper's dog alone killed fifty-nine in a single day. Regardless, the keepers and their dogs simply could not keep up with the growing population of rats. The rats decimated the bird population, most particularly the puffins, which nest in burrows on the ground where their eggs and chicks make easy prey for a hungry brown rat. Eventually, the puffins simply gave up and completely abandoned Ailsa Craig as a nesting site.

In the early 1990s, scientists set out to eradicate the brown rats, save the few remaining resident birds, and entice the puffins to return. They placed five tons of wheat laced with Warfarin in cracks and crevices all over the entire island, where it was accessible to the rats but out of reach of the birds. Within a year, all of the rats were dead. The last live rat sighting on Ailsa Craig was on April 15, 1991.

The puffins did eventually return, but it took more than a decade. The first successfully mating puffins were reported in 2002, eleven years after the last rat was killed and sixty-seven years after the rats had forced them to flee Ailsa Craig. There were ten pairs of puffins in 2004, 130 pairs by 2015, and hundreds more now.

Today, in addition to the puffins, there are reported to be twenty-five pairs of black guillemot; eighty pairs of fulmar; eighty pairs of great black-backed gulls; 140 pairs of shag; 200 pairs of lesser black-backed gulls; 300 pairs of herring gulls; 900 pairs of kittiwake;

1,200 pairs of razorbills; 12,000 pairs of guillemot; and 40,000 pairs of gannets. Having finally been lured back to Ailsa Craig with the elimination of the rats, the birds may soon be forced to leave yet again as the water temperatures rise in the firth and the North Atlantic Ocean, chasing the birds' food supply of herring, hake, and capelin farther north.

Chapter 10

The Castle, Caves, Chapel(s), and Quarries

A ilsa Castle, sitting atop a rock ledge 300 feet above the sea, was built in the 1500s on the eastern side of Ailsa Craig, facing mainland Scotland. No one seems to know exactly when the castle was built, most likely in the early part of the century, or even why it was built, but it was later used to protect the island from a possible invasion by King Philip II of Spain, who had designs on making Scotland a Catholic nation. The feared invasion never happened, though. Today, the only way to approach what remains of the castle, and not much of it remains other than the tower, is via a steep, narrow footpath. Even though the castle sits on a rock island in the sea ten miles from shore, there are two freshwater springs nearby – the Castle Well, which serviced the castle and the Horse Well, which served the lighthouse.

Remnants of the castle tower are the only part of the castle still relatively intact, reaching a height of thirty-nine feet at the wall walk. There was once a kitchen in the basement of the castle, as well as a spiral staircase which wound up through the castle's tower, and there was an adjoining building on the north side. Three cinquefoils, or five-sided coats of arms, remain on the tower, indicating that the castle belonged to the House of Hamilton in the 1580s.

Other than to protect the island from King Philip II, very little is known about the castle's history. Since the island of Ailsa Craig served as a prison at times during the 18th and 19th centuries, part of the castle was likely used to house the prisoners. One of the reasons that so little is known about the castle's history is that Ailsa Craig has never been inhabited, other than by the lighthouse keepers, some seasonal quarrymen, smugglers, and the prisoners, none of whom had much motivation to keep detailed records about the history of a crumbling castle.

In 1597, not long after the castle was built, the island was seized by Hugh (or Hew) Barclay of Ladyland, a Roman Catholic who was clandestinely involved in the scheme to aid King Philip II in re-establishing Catholicism in Scotland. The plan involved using Ailsa Craig as a waypoint and supply depot for the king's eventual invasion of Scotland. Andrew Knox, the Protestant Minister of Paisley, got wind of the plot and took a party of twenty men to Ailsa Craig to confront Barclay. In the confrontation, Barclay either accidentally fell into the sea and drowned, or, in some tellings, jumped into the sea to kill himself. Either way, Barclay was gone and Ailsa Craig was saved from serving as part of King Philip's plot.

There are dozens of small and large caves all around Ailsa Craig, including Water Cave, Goat Cave, Mermaid's Cave, and Swine Cave. The most famous, MacNall's Cave, on the south side of the island, was allegedly home to a notorious smuggler named MacNall, or MacAnall. It is a large cave, more than one-hundred feet long and twenty feet high, perfectly suited and well-located for concealing contraband. MacNall used it to hide and then transport smuggled goods to the Scottish mainland.

In the mid-1800s, a group of men were shoveling years' worth of guano from MacNall's Cave. There are two reasonably plausible explanations for exactly why people would be shoveling guano from an island cave. The first is that guano had been discovered to be an excellent fertilizer, due to its high nitrogen, potassium, and phosphate content, and the men were collecting it for sale as part of the thriving global guano trade. The second is that guano can be used to make gunpowder, which would have been very useful to those mining the quarries on Ailsa Craig. While collecting the guano, the men uncovered two stone coffins containing skeletons. Reverend Lawson in his 1888 book speculates that one of them may have been MacNall himself, which makes for a nice tale, although there is little proof that the remains were actually his.

Goat Cave and Swine Cave were given their names for the animals penned there by the quarrymen and the lighthouse keepers, who used the animals for meat and milk. How Mermaid Cave got its name remains a mystery, for surely there were no mermaids to be found on Ailsa Craig.

There still exist the ruins of at least one, and possibly two, chapels on Ailsa Craig. The first is on lower ground, not far from the lighthouse, and there, too, were found human remains. In the late 1800s, four stone coffins containing skeletons were discovered at the chapel. It is rumored that two of the skulls were sold to curiosity seekers. The second chapel, near the summit, was most likely used as a place of prayer by seamen and fishermen setting out on, or returning from, their journeys. From the summit, one can see the firth to the east, the Atlantic Ocean as far as the eye can see to the west, and the firmament stretching into the heavens above. Little is left of this second chapel, but one can imagine the prayers offered for those who never returned from the sea. Reverend Lawson did not mention this second chapel or record it as he mapped the island.

Although Reverend Lawson did not record the chapel atop the island on his map or in his book, others fervently maintain that it was real and was used centuries ago. Even if it is not a chapel, which I truly believe that it is, it is most assuredly a sacred and holy place, at least to me. I had to see it for myself.

Other than the castle, the chapels, and the lighthouse and quarry infrastructure, Ailsa Craig is seemingly not much more than a small granite island with a few weeds, wildflowers, and hundreds of thousands of birds. It remains largely what it has been for millions of years since the volcano cooled.

The intersection of curling and Ailsa Craig is found in the two quarries currently located on the island. It is universally agreed that the best curling stones in the world all originate from those quarries – one on the north side and the other on the south side of the island. Those quarries have yielded the blue hone and common green granite used to make curling stones for at least two centuries. No one knows who first discovered that Ailsa Craig granite was perfect for making curling stones, but curlers around the world owe an enormous debt of gratitude to whoever it may have been.

The first known mention of Ailsa Craig curling stones that I found in my exhaustive research into curling's history is in Sir Richard Broun's book, *Memorabilia Curliana Mabenensia*, published in 1830, which references 200 Ailsa Craig curling stones being shipped to Canada, where by that time they were the preferred stones. In 1833, John Cairnie referred to harvesting granite for curling stones from Ailsa Craig in his *Essay on Curling and Artificial Pond Making*.

Curling stone production increased dramatically in the 1880s as the sport, and especially the stones that it is played with, became standardized after the formation of the Royal Caledonian Curling Club and the adoption of uniform rules. During this time, the quarries were leased to Andrew Girvan, who aggressively produced and marketed Ailsa Craig curling stones. By 1890, Andrew Girvan was manufacturing between 1,000 and 1,400 stones per year from Ailsa Craig granite. Andrew Girvan would cut the granite into cylindrical blocks, called cheeses, fourteen inches in diameter and weighing eighty to one-hundred pounds each, and ship them ashore for finishing and polishing. Andrew Girvan leased the quarries and harvested the granite for more than six decades, until 1952, employing up to thirty men in the quarries during the summer months, when they would live on the island. Although the Ailsa Craig granite is most uniquely suited to making curling stones, in the past it was also used in church buildings, paving, and walls. Today, it is far too valuable and scarce for such pedestrian uses.

When Andrew Girvan stopped his quarrying operation in the 1950s, the quarrymen took their leftover dynamite and leveled their living quarters before departing the island. Not all of them left, though, at least according to legend. It is said that one man – Ben Gunn – refused to leave with the others and lived out his remaining days on Ailsa Craig as a hermit. Curiously, it was the character Ben Gunn who was marooned in *Treasure Island,* the classic novel by Robert Louis Stevenson, author and member of the Stevenson family, the most famous lighthouse engineers in the world and the builders of the lighthouse on Ailsa Craig.

In the early days of quarrying on Ailsa Craig, nature did much of the work. Sufficient boulders and blocks of granite had fallen from the cliffs to the shore below so that no blasting or working away at the cliffs by man was necessary. All that the quarrymen needed to do, which in itself was very difficult and dangerous work, was to harvest the granite which nature had deposited on the ground. Large boulders were split by hand using a "plug and feather" technique, which experienced quarrymen used to split the boulders into a more manageable size.

Quarrying on Ailsa Craig was a seasonal activity which was conducted in the warmer months and continued to be such into the 1960s. Larger stones were lifted by crane onto bogies, while smaller ones were loaded by hand, for transport along one of the two primitive railways on the island, mostly powered by men and horses. All of the annual quarrying stopped by 1971. During the time when annual quarrying was still taking place, the quarrymen lived on Ailsa Craig in stone quarters, with married men living in one building and single men living in another. For the past seventy years, Andrew Kay & Company Ltd. has owned the exclusive rights to harvest Ailsa Craig granite, with blue hone granite harvested from the North Quarry and common green granite from the South Quarry.

Today, quarrying is only conducted between the months of September and November in order to avoid breeding seasons and endangering the avian and seal populations, and granite is only harvested over the course of a week or two roughly once a decade. Only a predetermined quantity of granite is to be harvested each time. The most recent harvest occurred in late 2022, when Kays Curling harvested 600 tons of granite, more common green than blue hone, enough to meet projected curling stone demand for the next decade. For the first time since 1970, the granite had to be blasted from the cliffs rather than simply picked up from the shore. Blasting was by deflagration, a far less explosive method than detonation, to less disturb the wildlife. The next granite harvesting will not take place until sometime around the year 2030.

Having learned about the granite harvesting, I needed to learn how an Ailsa Craig curling stone is actually made. As I came to learn, making an Ailsa Craig curling stone is not as simple as one might think. You can't just take a chunk of granite, machine and polish it until it's round, and have a curling stone. In fact, you need two pieces of granite to make one proper Ailsa Craig curling stone – one piece of blue hone and a larger piece of common green.

Blue hone granite is the most impervious to water penetration and is used to make the running surface of the stone, which is the part that actually comes into contact with the ice. It is machined and inserted into the base of the larger piece of common green, which makes up the bulk of the curling stone. The blue hone insert in the base of the stone is actually concave, so that only a round band, less than one-half of an inch wide, actually touches the ice, resulting in far less friction than if the entire bottom of the stone touched the ice. The running surface of a curling stone appears very similar to the bottom of a coffee cup. The common green granite, on the other hand, is the part of the stone making contact and absorbing tens of thousands of collisions with other stones over the course of a stone's thirty, forty, or even fifty-year lifetime.

Ailsa Craig granite is not the *only* granite used for making curling stones, although it is considered to be the finest. In fact, the only stones which are allowed at the Olympics and in sanctioned World Curling Federation events are Ailsa Craig stones. Nonetheless, other granite can make a passable curling stone. Trefor Quarry in Wales, for example, is also a source of granite for some of the curling stones being made today. There have been upwards of a dozen quarries in Scotland providing granite for curling stones over the decades. The quarry at Craighead Farm, for instance, produced granite which at one time was used for curling stones. James Brown, however, in his *History of the Sanquhar Curling Society*, wrote of Craighead curling stones, "A great drawback to their general adoption is their great brittleness. Some do stand well; but, as a rule they are easily broken."

Just as different kinds of granite have been used to make stones, so, too, have there have been different manufacturers. Kays Curling was by no means the only curling stone maker in Scotland. In the very early 1900s, Thomas Thorburn was making curling stones in Beith, which he claimed in his advertising were, "known all over Canada and [the] United States, and at home his Stones are known and admired by all curlers in every little town and village, and played with by LORDS AND LADIES."

Kays Curling, however, with a monopoly on the finest curling stone granite in the world, dominates the market. Kays stones do not come cheaply. Nor do any other curling stones, for that matter. Sixteen stones, enough for two teams to play a game, cost upwards of $12,000 for a single set. Olympic quality stones cost a hefty $16,000 per set.

In May 2011, the castle, and indeed the entire island of Ailsa Craig, was placed for sale for 2.5 million pounds, or approximately 4 million dollars. Two years later, finding no takers, the asking price was reduced to 1.5 million pounds. There were still no takers, and Ailsa Craig today remains the property of David Kennedy, the 9th Marquess of Ailsa and the hereditary Clan Chief of the Clan Kennedy, except for the five acres which comprise the lighthouse grounds, which are owned by the Northern Lighthouse Board.

Chapter 11

The Wickies

Some men found serenity and peace as lighthouse keepers, some men found something else. And it was almost exclusively men who served as lighthouse keepers. Even more specifically, it was usually married men who were keepers. The Northern Lighthouse Board in Edinburgh, which regulated all of the lighthouses in Scotland, preferred married men as lighthouse keepers, believing that they were of a more stable and reliable character than single men. Bachelors were only occasionally admitted into the fraternity, mostly out of necessity.

After the Ailsa Craig Lighthouse was completed in 1886, the lamp burned oil for the first twenty-five years, before converting to incandescence. Before automation took over a century later, rendering the lighthouse keepers obsolete, the lighthouse had to be staffed twenty-four hours a day, every single day of the year. Lighthouse keepers, who were known as "wickies," had the often lonely and always difficult job of seeing that the light shone brightly every single night. They came to be called wickies because one of their main jobs was to trim and maintain the wick which burned the oil, so that it burned cleaner and more efficiently. A properly tended wick meant that less soot would cloud the enormous windows and lenses in the lantern room atop the lighthouse tower.

The lighthouse on Ailsa Craig was usually staffed by two, or even three people at a time, at least in the months when the nights were long. In December, there is as little as seven hours of daylight on Ailsa Craig between the 8:45 a.m. sunrise and 3:45 p.m. sunset. Since Northern Lighthouse Board regulations required that the light burn from before sunset until after sunrise, on the longest nights that meant more than seventeen consecutive hours of maintaining the light – an impossible task for a single man and a herculean one even for two. In the summer months, though, the night lasted just six-and-a-half hours, meaning that the light only had to be burning for seven hours, which could be managed by a single, diligent, experienced wickie.

The duties of the wickies on Ailsa Craig were repetitive, difficult, and often dangerous, as they were at all lighthouses. These duties were basically the same as at lighthouses all around the world. One might think that a keeper could simply flip a switch and the light would come on and rotate, but that was very far from the case in the late 1800s. In addition to the constant trimming of the wick, wickies had to replenish the oil; clean and polish the lenses every day, since the smoke from the fire left them covered in soot; clean the windows of the lantern room every day; raise and lower the lantern room blinds; and wind the clockworks which spun the lenses. In addition to all of the duties related to the light itself, the wickies had to tend to the two foghorns, polish the brass, sweep the floors and stairs, paint the lighthouse tower as needed, make any repairs to the roof and buildings, clean and maintain chimneys to avoid fires, clean and lime the privy, prepare their meals, and keep detailed and accurate logs of the weather and supplies. Above all else, and without exception or excuse, a lighthouse keeper was required at all times to "keep a good light." Failure to do so was the most egregious dereliction of duty.

One of the reasons why lighthouses always had to have a keeper on watch and awake was to wind the clockworks, which are much like the mechanism in a grandfather's clock. Attached to a chain, and hanging like a pendulum, was a heavy weight, usually made of iron. The chain itself wrapped around a barrel, or spindle, and gravity did the rest, spinning the gears which drove the lenses to rotate. In order to reduce friction, Fresnel lenses, like the one at the Ailsa Craig lighthouse, used a pool of mercury upon which to rotate. Depending in part on the height of the lighthouse and in part on the corresponding length of the clockworks chain, the clockworks had to be wound every thirty or forty minutes at most lights in order to keep the lamp spinning. By constructing the lenses with different patterns and by controlling the rate at which the clockworks spun the lenses, each lighthouse created its own unique characteristic, enabling ships to identify exactly which lights they were seeing and precisely where they were.

In some lighthouses, like the one at Skerryvore in Scotland, the chain hung straight down through the center of the tower, through the kitchen and bedrooms. In others, it hung down a shaft in the lighthouse tower wall. One of the reasons that lighthouses had to be tall, in addition to making them easier to see from greater distances, was to accommodate the clockworks.

Daily weather checks were required to be sent from all rock and island lighthouses to the nearest on-shore station. Lighthouse keepers were some of the best weather forecasters in the world and had to learn a strict numeric system for reporting winds ranging from dead calm to hurricane force. They learned to read the clouds, sea conditions, and the dreaded fog.

Throughout Scotland, most lighthouses are within sight of at least one – and usually several – other lighthouses. Every night at midnight, in the days when keepers still tended the lights, the keeper on watch was required to check every other lighthouse within eyesight to confirm that it was lit and had to enter the information into the log. That way, not only was the operation of a particular light confirmed, but the vigilance of each keeper was also monitored. If two keepers reported a light to be off, and one reported it to be on, the Commissioners would know that one of the keepers hadn't really checked and was derelict in his duties. Such an offense would lead to swift discipline or termination, for the Commissioners would know that such a man could not to be trusted to faithfully perform his duties.

Some of the greatest dangers to keepers, of which there were many, came with snow, ice, sleet, and freezing rain. Since there could never be any obstruction of the light, nor any diminishing of its intensity, keepers were required to go outside to the narrow gallery walkway which encircled the lantern room and remove any snow or ice from the enormous window panes. With one hand holding the railing and the other scraping away at the snow and ice, the keeper slowly made his way around the tower, usually at night and in the face of fierce wind. In a great storm, no sooner had the keeper navigated around the tower clearing the windows than he would have to start around again, repeating the process.

The Northern Lighthouse Board in Edinburgh was established in 1786 to protect those navigating the waters around Scotland and the Isle of Man. The Board operates and maintains more than 200 lighthouses. Wickies of old derogatorily referred to the Northern Lighthouse Board as "84," a reference to its address at 84 George Street in Edinburgh. Rightly or wrongly, most keepers were absolutely convinced that a Commissioner would not survive even twenty-four hours working as a wickie.

The Board has preserved hundreds of thousands of photographs, drawings, plans, logs, and other records from its lighthouses, including the lighthouse on Ailsa Craig. One of the documents is a list of all of the keepers of the lighthouse on Ailsa Craig.

Some worked very briefly, others over a much longer time. The first three were Malcolm Campbell (1886-1888), Cuthbert Urquhart (1888-1889), and Alexander Thomson (1889-1926).

Alexander Thomson was certainly the most noted and revered keeper of the Ailsa Craig lighthouse. He was the Principal Lighthouse Keeper on the island of Ailsa Craig for more than three decades, a remarkable service record for anyone at any light, particularly an offshore one. He succeeded Cuthbert Urquhart in the summer of 1889, under extremely difficult and unusual circumstances. Thomson was the first man known to have gotten married on Ailsa Craig. A sober man of upright and stoic bearing, he was inclined to neither lengthy discourse, imaginations, fancy, nor exaggeration. If he said it or wrote it, he believed every word to be absolutely true.

Alexander Thomson was renowned, at least in the world of lighthouse keepers, for his minutely detailed, elegantly written, keeper's logs. On August 7, 1909, he wrote of being startled at 0320 hours, while in the lantern room, by noises which seemed to come from the kitchen two floors below the light. Thinking that it was simply the wind, or perhaps the dog, he continued meticulously trimming the wick, as he did several times every night. The light was his first priority, not investigating a random noise.

Minutes later, he heard what he thought was the sound of metal crashing to the floor from below. Startled once again, but now finished with the more immediate and important duty of tending to the wick, he made his way down the spiral stairs to the tower's small kitchen. Descending the final steps, he wrote of coming upon a "specter of what appeared to be a young maiden, sobbing, and cleaving to several red flowers, appearing to be roses."

"I felt no fear," he continued, "but rather an abiding sense of sorrow and pity. She said nothing and then she was gone, I know not where to, even before I alighted from the stair." Thomson knew that anyone reading his log might suspect that he was mad, but he recorded everything in his logs, and he recorded everything accurately. If anyone actually bothered to read the logs and thought him to be mad, so be it. He had seen what he had seen.

Thomson had been a keeper long enough to have heard all of the haunted lighthouse stories. Nearly every lighthouse in Scotland, and in England, Ireland, and Wales, for that matter, was rumored to be frequented by spirits, ghosts, bogeys, or wraiths of some kind. Thomson gave little credence to any of it. The most notorious haunting is of the lighthouse on Eilean Mor, which is reportedly frequented by the ghosts of three wickies who disappeared without a trace in December of 1910. Subsequent keepers reported hearing voices crying out the names of the three doomed men. What happened to the three keepers on Eilean Mor is unknown to this very day, although plenty of theories still abound.

On December 15, 1910, the *Archtor*, on a passage from Philadelphia to Edinburgh, made a notation in its log that the Flannan Isles Lighthouse on Eilean Mor stood dark. Upon docking, the crew of the *Archtor* reported the Flannan Isles Lighthouse situation to the Commissioners of the Northern Lighthouse Board. At the time, the light was kept by three men – James Ducat, Thomas Marshall, and Donald McArthur – good, sober, and reliable keepers all. It was not until the day after Christmas that the lighthouse tender vessel the *Hesperus* was able to finally reach the island, having been unable to sail due to dangerous weather and seas. There was no flag on the lighthouse flagpole and none of the keepers were at the dock to greet the *Hesperus*, as would have been the proper protocol. The captain of the *Hesperus* blew the whistle and fired a flare. There was still no response.

The relief keeper, Joseph Moore, reluctantly went ashore to investigate. He found that the gate to the lighthouse compound was closed, but unlocked, as was the door to the lighthouse itself. Inside, he found all of the beds unmade and the clocks unwound. One set of oilskins was found, belonging to McArthur, who had obviously left the lighthouse without them. A meticulous search of the island revealed not a trace of any of the three keepers. Their sudden and complete disappearance from the island has never been fully explained. Perhaps a rogue wave had taken all of them, or pirates had kidnapped them, or a sea serpent consumed them, or perhaps they had fled the island together of their own accord. The story of the mysterious vanishing was recorded in verse by the poet Wilfred Wilson Gibson:

Flannan Isle

Though three men dwell on Flannan Isle
To keep the lamp alight,
As we steered under the lee, we caught
No glimmer of the night!

A passing ship at dawn had brought
The news; and quickly we set sail,
To find out what strange thing might all
The keepers of the deep-sea light.

But, as we near'd the lonely Isle;
And look'd up at the naked height;
And saw the lighthouse towering white,
With blinded lantern, that all night
Had never shot a spark
Of comfort through the dark,

So ghastly in the cold sunlight
It seem'd that we were stuck the while
With wonder all too dread for words.

And, as into the tiny creek
We stole beneath the hanging crag,
We saw three queer, black, ugly birds -
Too big, by far, in my belief,
For guillemot or shag –
Like seamen sitting bold upright
Upon a half-tide reef;
But, as we near'd, they plunged from sight,
Without a sound, or spurt of white.

And still too mazed to speak,
We landed; and made fast the boat;
And climb'd the track in single file,
Each wishing he was safe afloat,
On any sea, however far,
So it be from Flannan Isle.
Yet, all too soon, we reached the door –
The black, sun-blister'd, lighthouse door,
That gaped for us ajar.

Yet, as we crowded through the door,
We only saw a table, spread
For dinner, meat and cheese and bread;
But all untouch'd; and no one there:
As though, when they sat down to eat,
Ere they could even taste,
Alarm had come; and they in haste

Had risen and left the bread and meat:
For on the table-head a chair
Lay tumbled on the floor.
We listen'd; but we only heard
The feeble chirping of a bird
That starved upon its perch:
And listening still, without a word,
We set about our hopeless search.

We hunted high, we hunted low,
And soon ransack'd the empty house;
Then o'er the island, to and fro,
We ranged, to listen and to look
In every cranny, cleft or nook
That might have hid a bird or mouse.

Aye: though we hunted high and low,
And hunted everywhere,
Of the three men's fate we found no trace
Of any kind in any place,
But a door ajar, and an untouch'd meal
And an overtoppled chair.

And, as we listen'd in the gloom
Of that forsaken living-room –
O chill clutch on our breath –
We thought how ill-chance came to all
Who kept the Flannan Light;
And how the rock had been the death
Of many a likely lad;
How six had come to a sudden end

And three had gone stark mad:
And one whom we'd all known as a friend
Had leapt from the lantern one still night,
And fallen dead by the lighthouse wall:
And long we thought
On the three we sought,
And of what yet might befall.

Like curs a glance has brought to heel,
We listen'd, flinching there:
And look'd, and look'd, on the untouched meal
And the overtoppled chair.

We seem'd to stand for an endless while,
Though still no word was said
Three men alive on Flannan Isle,
Who thought on three men dead.

While the Flannan Isles Lighthouse has the most mysterious past, Wicklow Head Lighthouse in Ireland is also famous for its haunting. Wicklow Head is supposedly frequented by a headless woman roaming the grounds. It is rumored that the woman's boyfriend beheaded her with a slash hook or scythe when he discovered that she was in love with another man. At Kinneard Head Castle Lighthouse in Scotland, the owner, Alexander Fraser, Laird of Philorth, had one of his servant pipers imprisoned below the castle in the Selches Hole after the laird's daughter, Isobel, fell in love with him. When the piper drowned in the prison below the castle during a storm, Isobel, overwhelmed with grief, jumped to her death from the castle wall. Some visitors now claim that they hear the piper playing in his cell and others report seeing Isobel herself. Of course, despite all of the stories and sightings, we all know that lighthouses aren't really haunted. Or at least we're fairly sure that they aren't.

Most of the stories of lighthouse keepers going mad from the loneliness and the solitary life on a rock or island are apocryphal. It was a hard life, for sure, and at times a very lonely life, but those who kept the lights were made of pretty stern stuff for the most part. And most didn't serve at lighthouses alone. Those who served on shore or on larger islands usually had their families with them, and those who served on rocks or uninhabited islands were usually there with one or two other keepers and on relatively short stints of two or four weeks at a time. The far greater danger came from being injured or killed in a fight with a fellow keeper, or from an accident, or from mercury poisoning, not from madness, although a few did, indeed, go quite mad. The galleries atop lighthouse towers made enticing and ultimately irresistible jumping points for those who could no longer cope.

After World War II, the Northern Lighthouse Board drew up detailed instructions for keepers to follow in the event of a nuclear war. The instructions were kept in safes at the lighthouses, with only the Principal Lighthouse Keeper at each lighthouse knowing the combination. The keepers were under strict orders not to look at the instructions unless there actually was a nuclear war, and they were required to sign a document confirming that they would comply with the Official Secrets Act. How many keepers, overcome by a morbid curiosity on a late night, or after one last whiskey, have secretly read the instructions, no one knows. None have ever dared to reveal their contents.

During the latter part of the twentieth century, lighthouses were increasingly being automated and operated remotely, including the lighthouse on Ailsa Craig. Perhaps this is a safer, more efficient, and more cost-effective way to operate them, perhaps not. Lighthouses are also increasingly being abandoned, rendered obsolete by GPS and satellite navigation. Some have been demolished or have become ruined through neglect. Many have been lovingly and painstakingly preserved by nonprofit lighthouse foundations. With their automation, abandonment, and ruin, a way of life has been lost forever to the past.

The wickies are all gone now. No modern lighthouses need to have their oil replenished, their wicks trimmed, or their clockworks wound. Wickies are a thing of the past, a vestige of a different time and place and way of life, rendered forever obsolete by the relentless advance of technology and automation. Their stories and legends now live on mostly in poems, books, and museums. A few former wickies are still with us to tell their stories, but the last of them will soon be gone, too. Whether or not the consignment of the wickies to history is a good thing will be left for the historians and philosophers and poets to debate. On March 31, 1988, the last lighthouse keeper in Scotland, a man named Bill Gault, manually turned off the light at Fair Isle South Lighthouse for the final time.

Chapter 12

The Ailsa Craig Lighthouse

M olly and I loved the lighthouses in Maine and visited them as often as we could, sometimes planning entire days around lighthouse visits. We cherished their beauty and majesty and their silent, constant vigilance in protecting those at sea. They spoke to us of a different time and a different way of life. Of course, we also thoroughly enjoyed the tales of hauntings, despite our mutual skepticism about the veracity of those tales. After Molly was gone, learning about the lighthouse on Ailsa Craig and the history of Scottish lighthouses fascinated me. In particular, it was the one recorded mention of the Ailsa Craig lighthouse's haunting, by keeper Alexander Thomson, and his encounter with the spirit of an anguished young maiden on the night of August 7, 1909, that stayed with me.

In 1881, the Scottish Shipmasters Association formally requested that the Commissioners of Northern Lighthouses, also known as the Northern Lighthouse Board, build a lighthouse and install two fog signals on Ailsa Craig. Following the Commissioners' approval, five acres on Ailsa Craig were purchased by the Commissioners and construction of a lighthouse began the next year. Construction was under the supervision of legendary lighthouse engineers Thomas and David Stevenson. The Stevensons were the premier lighthouse builders in Scotland, if not the world, throughout the 1800s and early 1900s. Of Scotland's more than 200 lighthouses, half are

Stevenson family lighthouses. Thomas Stevenson was also the father of Robert Louis Stevenson, the Scottish writer best known for his books *Treasure Island, Strange Case of Dr. Jekyll and Mr. Hyde,* and *Kidnapped.* Some of Robert Louis Stevenson's inspiration for his writing came from time spent at remote locations at sea with his father.

The Stevensons earned their reputation in part by successfully building the oldest rock lighthouse in Great Britain in the early 1800s. A rock lighthouse is one which sits not along the coast or on an island, but on an outcrop of rock in the sea. Robert Stevenson, the patriarch of the Stevenson family lighthouse dynasty, was the engineer who oversaw construction of the Bell Rock Lighthouse, also known as Inchcape Lighthouse, twelve miles east of Dundee in the North Sea. Construction of the 115-foot-tall lighthouse was immensely complicated by the fact that the rock on which it was built was only exposed at low tide and for just four hours per day. At all other times, it was under water and virtually invisible, which is what made the rock so treacherous to ships and had caused so many to wreck. Nonetheless, Stevenson successfully constructed the lighthouse, an engineering marvel which still stands today. Bell Rock Lighthouse was first lit on February 1, 1811. It took brave, hard men, some of whom were lost in the effort, three years to build Bell Rock Lighthouse.

A series of shipwrecks at Ailsa Craig had sparked the request for the Stevensons to build a lighthouse and install foghorns. On January 19, 1870, the paddle steamer *Duke of Edinburgh* ran aground at Ailsa Craig, although no lives were lost. The cargo ship *Clan Campbell* wrecked on January 18, 1881. The *Barbalta*, the *Ariel*, the *Nith*, the *Cynthia*, and the *James* had all wrecked at the island before the lighthouse was built.

On October 15, 1884, while the Ailsa Craig lighthouse was still under construction, the cargo ship *Austria* wrecked on the island. According to one account, "Between the dodgy course set by Captain Helig (who retired below to keep company with a bottle) and the smoke from the funnel impairing the vision of Second Mate James Morris, who had been left in charge, the catastrophe was only a matter of time." Some speculate that the first rats swam ashore from the *Austria*, or maybe they came later, from another wreck, but they came.

On the night of June 15, 1886, the lighthouse on Ailsa Craig was put into service for the first time. At first, it burned gas from coal, and later paraffin, until it converted to incandescent in 1911. The gas was manufactured right on the island and was stored in two nearby gasometers. Thomas Stevenson's original light shone on Ailsa Craig for nearly twenty-five years, although Stevenson himself passed away less than a year after the lighthouse went into service.

The lighthouse on Ailsa Craig was originally fitted with a third-order Fresnel lens. Fresnel lenses were invented by French physicist Augustin-Jean Fresnel in the 1820s, and consist of a ring of prisms arranged in a dome which reflects refracted light. The creation of the Fresnel lens was undoubtedly the single greatest advancement in the history of lighthouse technology. Many lighthouses today still employ their Fresnel lenses. So beautiful and groundbreaking were Fresnel lenses that hundreds have been preserved in lighthouses and museums around the world.

A third-order Fresnel lens, such as the one installed at Ailsa Craig, consists of 252 cut glass prisms, is enormous – five feet tall and seven feet in diameter – and weighs more than two-and-a-half tons. First and second-order Fresnel lenses are even larger. A third-order beam can be seen all the way to the horizon, twenty miles away. Fresnel lenses were in wide use in lighthouses for nearly a century, with virtually every lighthouse in the world at some time employing a Fresnel lens. The original Ailsa Craig third-order Fresnel lens now resides at the Museum of Scottish Lighthouses in Fraserburgh. After Molly's death and my introduction to the world of curling, I made a special trip to Fraserburgh to see the original Ailsa Craig Fresnel lens, although it was much more than idle curiosity which led me there.

The other significant innovation of the Fresnel lens was its ability to produce a variety of patterns, known as characteristics, depending on the speed at which the clockworks rotated the lens and the number of flash panels in the lens. With each lighthouse utilizing a Fresnel lens designed to have a different characteristic, mariners could tell exactly where they were from a great distance away. Individual lighthouse characteristics included the number of flashes per minute, the number of beams, and the color of the beams. All of the characteristics relating to the light itself are referred to as the nightmarks. The patterns painted on the towers and the towers' shapes, recognizable in the daylight, are known as the daymarks. The Fresnel lens has been called "the invention that saved a million ships."

One of the two foghorns which were installed along with the lighthouse was placed on the northern end of Ailsa Craig, near Swine Cave, while the other was installed on the south end, at East Trammins. The foghorns were massive, taller than a person, and were powered by compressed air from gas engines located near the lighthouse. The same two foghorns were used until 1966, when they were retired in favor of a single Tyfon horn, located to the southeast of the lighthouse. The Tyfon horn itself was ultimately discontinued in 1987, when modern navigational equipment rendered a foghorn on the island unnecessary. Both of the original foghorns now stand silent, rusting, and abandoned on Ailsa Craig, as do the compressed air cylinders, their decades of faithful service no longer required.

One of the pipelines, which fed the compressed air to the northern foghorn near Swine Cave, still survives as well.

On January 24, 1911, the beacon at the lighthouse was converted from oil-burning to incandescent, at the same time that the two compressed-air fog signals were converted from gas to oil-powered engines. The foghorns sounded in bursts of three three-second blasts every forty-five seconds, giving the foghorns, like the beacon, their own unique characteristic, recognizable to nearby ships.

Of all the tribulations that lighthouse keepers had to endure, and there were many, fog may have been the most maddening and unwelcome. With fog meant foghorns, sometimes sounding day and night for hours, or even days, on end. There was no way to escape the noise. Peter Hill, in *Stargazing: Memoirs of a Young Lighthouse Keeper*, describes the rhythm that keepers learned in order to have a conversation while foghorns were blasting. So loud were the two horns on Ailsa Craig that the residents of Girvan, ten miles away across the firth, regularly complained to the Northern Lighthouse Board about the noise.

The lighthouse was completely automated in 1989, and the lighthouse keepers left for good, leaving Ailsa Craig uninhabited, save for the birds and seals. Finally, years after keepers were no longer needed, the lighthouse was converted to solar power in 2001.

Before telephonic communication between the island and the mainland was established in 1935, the lighthouse keepers and the quarrymen relied largely on pigeons to communicate with the mainland. However, if the pigeons couldn't fly because of bad weather or some other exigency, a more primitive system utilizing fires was used to communicate. A single fire built to the south of the lighthouse meant that a doctor was needed at the lighthouse, a single fire built to the north of the lighthouse meant that supplies were needed, and two fires meant that a doctor was needed at the quarry. It was not the fastest way to summon help, but it was the available way.

The modernized Ailsa Craig Lighthouse tower today stands thirty-five feet high and requires thirty-seven steps to ascend. The lighthouse is located at Latitude $55^{\circ}15.109'$N and Longitude $005^{\circ}06.520'$W, its base resting fifty-nine feet above sea level. The beacon flashes a white light every four seconds, with a range of seventeen nautical miles. The rusting remains of a narrow-gauge railway run from the small pier to the lighthouse and to the quarries.

The entire island of Ailsa Craig today is owned by David Thomas Kennedy, the 9th Marquess of Ailsa, and is leased through 2050 to the Royal Society for the Protection of Birds, with the exception of the five acres comprising the lighthouse grounds, which are owned by the Northern Lighthouse Board. Kays Curling owns the exclusive rights to harvest granite from the island, but only under very strict conditions.

Although Ailsa Craig Lighthouse is historic and interesting unto itself, I became far more interested in the men who had served there. One particular man, to be more specific.

In spite of everything that I had learned in my studies of Ailsa Craig – the chapels, the castle, the rats, the birds, the lighthouse, the Stevensons, Fresnel lenses, the smuggler McNall, Hugh Barclay, blue hone granite, the quarrymen, the wickies, the shipwrecks, the foghorns, and the clockworks – I nonetheless knew that my education was far from complete. I knew that there was something more that I needed to learn; that I was *meant* to learn. It was something dark, something maleficent, yet altogether necessary for me to complete my journey.

I was being led to whatever it was that I was destined for. It was neither willful nor against my will; neither intentional nor accidental. It must have been like what a prophet, or even a Chosen One, feels upon realizing that something beyond their control or understanding lay ahead. I accepted what was surely my destiny and waited for it to be fully revealed.

Chapter 13

The Hero

As the Principal Lighthouse Keeper on Ailsa Craig in the summer of 1889, Cuddy Urquhart had little time to interact with the quarrymen. Without an assistant or apprentice, his job had become more difficult, but not unmanageable for the twenty-nine-year-old wickie. With a well-thought-out routine and great discipline, Cuddy was more than able to keep a good light. He was even able, on a few occasions, to take his self-made sailboat, the *Lottie*, out into the firth and sail around Ailsa Craig. From the water, the island seemed far steeper and much more imposing. At his father's request, the Northern Lighthouse Board had delivered the *Lottie* to Ailsa Craig for the summer as a surprise for his son.

Most of Cuddy's waking time was at night, tending to the light, while the quarrymen labored by day, usually in either the North Quarry or the South Quarry. Cuddy's eating and sleeping patterns were also very different from the quarrymen's. The quarrymen prepared their own meals, while Cuddy prepared his own and ate on an entirely different schedule.

On the afternoon of June 10, 1889, just ten days after the Commissioners had left Cuddy to tend the Ailsa Craig lighthouse alone for the summer, the lives and fates of Cuddy Urquhart and the quarrymen intersected. Because the solstice was approaching, with just eight hours of darkness, Cuddy had been left to work the lighthouse alone. The assistants would return in August, when the nights would be getting longer and it would again require more than one man on the light. Cuddy was awakened from his sleep at around three-thirty in the afternoon by the shouts of men running toward the lighthouse from the North Quarry. One of the quarrymen was trapped under a boulder of granite which had rolled onto his left leg, crushing it in a gruesome fashion. Cuddy grabbed the first aid equipment which was issued to every lighthouse by the Northern Lighthouse Board and ran back toward the quarry with the men. The rudimentary first aid kit would prove to be no match for the severity of the man's injuries.

On one of Cuddy's early stints as an apprentice, he was assigned to Girdle Ness Lighthouse in Aberdeen, a Stevenson lighthouse built following the wreck of a whaling ship which killed forty-three of the forty-five men aboard. At Girdle Ness, Cuddy was under the command of a principal keeper who he didn't much care for and had befriended an assistant keeper who he liked very much, John Kincaid. Kincaid was always looking for someone to talk about medicine with at his lighthouse assignments, usually finding absolutely no interest. Cuddy, though, with an intellectual curiosity cultivated mostly by his father, was more than willing to play the student while apprentice John Kincaid was thrilled to have someone who shared his interest in medicine.

John Kincaid had begun his first year of medical studies at the University of Aberdeen School of Medicine, but felt compelled to withdraw after his girlfriend found herself quite unexpectedly expecting. Kincaid signed on with the Northern Lighthouse Board as an apprentice keeper, the first job that he was offered, ending his much-anticipated medical career before it really even started. In the end, Kincaid ended up tending lighthouses for more than forty years and being happily married for fifty. The son whose birth had cut short Kincaid's own medical career grew to become a prominent physician and professor at the University of Aberdeen.

Kincaid took to playing the professor and Cuddy to playing his student. Kincaid always traveled to his lighthouse assignments with his small library of medical texts and journals, hoping to find someone – anyone – interested in discussing medicine. Before meeting Cuddy, Kincaid had never met any keeper, assistant, or apprentice even remotely interested in being his personal medical student. He was thrilled to meet Cuddy, who seemed to enjoy the rigor of studying and learning. Kincaid assigned various readings to Cuddy, who used his solitary time in the lantern room while tending the light, or his little bit of free time during the day, reading, studying, and writing down questions for his "professor." Kincaid excelled as the teacher and Cuddy as the student.

The medical reading and Kincaid's tutoring kept Cuddy's mind occupied with things other than wicks, oil, brass, glass, and clockworks, and he found it to be a welcome intellectual challenge. He particularly enjoyed studying anatomy, dealing with the structure and functions of the human body. It felt like he was actually preparing for a medical career, although it was really no more than an interesting little pastime for two assistant keepers who both hated the arrogant bastard who was serving as the Principal Lighthouse Keeper. The Principal Lighthouse Keeper, for his part, thought them to be fools.

John Kincaid and Cuddy remained friends throughout their entire lives. When Cuddy passed away in 1941, Kincaid, although himself quite frail, escorted his friend to his final place of rest in the Canongate Kirk Graveyard in Edinburgh, where he was buried beside his parents, Bryson and Lottie, and not far from the grave of Bryson's hero, Adam Smith. Also nearby was the resting place of Ebenezer Scroggie, the inspiration for Charles Dickens' character

Ebenezer Scrooge in *A Christmas Carol*. Dickens had noted the gravestone of Ebenezer Scroggie on a visit to the Canongate Kirk Graveyard and had changed the name to Scrooge for his story.

Cuddy's medical "training" proved very valuable, indeed. Upon reaching the injured quarryman, Cuddy immediately knew that summoning a doctor from the mainland by setting two fires as a signal or sending a messenger pigeon and waiting hours for a doctor to arrive would take far more time than the unfortunate man had. Everything about Cuddy's decision was binary – let a man die, or give him a chance; abandon the light, or stay; damn the rules, or obey; do what was right, or what he had been taught. Cuddy instantly made his decision, knowing that he would soon face the unpleasant consequences. He abandoned his light, an unforgivable act which would no doubt cost him his young, very promising career as a wickie.

Several of the quarrymen, using makeshift pry bars, finally freed the man, who was screaming from pain and fright, from under the boulder. Cuddy fashioned a splint, of sorts, from pick handles and strips of cloth, and stabilized the grotesquely shattered leg as best as he could. As he was applying the splint, he shouted instructions to the quarrymen to rig some kind of stretcher. They quickly made one from two poles and a piece of canvas tarpaulin.

Cuddy ran ahead to the dock to prepare for the trip to the mainland while four quarrymen carried the injured man onto the small wooden smack which served as tender for the lighthouse on Ailsa Craig. They shoved off as quickly as they could and headed east across the firth for Girvan, ten miles away, to get medical attention for the dying man. A carrier pigeon had been dispatched to the mainland to request a doctor at the pier.

The sun was getting lower, and Cuddy knew that he should have been preparing to light the beacon, but he was steering the *Whalsay* toward the mainland, far more concerned for the quarryman than for the light. Cuddy had never seen anyone die, nor did he care to. As he was piloting the boat, he was also giving instructions to the two quarrymen who were attending to their friend, who was in a deep shock, cold and pale; his breathing labored and shallow; his pulse weak; and his pupils dilated. Over the noise of the engine, Cuddy instructed the two quarrymen to keep the man still, loosen his clothing, cover him with a blanket, and to continue to apply pressure to the bleeding.

Against long odds, they reached shore in time. Although the injuries cost the man his left leg, he survived. Doctors later told the quarrymen that the man would surely have succumbed to his injuries had he been left on the island to await help. Cuddy Urquhart had managed to save the man's life, but the Ailsa Craig lighthouse had been allowed to stand dark for the first and only time that night, a lighthouse keeper's most egregious and unforgivable sin. He would do the exact same thing again, Cuddy thought to himself, although he would dare not tell that to the Commissioners, who would soon demand Cuddy's appearance at 84 George Street in Edinburgh.

In the early 1800s, Robert Stevenson, who was then the engineer to the Northern Lighthouse Board and who was the premier lighthouse engineer in Scotland, set the standards for the job duties, personal attributes, and behaviors of keepers. Included in those standards was the following:

The lamps shall be kept burning bright and clear every night from sunset to sunrise; and in order that the greatest degree of light may be maintained throughout the night, the Wicks must be trimmed every four hours or, oftener if necessary; and the Keeper who has the first watch shall take care to turn the oil valves so as to let the oil flow into the Burner a sufficient time before lighting.

The Principal Light-keeper is held responsible for the safety and good order of the Stores, Utensils, and Apparatus of what kind soever, and for every thing being put to its proper use, and kept in its proper place. He shall take care that none of the stores or materials are wasted, and shall observe the strictest economy, and the most careful management, yet so as to maintain in every respect the best possible light.

The Light-keepers are also required to take notice of any Shipwreck which shall happen within the district of the Lighthouse, and to enter an account thereof – according to the prescribed form, in a Book furnished to each Station for this purpose; and in such account shall state whether the Light was seen by any one onboard the shipwrecked Vessel.

The Light-keepers are also directed to take care that no smuggled goods are harboured or concealed in any way in or about the Lighthouse premises or grounds.

The Light-keepers are required to be sober and industrious, cleanly in their persons and linens, and orderly in their families. They must conduct themselves with civility to strangers.

The Light-keepers are to appear in their Uniform-dress when any of the Commissioners or Principal Officers visit a station, and also on Sunday; on which day, at noon, the weather permitting, the Lighthouse flag shall be hoisted by the Assistant Light-keeper, or in his absence by the Principal Light-keeper, when it shall remain displayed until sunset.

It is recommended that the Principal Light-keeper shall, every Sunday, perform the service pointed out for the inmates, by reading a portion of the Scriptures, and any other religious book furnished by the Board, and the prayer composed for their use by the Rev. Dr. Brunton.

Notably, and quite purposefully, the duty to save lives was never considered to be part of a wickie's job. Keepers were to keep the light burning, under any and all circumstances, as a warning and as a guide to those at sea. Keepers were actually enjoined from helping those who may have shipwrecked, because it might entail abandoning their light. The rationale, rightly or wrongly, was that many more lives would be endangered if the light were to stand dark than would be saved in a rescue attempt for a single ship. Cuddy knew all of this very well, of course, but nonetheless chose to save the life of a single man.

The Northern Lighthouse Board did, in fact, immediately summon Cuddy to its offices in Edinburgh and supplied an Occasional keeper to Ailsa Craig, "Occasionals" consisting of mainly retired keepers who could be summoned to a light on short notice in case of an emergency. At the disciplinary hearing, Cuddy told the Commissioners exactly what he had done that day in tending to and transporting the injured man to Girvan, that there had been no time to summon help from the mainland, that as a result he knew that the Ailsa Craig light would not be illuminated that night, that he knew that his sole duty was to "keep a good light," and that he was prepared to accept whatever punishment the Board saw fit to impose. He did not take issue with the Board's rules, nor did he try to justify his decision. He knew that what he had done was right and was what he had to do. The foreman for the quarries testified as to how Cuddy had immediately directed the care being provided to the injured man, and how he had swiftly taken him ashore for medical care. The doctor who treated the injured man and amputated his left leg confirmed that the man would have surely died had Cuddy Urquhart not acted as heroically as he did.

The Commissioners, surprisingly, after longer-than-usual deliberation, suspended Cuddy's keeper's license for only thirty days. They would have been completely justified in revoking it permanently, of course, for such a knowing and brazen dereliction of duty. There were several factors, though, some more significant than others, that ultimately influenced their decision. First, they noted that Cuddy had an exemplary record during his tenure at Ailsa

Craig and at all of the other lights where he had served; second, although he had abandoned his light, a man's life had indeed been saved; third, the Board was finding it difficult to recruit, train, and retain keepers, and Cuddy was an otherwise exemplary and reliable one, notwithstanding his recent lapse in judgment; fourth, it was the Commissioners' decision to have only one keeper at Ailsa Craig in the summertime; and fifth, Cuddy was, after all, Bryson Urquhart's son, although the Commissioners neglected to mention that important fact in their findings.

After serving his thirty-day suspension, Cuddy was taken back to Ailsa Craig on July 14, 1889, to relieve the Occasional and to resume his duties there as Principal Lighthouse Keeper. The quarrymen greeted him at the dock and welcomed him back as a hero. He was one of them now, and would remain so forever. The Commissioners would not have approved of the fuss being made by the quarrymen over Cuddy's return to Ailsa Craig.

Although Cuddy didn't know it when he first returned to resume his duties, there was a new resident living on Ailsa Craig. A woman.

Chapter 14

The Broomspiel

S ure enough, the Nae-Sayers were there for the Broomspiel at Broomstones Curling Club in Massachusetts in March, all dressed in their Scottish finest. It had been just one year since I began curling. The annual Broomspiel was both a high point and a low point for curlers in the northeast, a high point because everyone loved curling at Broomstones and a low point because, with the warmer weather approaching, most curling clubs would soon be taking out their ice until the fall. Both my team, the Stoneheads, and Skye's team, the Nae-Sayers, had draws at six o'clock on Friday night, but against different opponents on opposite sides of the ice. We were soundly defeated by the Hearts of Stone from the Cape Cod Curling Club, while the Nae-Sayers made easy work of an arena curling club from Vermont.

We were sitting with the Hearts of Stone, enjoying our complimentary post-game beer and recounting the painful details of our game, which included me, unfortunately, knocking one of our own stones out of the house, thereby gifting the Hearts of Stone two points in the third end. It was not at all uncommon for someone on my team to gift points to our opponent with a terrible shot. I was chatting with the Cape Cod curlers and my teammates, but what I really wanted was to be with Skye Brodie again.

Skye was sitting with the Nae-Sayers at another table in the warm room and treating the Vermonters to their post-game beer when our eyes happened to meet. "Happened to meet" isn't entirely accurate, since we were obviously looking at each other, not merely surveying the room. We hadn't even said hello yet, since we had immediately gone about preparing for our games when we arrived at the club. Finally, Skye got up and came over to chat. We talked about our respective matches, and then she told me that she had brought a copy of her family tree with her and would give it to me in the morning, along with an explanation of its meticulous and elaborate layout and color-coding. I thanked her for remembering and told her that I had been looking forward to seeing it, and to seeing her, as well, a little bit flirtatiously. We talked for a few minutes about the bonspiel and about our curling seasons, which were quickly coming to an end. It really was good to see her again.

The next morning, my team had an early eight o'clock draw in the losers' bracket, a familiar place for us. The Nae-Sayers were more fortunate, not having to get up and play until their ten o'clock draw in the winners' bracket. I said hello to Skye as I stepped off of the ice after our game and she stepped on for hers, after our surprising 8-6 win over the same Vermont arena club team which the Nae-Sayers had easily dispatched the night before. I sat in the warm room nursing a breakfast stout with my teammates and watching the Nae-Sayers' match, along with the other three matches, that were being played on the ice below. Skye was the vice-skip for the Nae-Sayers and was a very good player. I was reminded once again of how nice she looked in her kilt and couldn't help but notice how much she seemed to love playing. Surprisingly, the Nae-Sayers lost their match, surrendering two points in the eighth and final end.

Skye and the rest of the Nae-Sayers found an empty table and sat down with their victorious opponents, in the largely unfamiliar position of being treated to drinks. I sat in the gallery with Rich watching as the next matches began on the ice below. Eventually,

Skye came over and sat next to me, which was not at all an unwelcome event.

"Are you ready to take a look at my amazing family tree?" she asked.

"Sure," I answered. "And I'm sorry you lost your game."

"Let's not talk about that, OK?" she said, "I'm a sore loser." It was said partly in jest, but I could tell that Skye took her bonspiels a lot more seriously than Rich and I took ours.

She went downstairs to the locker room to retrieve her family tree. When she returned, we found an empty table and sat down. Skye unrolled her masterpiece. It was, indeed, something of a work of art. Skye had somehow managed to fit more than 200 names onto a single sheet of poster-sized paper. Almost every entry had a name, date and place of birth, date and place of death, maiden name for the married women, immigration status, and there were even pictures for some of the people. Direct descendants had vertical connecting lines; aunts, uncles, cousins, half-siblings, and assorted other indirect relatives had other connecting lines; each category of relationship had a different color code; and some relatives were traced back more than ten generations into the 1600s. Almost all of them lived in Scotland until some began leaving Europe for the prospect of a better life on the other side of the Atlantic.

I had never realized how important Scottish immigration to the United States was until Skye began educating me. She was unabashedly proud to be Scottish. One-third of the signers of the Declaration of Independence were of Scottish ancestry, she told me. Nine out of the first thirteen governors were also Scottish. Upwards of half of the soldiers in the Revolutionary War were, too. Without Scotland, there would be no United States, she professed. I did not doubt or challenge her. I was happy just to sit next to her and listen.

I wasn't really focusing much on the individual people in Skye's family tree. I was more mesmerized by the meticulous layout, colors, and lines. Skye told me some stories about a couple of the people in recent generations, like her parents and grandparents, how they had ended up in New Brunswick, and how just about every one of them was an accomplished curler. Her family tree was quite different-looking than my collection of names, dates, and notes, and was obviously a labor of love for Skye.

After she finished explaining the layout and structure of her family tree, she rolled it back up, rubber-banded it, placed it back into its cardboard tube, and handed it to me. I didn't notice whether anyone was watching us, but no one had stopped by to see what we were doing, other than a couple of my teammates who stopped to say that they were heading back to the hotel for a couple of hours. Once they left, Skye asked me how my research into my wife's genealogy was going. "By the way, I don't think you ever told me your wife's name," Skye said.

"Molly," I told her. "Her name was Molly." It felt odd to say it.

"I love that name," Skye replied, although her reply seemed off by just a beat, perhaps picking up on my use of the word "was."

I really enjoyed talking to Skye and it felt like there was some kind of commonality with us, a kinship, although that may have simply been a creation of my imagination and loneliness. I admired not only her curling skill, which far exceeded my own, even though I had been practicing diligently, but also her focus, intelligence, and genuine warmth. It had been a long, long time since I had spoken out loud about Molly, and I certainly didn't start the day planning to do so, but in that moment, with just the two of us sitting side-by-side at the table, I told her why I was working on studying Molly's family history. "It just feels like a way of keeping her alive," I said. Skye seemed genuinely surprised. I was really enjoying Skye's company in the moment, and for whatever reason, I felt like she deserved to know the truth. I spared most of the painful details about losing someone to brain cancer. When I finished my monologue, Skye's eyes were moist. There was a genuine sadness, although not pity, which I greatly appreciated. It was the first time in a long time that I had told the story of losing Molly. Finally, I said to her, "This isn't something that I like sharing with anyone, so it's OK if we keep this between us." She seemed to understand. I trusted her.

By now, it was almost two-thirty in the afternoon and I had been at Broomstones for nearly seven hours. I didn't have my next match until seven-twenty that night, so I excused myself to head back to my hotel for a little nap. I thanked Skye for giving me the copy of her family tree and for being a good listener. She still seemed a little bit unnerved by my surprise revelation. As I got ready to leave, she gave me a hug and simply said, "I'm sorry." All I could manage was, "Thank you," since I, too, was a little shaken after telling Molly's story. It was the first hug that didn't feel perfunctory, and one that I actually appreciated, in a long time.

I found Rich and told him that I was heading back to the hotel for a little break. "What was that all about?" he asked.

"What was what all about?" I asked in return.

"You and Skye," he answered.

"Oh. Well, you know that I've been researching Molly's family tree for a few months. Skye's kinda into all that genealogy stuff and all the Scottish connections. At the Pumpkinspiel she told me that she would show me how she constructed her family tree and we were just looking at it," I explained.

"I meant the hug," Rich said, just to be a smart-ass. I had no intention of humoring him with an answer.

"See you tonight," I said over my shoulder as I headed out.

I didn't even bother to open the tube with Skye's genealogy when I got back to the hotel. All of my research was back in Belfast, and there wasn't any reason to look at it in a hotel in Wayland, Massachusetts, so it just stayed in the trunk of my car. I would study it more closely after I got home. I lay down on the hotel bed and fell asleep while thinking about Skye Brodie. "Maybe there's something there," I thought to myself. I felt guilty for even thinking it, but the thought wouldn't go away. It had barely been a year without Molly, and I knew that I just wasn't ready. If, and when, I ever was, though, Skye Brodie was an intriguing possibility.

It was after five-o'clock when I finally awoke. I changed back into my curling clothes and headed back to the club for the Saturday night banquet, where I found the table with Rich Scamman and my teammates, who had saved a seat for me. It was a pretty informal event, just a buffet prepared by Broomstones' members.

With a belly full of chowder, cornbread, and a local New England IPA, I stepped onto the ice for our seven-twenty match with a team from the Nutmeg Curling Club in Bridgeport, Connecticut. On the next sheet, the Nae-Sayers were taking on one of their biggest rivals, a local team from Broomstones. I wished Skye "good curling" before her match began. Our match ended poorly, an embarrassing 12-2 loss in seven ends, while the Nae-Sayers bested their rivals by winning the tie-breaking "draw to the button," which consists of each team's skip throwing one stone, with whoever comes closest to the button winning the game. Nearly everyone upstairs in the warm room was watching the deciding shots between the Nae-Sayers and the locals. I suspect that a few friendly wagers were placed by the spectators.

There was a small dance floor with a Broomstones curler serving as emcee and DJ. Since most of the people at the Broomspiel were no longer kids, to state it kindly, the music tended toward "classic" pop and rock, with an unfortunate smattering of disco and line dances.

I was sitting back at my table with the Nutmeg team, yet again being treated to the losers' customary free beer. As Skye and the rest of the Nae-Sayers walked by, we gave each other a quick smile. She looked so happy, basking in the glory of their big win. I was truly happy for her. By this point in the evening, some folks, who had enjoyed more than a single post-match drink, were on the dance floor. Some were great dancers, particularly some of the husband and wife teammates who had also been dance partners for decades. I, on the other hand, can't dance worth a damn. I am, though, self-aware enough to own it.

As the night was getting late, and with one final nine o'clock draw awaiting in the morning, I was ready to head off to my hotel. As I was contemplating that, Skye came over and motioned her head toward the dance floor. I must have made a disapproving face of some kind, as I have done my whole life when anyone dared ask me to dance. She nodded toward the dance floor again, as if to say, "Get out here, old man," even though I knew, from sneaking a peek at the birth date on her family tree that morning, that she was only a year younger than me. There was no way to graciously decline without being impolite or embarrassing her, so I stood up. She took my hand and bounced onto the dance floor, like a teenager. It was very sweet and endearing, and quite innocent, I supposed. I made sure to tell her that I was a terrible dancer, and she responded, "But at least you have a good partner!" I didn't disagree with that. I couldn't tell whether she had asked me to dance because she actually liked me, or was interested in me, or because she was just trying to be kind. Certainly the latter, I decided. Almost certainly.

Mercifully, the song ended, and I turned to head back to my table. One dance was more than enough for me, even with the increasingly captivating Skye Brodie. As I started to leave, the opening piano notes of Skeeter Davis's "The End of the World" came over the DJ's sound system. There was a tug from behind on my sleeve. It was Skye, of course. Having now seen me dance, she said, "I'll lead," with an adorable and irresistible little smile. Not the best song for a widower of just a year, but I did dance, trying not to hear the lyrics:

> *Why do the birds go on singing?*
> *Why do the stars glow above?*
> *Don't they know it's the end of the world?*
> *It ended when I lost your love.*

It was sweet of her. Perhaps she was just trying to say that she cared. It was maybe a little bit flirtatious, and it actually felt good to meet someone new. I felt a little smitten, if that's the right word to apply to a fifty-one-year-old man. It was the first time that I had felt warm in a long, long time. I didn't know if Skye was thinking of anything beyond simply trying to show kindness to a somewhat lost soul. Probably not, but maybe. After the dance, I gathered my things, said goodnight to my teammates, and headed for the door. I stopped at Skye's table, put a hand on her shoulder, and said, "Thank you."

Riding back to the hotel, and alone in my room that night, I thought a lot about Skye Brodie. In fact, I didn't think of much else. Random, dissociated thoughts. What color her eyes were, her Maritimes accent, the tartan of her kilt, whether she was flirting or just trying to be nice, how far away she lived, whether Molly would have liked her, and what Molly would have thought about me thinking about Skye Brodie. I wondered whether Skye was thinking about me, too. If, possibly, she was, what exactly might it be that she was thinking?

We only saw each other very briefly on Sunday morning. As I was entering the warm room after our loss to an Ocean State Curling Club team, Skye was getting ready to head down to the ice for the Nae-Sayers' final match. I said hello and told her that I was heading back to Belfast. To my surprise, she asked, "You got a passport?" I paused for a second, caught off guard by the unusual question. Finally, I said, "Of course."

"You should use it," she said, winking, and then she headed off for her game. She had to know that I was watching her as she walked away.

Now, I'm not the most intuitive person or the best at deciphering cryptic meanings and messages, but this one seemed pretty clear to me, even though I was decades out of practice at reading clues from women. I sat with Rich and watched the first three ends of the Nae-Sayers' game, after which they led 4-1. With a 220-mile drive awaiting and some thinking to do, I elected to let our victors get me a coffee rather than the usual beer. I found a pen and a piece of paper, wrote a note, and folded it, intending to leave it in Skye's plaid equipment bag, which was one of dozens scattered around the warm room. "Give me some time to think about that passport thing," I wrote. "Thanks for everything."

I changed my mind. I decided not to leave the note for Skye, instead putting it into my pants pocket. I would call her in a day or two to tell her in person.

Four hours later, I was back home in Belfast. I had spent the entire ride thinking about Skye, and, to a lesser extent, about Molly. It was more like fantasizing, really, but not in a creepy kind of way. I was trying to imagine a life with someone other than Molly. Could I do it? Should I do it? Would I do it? In truth, I barely knew Skye Brodie, and it was stupid to even be thinking these thoughts. They rolled and tumbled through my head in no coherent way, one just leading to the next without any control on my part. I was like a schoolboy with a crush. I wondered what Molly might think of all of this. I wasn't even sure what *I* thought of it.

I told the truth in my undelivered note to Skye – I did need time to figure things out. I didn't know whether I was ready for a simple date, let alone any kind of relationship, nor did I know if I would ever be ready. Maybe the answer would come in its own time.

———◆———

My research into Molly's family tree had taken me back as far as eight sets of great-great-grandparents, but still there was nothing nearly as interesting as her great-great-grandaunt, Darcie Gilday Ross, and her premature death at the age of twenty-three. I had finally learned about her death, and a little about her life, after reading the 1889 and 1890 accounts of her life and death in *The Scotsman*.

I remembered that I had the copy of Skye's family tree in the trunk of my car. I went outside to get it, brought it inside, took it out of its tube, and flattened it out on my dining room table, which a year later was still covered with pictures, index cards, and notes from the project which I had begun shortly after Molly's death. Skye's tree really was a work of art. I would study it more closely tomorrow, after a good night's sleep. Why not learn more about the lovely and charming Skye Brodie, I thought. Maybe I would actually summon up the courage to contact her.

Chapter 15

The Late Darcie Ross

Father O'Shaughnessy at the Sacred Hearts of Jesus and Mary Catholic Church in Girvan learned in the spring of 1889 that the quarrymen on Ailsa Craig were interested in employing a cook who could alleviate their burden of having to prepare three meals a day for twenty men. His thoughts immediately turned to the young widow, Darcie Ross. Father O'Shaughnessy was well-acquainted with her unhappiness living amongst the glances and the whispers in Glasgow after Murdock's death, and then again in Girvan. He believed that some time away might prove to be a blessing to her. Perhaps his prayers for Darcie were being answered. One Sunday in May, after mass, he sought her out and asked if she would be interested in living on Ailsa Craig during the summer months, cooking for the quarrymen. Darcie immediately said that she would. She would have done almost anything to get away.

As the oldest girl in her family, Darcie was the one who had helped her mother prepare the family meals. She learned to make dough and bread, how to chop and dice vegetables, how to let nothing go to waste, and how to time and cook dishes of beef, lamb, chicken, and fish. Preparing meals for a family of six helped to prepare her, in at least some small way, for cooking for the quarrymen. She had also learned how to tend to a vegetable garden, as her mother had planted one in the yard of their home. For eleven short months, she had prepared all of the meals for herself and Murdock.

Many of the quarrymen were known to Father O'Shaughnessy, some of them quite well, including John Greenlaw, the foreman in the quarries on Ailsa Craig. Before he had even approached Darcie Ross with the notion of going to Ailsa Craig, Father O'Shaughnessy had spoken at length with John Greenlaw about the idea of a young woman living on the remote island with a group of men. "Perhaps it would be better to find a man to cook for them," Father O'Shaughnessy offered. Greenlaw assured Father O'Shaughnessy that all of the quarrymen under his charge were good, decent, God-fearing, family men who would see to it that Darcie Ross was protected and safe. Father O'Shaughnessy asked about the young lighthouse keeper and was told the story of Cuddy Urquhart risking his own career to save the life of a single quarryman whom he didn't even know. Greenlaw had nothing but the utmost praise for Cuddy. Father O'Shaughnessy, of course, already knew the story of Cuddy's selflessness and heroism. He also knew the quarrymen's employer, Alec Garrie, and he secured Garrie's personal assurances that none of his men would ever allow any harm to befall Darcie Ross.

Despite receiving the assurances of John Greenlaw and Alec Garrie, Father O'Shaughnessy insisted upon meeting all of the quarrymen himself and obtaining their individual assurances, as well. He asked Alec Garrie if they could sail together to Ailsa Craig to address the men prior to Darcie's arrival. Garrie agreed to the request, for he had great respect for both his men and the priest. When Father O'Shaughnessy and Alec Garrie arrived on Ailsa Craig, the quarrymen were finishing their lunch and preparing to return to the North Quarry. They were surprised and nervous upon seeing their employer and the priest, who many of them recognized, waiting outside. They braced themselves for what they feared must surely be bad news.

Garrie addressed the men first, informing them that he intended to honor their request to have a cook come to Ailsa Craig to prepare their meals, and that he had someone quite capable and willing to take on the job in mind, upon certain conditions being met. He then asked Father O'Shaughnessy to address the men. Father O'Shaughnessy told the men about Darcie Ross, leaving out the details about Murdock Ross and Darcie's widowhood, even though some of the men already knew them. Father O'Shaughnessy made each of the men promise to him and to God that they would respect and honor Darcie Ross and would take care of her as if she were a daughter. Each man did exactly that. Father O'Shaughnessy was pleased to see such a fine and faithful group of men. The only person who would be living on Ailsa Craig who was not there to hear Alec Garrie and Father O'Shaughnessy was Cuddy Urquhart, who was serving the remainder of his thirty-day suspension ashore in Edinburgh at his parents' home.

When Darcie Ross arrived on Ailsa Craig the following week, on June 20, 1889, she was greeted at the dock by foreman John Greenlaw and the quarrymen, who stood in a single row with their hats removed, to welcome her. As she walked from the dock, with Father O'Shaughnessy walking behind, each and every man nodded, smiled, and said, "Hello, ma'am. Welcome to Ailsa Craig." Two of the quarrymen carried her belongings up the hill to her quarters, which were spotless and in which the quarrymen had placed a vase of flowers, fresh cut from their garden. Yes, Father O'Shaughnessy thought, living on Ailsa Craig for the summer just might be a blessing for Darcie. The quarrymen, for their part, were thankful to have someone who would prepare their meals. They fully intended to honor their vows to keep her safe.

Darcie didn't bring many possessions with her to Ailsa Craig. She brought her Bible, of course, as well as her rosary beads. She brought three cookbooks, including *The Practice of Cookery and Pastry*, and several of her mother's best recipes. She also brought her embroidery, yarn, thread, and needles, as well as three aprons which she had made for herself, each embroidered with red roses, just like the roses that Murdock used to bring home to her each Saturday after work. Her room was quite small, but immaculately prepared for her, and she was pleased. She looked forward to the peace, quiet, and solitude of life on the crag, where she would be able to fully embrace her grief. She was already relieved to be away from the streets of Girvan and from the strangers who whispered about her. John Greenlaw had to return to the quarry, but before he did, he said to Darcie, "Anything at all that you need, ma'am, you come right to me. Anything at all. Welcome again, ma'am." Darcy smiled, something which she had rarely done over the past year, and said, "Thank you, sir. I will."

Greenlaw assigned two of his most righteous and upright married men to introduce Darcie Ross to the island. They showed her the castle ruins, the quarries, the wells, some of the caves, the bird nesting sites, and then walked her to the top of Ailsa Craig to the chapel ruins. She asked about the ruins, and the men told her how seamen used the chapel to pray for those starting their voyages and for those who had been lost at sea. There was an awkward silence. Darcie would visit the chapel ruins as often as she could to pray for Murdock, she thought. At the summit, she asked her guides, "Could you show me where Skelmorlie is?" The men pointed north-northeast across the firth, past the coast of the Isle of Arran, but told Darcie that it could not be seen from that distance. When they returned from the summit, Darcie was shown the quarrymen's garden, the kitchen, and the storeroom where the food was kept. The first rat had not yet been sighted on Ailsa Craig, but would be soon, so the food in the storeroom was secure. Darcie would begin her cooking duties in two days, after she settled in, rested, and became accustomed to life on Ailsa Craig.

Darcie was pleased to learn that the quarrymen maintained a garden, which made her think of her mother, although it seemed odd to her that such hard men nurtured such a beautiful space. In fact, though, it was quite common for men such as lighthouse keepers or quarrymen to maintain gardens for very practical reasons. Most importantly, gardens provided a reliable source of fresh vegetables, which was very helpful in locations where deliveries were made only every few weeks. Working the soil was also a hobby which many of the men enjoyed, since many of them came from generations of farming families. There was plenty of guano on the island to use as fertilizer. Darcie looked forward to tending the garden, like she had been doing with her mother ever since she was just a child.

Preparing three meals a day for twenty men was not easy work, but Darcie didn't mind work. It was not only hot, hard work in the summer months, but it also required meticulous planning and timing, so Darcie maintained a list of what would be needed when the weekly supplies arrived. After taking note of the food that was on hand in the storeroom, she prepared a list of what would be served at each meal. She asked Mr. Greenlaw what the men's favorite foods were, and learned that they were particularly fond of fish, lamb, stew, and especially warm, freshly-baked bread. Mr. Greenlaw also told her that some of the men would occasionally catch lobsters in the waters around Ailsa Craig, although never enough to feed all of them at the same meal. The men, Mr. Greenlaw assured her, would determine amongst themselves who would get to eat the lobsters.

Cuddy Urquhart returned to Ailsa Craig on July 14, 1889, after serving his thirty-day suspension for abandoning his light to save the injured quarryman. He was unaware that Darcie Ross was now living on the island and cooking for the quarrymen. The first time that he saw her was on the evening of his first day back at the lighthouse, when he was in the lantern room preparing to light the beacon. He noticed her walking down the path from the summit and the chapel ruins, carrying something. Cuddy had never before seen a woman on Ailsa Craig, nor did he expect to ever see one, particularly one so young and beautiful. For an instant, he thought that she must be an illusion. He stood in the lantern room transfixed, frozen in place, and followed her every step until she opened the door to her room and disappeared inside. She had not noticed Cuddy staring at her from above. That would happen later. Cuddy had no idea who she was – a quarryman's wife, perhaps – or why she was there. Cuddy spent the entire night in the lantern room watching Darcie's door and hoping for another glimpse of her, but there was none.

Darcie Ross walked up to the chapel ruins atop Ailsa Craig with her Bible and rosary beads two, three, or even four evenings each week, depending on the weather and the dinner schedule. She enjoyed her work cooking for the quarrymen, and they respected her by keeping their distance and affording her privacy, as Father O'Shaughnessy had requested. The quarrymen tried their best not to cuss during meals, although some would have to offer an occasional, "Sorry, ma'am." The quarrymen had even taken to washing the dishes, pots, and pans after meals to allow Darcie some extra time for her walks before the sun set. What she enjoyed the most about being on the crag were the solitude and her time alone atop the island at the gloaming, when she would read her Bible and pray for Murdock's soul. She was aware that the lighthouse keeper was named Cuddy, having occasionally heard the name during meals, but they had neither met nor spoken, except for one time.

Three days after he had arrived back on the island, Cuddy found a reason to walk past the garden at the precise time that Darcie was picking vegetables. He wanted to see her up close, having studied her only from a distance every day, and he offered a "G'Day, ma'am," as he walked slowly by. "I'm Cuddy Urquhart, the lighthouse keeper." He stopped, awaiting her reply.

She offered only a slight smile back, looked up for just an instant, and said, "G'Day, sir. I'm Darcie Ross, the cook for the men." She immediately returned her attention to the garden. To Cuddy, she was even more beautiful and delicate than he had imagined when only staring at her from the lighthouse tower.

Cuddy grew infatuated with Darcie Ross, even though he knew nothing about her. He certainly knew nothing of the late Murdock Ross and Darcie's widowhood. When she was outside tending to the vegetable garden or to her laundry, he would find a chore to do such that he could watch her. He altered his routine to increase his chances of catching even a momentary glimpse of her gardening, doing her laundry, or climbing the path up to the chapel ruins. Every single night, he made sure to be in the lantern room when the quarrymen's meal ended, just in case Darcie should happen to appear. He was discreet, he thought, but once or twice she had caught him watching, and he quickly averted his eyes and returned to some supposed task. Cuddy was quite certain, though, that Darcie had again smiled at him one time before returning to her chores. The lantern room and gallery offered the best chances to watch, and Cuddy found himself there even when he had no real reason to be, other than to catch any fleeting glimpse of her. He also found himself paying much more attention to his own small vegetable garden, which was not far from Darcie's.

Every evening, Cuddy found his way to the lantern room or gallery earlier than truly necessary, increasingly desperate to see Darcie making her way up to the chapel ruins. He had changed the routine at the lighthouse upon discovering that Darcie enjoyed evening walks to the summit, such that cleaning the inside and outside of the lantern room windows would be done in the evening, when it would be possible to study Darcie as she took her walks. He always wished for good weather, both because it made the cleaning easier, but more so because it meant that he was more likely to see her. Cuddy was now quite convinced that Darcie, too, had changed *her* routine to allow him to watch her more often. She hadn't done that, of course, but what mattered was that Cuddy was convinced that she had. Emboldened by the knowledge that Darcie loved and encouraged having him watching, Cuddy took to watching her, very discreetly, of course, using the binoculars issued by the Northern Lighthouse Board.

To Cuddy, Darcie was of another world. She was more beautiful than any woman he had ever seen. She often wore a simple cotton dress, which caught the breeze as she walked. It seemed to Cuddy as if her feet barely touched the earth, making her, to his mind, more of an angel than a mere mortal. He would come to know her, he was quite certain, and they would fall deeply and completely in love. Perhaps they already *were* in love, he imagined, remembering the smiles he fancied her giving him from the garden and how she now arranged her life so that Cuddy could watch her more often. All that they needed to do now was to confess their love for each other and begin their life together.

Hour-by-hour and day-by-day, Cuddy's obsession with Darcie deepened and his longing for her grew. He now lived to catch even the briefest peek at her. If, for some reason, such as bad weather, she didn't come outside during the day, Cuddy was devastated. He spent those days pacing incessantly, obsessively, unable to concentrate on anything and cursing the weather. It was especially difficult when she didn't take her walk to the summit, for she was particularly beautiful then, in the soft light of the evening. He no longer even cared whether anyone, particularly Darcie, noticed him watching. Night after night after night, alone and tending to the light in the lantern room, he thought of nothing but her. They loved each other deeply, completely, and intimately.

After weeks of watching and incessantly dreaming of her, Cuddy was at last ready. He was certain that Darcie knew that he had been watching her from the beginning and that she welcomed – no – she desired it. She desired him just as surely as he desired her. She was desperately waiting for him. She longed for him to approach her, to touch her, to comfort and embrace her. Cuddy was convinced that she had been watching him, too. She planned her walks just so that he could watch. Working the light alone, awake all night in the lantern room, had provided more than enough time for his intrigue to turn into infatuation and then into obsession. He occupied a reality which existed only for him. Fate, or Divine Providence, had brought them together and would bind them together for all time.

On Wednesday, August 7th, destiny finally intervened and compelled Cuddy to follow Darcie up the path to the chapel ruins. The sun was getting low, but it still sat yellow and warm over the ocean. The water was calm and dozens of yachts and schooners glided on the water in the distance near the Scottish mainland, ten miles to the east. Only an occasional puff of wind stirred the air. It was as perfect a night as there could ever be on Ailsa Craig. A perfect night for Cuddy and Darcie to finally begin their life together.

Darcie was clutching her rosary beads, sitting on a flat rock which once was part of the chapel, consumed in prayer and thoughts of Murdock. She sat facing north, toward Skelmorlie, where Murdock had been lost when the *Princess of Wales* went down. Her Bible rested beside her, opened to the 103rd Psalm: *As for man, his days are as grass: as a flower of the field, so he flourisheth. For the wind passeth over it, and it is gone; and the place thereof shall know it no more.* Cuddy approached silently, reverently, enraptured by her. The closer he got, the more beautiful and angelic she became. He knew even then, before reaching where she sat, that this was the beginning of their destiny, their life together that was ordained to be. Fortune had surely led them both to this moment and this place. Cuddy would finally declare his love for her, and Darcie would likewise declare her love for him.

Darcie saw Cuddy approaching. She was startled, drawn from her prayers for Murdock. She wasn't afraid, for she knew that she had nothing to fear on Ailsa Craig. He sat down quietly beside her, even though he had not been invited to. For a long time he just sat and looked out over the sea, feeling the warmth of the setting sun on his face. He could feel her love. Darcie sat, too, the setting sun warming her, also, nevertheless confused by the presence of the virtual stranger sitting silently beside her. She knew neither why he was there nor why he didn't speak. She shivered. At last, Cuddy spoke. He had been practicing the words for days.

"I love you, Darcie, and I know that you love me," he said, looking directly into her eyes for the very first time. Her eyes displayed confusion, although not yet anger or fear.

Cuddy was confused. Why did she say nothing? Why did she not declare her unspoken love for him? He slowly reached out his hand to touch her arm, to assure her that everything was well. Darcie pushed it away, gently. Cuddy didn't, couldn't understand. He again gently reached for her arm to reassure her that everything was just as it was meant to be. Perhaps he had simply startled her, for there could be no other explanation. She loved him and longed for his touch. Their destiny and future together were finally upon them.

Darcie again pushed him away, this time harder and with both hands, stood, and took a step backwards. No one but Murdock was allowed to touch her or to love her. Her eyes flashed with a contempt and revulsion that Cuddy did not recognize. Her face was no longer soft and delicate, but hard and cold. How could she betray him like this?

"No – NO!" she admonished him, not screaming, but with a sternness of a kind often reserved for chastising a misbehaving animal. In an instant, Cuddy's feelings transformed from love to something else altogether, something with which he was completely unfamiliar. It wasn't hatred, because he loved Darcie Ross too deeply and completely. It was the shock of her betrayal of a sacred trust. Rage followed in an instant. It was not a *feeling* of rage so much as a *being* of rage which consumed him in the moment.

Cuddy stood, facing her. For the first time, her eyes reflected fear. He stooped down, perhaps in an act of contrition and to offer an apology, Darcie thought. Instead, without thinking, only acting, Cuddy grabbed a granite rock with his right hand. He struck her, swiftly and violently. He didn't strike her intentionally, really, for intent requires forethought and reflection. There had been no time to formulate an intent. It came from somewhere much deeper, somewhere more primitive, somewhere that he didn't know existed.

The cracking of Darcie's skull made a sickening sound, as it did again when it struck the granite bench on which they had been sitting. Cuddy didn't really hear the two cracks, such was his fury.

Nor did anyone else on Ailsa Craig hear them. It all happened so fast, so uncontrollably, and with such incomprehensible brutality. He stood silent and quivering over her, still holding a rock – *the rock* – in his right hand.

Cuddy couldn't tell whether she was breathing as she lay face-up on the ground. She was already ashen, though, and she didn't move. Blood trickled out of her left ear, mouth, and the wounds on her skull. Splatters of Darcie's blood were on the pages of her open Bible. Her eyes were open and unmoving, fixated upward toward the heavens.

Cuddy couldn't move. He could see what he had done, if not yet fully comprehend. The sun was nearing the horizon and the daylight fading. His instinct immediately turned to the most basic one of all, survival. No one had seen what he had done, as best Cuddy could tell. He started back down the path, hurriedly. The lantern had to be lit, and lit quickly, lest anyone suspect that something was amiss. He took the trail to the north of the lighthouse, out of the view of the quarrymen's quarters. On the way, walking by the shore, he tossed the rock, underhanded and gently, into the warm water of the firth, where no one would ever touch it again.

The setting sun had now reached the horizon. Cuddy hurried up the tower and managed to ignite the lamp, with trembling hands, as the sun finally dipped below the sea. It was a little bit later than usual or by protocol for the lantern to be lit. Cuddy prayed that no one on Ailsa Craig or elsewhere actually took any notice. From the gallery, he looked back up toward the top of the island where he had left Darcie. He saw nothing.

The quarrymen would find Darcie soon – if not this very evening, certainly in the morning, when they would find no breakfast awaiting them. Soon thereafter, the police would arrive and begin asking questions. Fortunately for Cuddy, sitting alone at the top of a lighthouse tower all night affords a person lots of time to remember, reflect, and plan. He knew that he had to be prepared.

The single greatest threat to Cuddy's freedom was the possibility that he had been seen ascending the island to the chapel ruins. He had harbored no fear of being seen then, having done nothing wrong and not intending to do anything other than to finally declare his love to Darcie. In fact, he had gone to the top of Ailsa Craig and the chapel ruins out of nothing but love for Darcie. Had anyone seen him, though, it would now have proven to be catastrophic. Whether or not anyone actually *had* seen him, no one would ever admit to seeing Cuddy between supper and the following morning when Darcie was found.

Alone in the lighthouse tower, Cuddy quickly came to understand that he had absolutely no control over what any of the quarrymen may have seen that evening. If there were witnesses, Cuddy was most likely spending his final night as a free man. If there were no witnesses, perhaps he had a chance. He focused his attention on what was still within his control.

Cuddy noted the blood on his clothes and hands – not a lot, but certainly enough to raise suspicion. His hands could easily be cleaned, but blood stains on clothing would be difficult to remove and even more difficult to explain. Nor could his clothes easily be hidden or disposed of on the tiny island except at great risk of being found. The police were certain to search every nook and cranny of the island for evidence, including caves, privies, wells, and fireplaces. Blood-stained clothing would be an easy and very incriminating find for the police. Fortunately for Cuddy, even should the police find his clothing with blood spots on it, which he made certain that they never would, they would not be able to prove that the blood belonged to Darcie Ross, since blood forensic science was still a decade away from that milestone and DNA analysis still a full century away. Nonetheless, the clothes were his biggest problem, in the absence of witnesses, Cuddy concluded.

There would be seven full hours of darkness before the sunrise. Seven hours alone in the lantern room. It was there, Cuddy decided, that the bloody clothes would be made to disappear. His pants and shirt were made of cotton, which helped immensely, since cotton burns easily and leaves virtually no ash. Cuddy secured a razor, scissors, and a small pan and took them up to the lantern room. Before he did, he added some coal to the stove and put a kettle of water on to make tea for the overnight watch, exactly as he did every night. Smoke coming from the stove stack throughout the night would raise no suspicions. In fact, it would be one small indication that everything was normal. In the lantern room, sitting on the floor, Cuddy began the painstaking project which would consume his entire night.

With a concentration born of fright and a primordial instinct for survival, Cuddy meticulously deconstructed the pants and shirt, one narrow strip at a time. He would cut a long strip of cloth from the garment and remove the threads, one by one, and place them in the pan.

Each time that Cuddy needed to wind the clockworks, he stopped in the kitchen for fresh tea and to dispose of the thread. Adding the cotton thread, bit by bit, to the coal in the stove would leave no discernible trace, so completely did it burn. It took the entire night to dispose of the bloodied clothing, thread by thread. When the spent coal was shoveled into the bucket for disposal in the morning, just as it always was, it was nothing but gray, dusty ashes. The buttons from the shirt were saved and simply added to the jar of buttons which was kept with the sewing kit provided by the Commissioners.

During the entire time that he was in the lantern room, Cuddy had been monitoring the quarrymen's quarters for any sign that something was out of the ordinary. At one point, three men stumbled out, but that was only to get some air during a break in their nightly card game and to clear their befogged heads from the whiskey and tobacco smoke. To all appearances, it had been nothing other than another beautiful summer night on Ailsa Craig.

——◆——

The next morning, foreman John Greenlaw released a carrier pigeon to fly across the firth to the mainland. It delivered the message, "Woman dead on Ailsa Craig. Send police and Father O'Shaughnessy. John Greenlaw." It took three hours for the message to be delivered and for the police and the priest to finally arrive. The investigation into the mysterious death of Darcie Ross began.

Chapter 16

The Trial

C uddy Urquhart's trial was short. He was acquitted of murdering Darcie Ross on February 12, 1890.

Nearly every newspaper in Scotland covered the story of Darcie Ross's murder extensively and enthusiastically, partly because of Darcie's tragic past, young age, and violent death, but mostly because the defendant was the only son of one of Edinburgh's most prominent citizens, Bryson Urquhart. *The Scotsman*, in particular, reported on the case almost daily in the weeks leading up to, during, and even after the trial. It was from the digital archives of *The Scotsman* that I learned most of what I would come to know about Darcie Ross, Cuthbert Urquhart, and Bryson Urquhart.

I learned that Scottish criminal law is unique in one very important way – a way that may have saved Cuddy Urquhart from a lifetime in prison, or worse. For centuries, Scotland has applied what is known as the "corroboration rule" to criminal cases. Few, if any, countries other than Scotland require corroboration in criminal trials. The corroboration rule requires that there be at least two independent sources of evidence to support each essential fact before an accused can be found guilty of a crime. The testimony of a single witness, with no other corroborating evidence, is insufficient. Even a confession is not enough to convict a person without some corroborating evidence to confirm its veracity.

Where the requirement of corroboration originated from, no one is really sure. Perhaps it came from *2 Corinthians 13:1* ("In the mouth of two or three witnesses shall every word be established.") Maybe it came from the Roman *Code of Justinian* ("We plainly order that the evidence of only one witness shall not be taken.") Wherever it came from, in 1890, it was the established law in Scotland.

Cuddy Urquhart's trial was held in the High Court of Justiciary, as were all murder trials in Scotland. Lord Judge William McCallum presided over the trial. In order to prove murder, which the Crown fully intended to do, it had to prove an *actus reus* (a wrongful act) and *mens rea* (a wicked intent). The two essential facts which the Crown had to prove to establish Cuddy's guilt and obtain a murder conviction – each with corroboration – were that a crime was committed, and that it was Cuddy Urquhart who had committed it. Each fact had to be proven beyond any doubt. In other words, the Crown had to convince the jury, beyond a reasonable doubt, that Darcie Ross was murdered, and that Cuddy Urquhart was the one who had murdered her.

No one saw Darcie Ross meet her end. The Crown Office and Procurator Fiscal Service had led the investigation into Darcie Ross's death and had almost immediately concluded that she was, in fact, murdered, and that it was Cuddy Urquhart who had murdered her. Actually proving those things would be quite another matter. The medical examiner relied on by the Crown concluded, based on an examination of the body, that Darcie Ross had died as the result of a massive trauma to her head just above her left ear, resulting in a cracked skull and cerebral hemorrhaging. A second, slightly smaller yet significant injury, occurred to the right side of her skull when she had fallen and struck her head. Based on the shape of the larger indentation in Darcie's skull, the most likely source was a single blow from a hard, irregularly-shaped object such as a rock. The medical examiner's testimony was convincing and quite accurate, even under scathing attack by Cuddy's barrister on cross-examination. The first injury, due to its great force, could not have been caused by an accidental fall, the medical examiner concluded. The defense was prepared to rebut this conclusion with its own expert medical testimony that Darcie's injury was most certainly the result of a tragic, accidental fall, should that testimony come to be necessary.

No murder weapon was ever found, even though the investigators spent several days painstakingly searching every inch of Ailsa Craig. How could anyone possibly find a single incriminating rock on an island that is nothing *but* rock? Had the investigators found that single rock, it would likely have done little to help their case, other than to confirm the medical examiner's conclusion as to the manner of death. In 1890, it was virtually impossible to get fingerprints off of rocks. Even if it were possible to do so, Scotland didn't admit fingerprint evidence in criminal trials until the 20th century, anyway. And there was surely no such thing as DNA evidence. The murder weapon stayed on the floor of the firth, tumbling with the tides.

The Crown had offered sufficient evidence to prove that a murder had occurred "beyond a reasonable doubt." It had produced a body and offered competent proof that the manner of death was, in fact, murder. Now, the Crown had the much more difficult job of proving that it was the defendant, Cuddy Urquhart, who had committed it.

No one had seen what happened, and the only people on Ailsa Craig at the time, other than Darcie, of course, were Cuddy and the twenty quarrymen. The procurator had interviewed each of the quarrymen separately the day after Darcie's death and again during the course of their investigation. Every one of them said exactly the same thing. No one had seen Darcie Ross since immediately after supper, nor had any of them seen Cuddy Urquhart. Each told the investigators that they had witnessed nothing unusual that evening or night. Two of the quarrymen testified that they had discovered Darcie's body the next morning, after they awoke to find no breakfast awaiting them and no sign of her anywhere. Their foreman, John Greenlaw, had directed his men to search the island in pairs, with one unlucky pair making the gruesome discovery.

Each of the quarrymen told the investigators that Darcie had prepared their meal of smoked fish chowder and bread as usual the night before, and that the lighthouse lamp had been lit at its usual time. The logs from the three lighthouses within view of Ailsa Craig all confirmed that the light was on at midnight when they did their routine checks. The lamps in the living quarters of the lighthouse had been lit at dark as usual. No boats had come or gone from the island that day. There had been no arguments or disagreements amongst the men and Darcie. They told investigators that it was not at all unusual to see Darcie climbing the path, alone, to the chapel ruins atop the island after supper when the weather was good and the sun still shone. Usually, they said, she took her Bible with her, although no one claimed to have noticed her doing so on the prior day. Their stories were identical. Perhaps a little too much so for the Crown's liking.

The quarrymen all believed that it was Cuddy who killed her, but none of them offered that opinion to the police. Who else could it have been? None knew of any possible motive for Cuddy to do so, although they admitted to knowing very little about him aside from his heroics in saving their injured friend.

Before the police first arrived, foreman John Greenlaw and the quarrymen met amongst themselves and agreed that it must have been Cuddy who had killed Darcie. The two men who found her body didn't need a medical expert to know that she had been struck, not fallen on a rock. The quarrymen could account for each other's whereabouts from supper until lights out, since they all bunked in a row of adjoining rooms and had spent most of the evening drinking whiskey and playing cards. The only person on the island who could not be accounted for on the night of the murder was Cuddy Urquhart. One of the quarrymen thought that he might have seen Cuddy walking back from the North Quarry around sunset, but wasn't certain. Another thought that he might have seen someone near the water's edge, north of the lighthouse. Neither man would tell the investigators those things.

John Greenlaw reminded his men of Cuddy's heroism in saving their friend only two months earlier. Cuddy had saved the life of one of their brethren, and now they would make their repayment by saving his. Greenlaw instructed them that there would be no mention that one of them may have seen Cuddy walking back from the North Quarry nor any mention of possibly seeing someone walking near the water's edge. Nothing at all was anything other than perfectly ordinary that night on Ailsa Craig, Greenlaw told them, even if the lantern had been lit a little bit later than normal. And Darcie Ross was, in the end, just an unfortunate young woman who cooked their meals for them. Whatever had happened, the quarrymen would never betray Cuddy Urquhart.

The Crown knew that it would need at least one of the quarrymen to testify against Cuddy Urquhart in order to establish Cuddy as the killer. One-by-one, each quarryman was called to testify in the hope that one of them would break from the story and somehow implicate Cuddy. The prosecutor became increasingly desperate and aggressive as the men all swore to the same things – that they had not seen Darcie Ross after supper; that she often climbed the path to the chapel ruins alone in the evening, carrying her Bible; that they had not seen Cuddy Urquhart that evening; that they had never seen Darcie and Cuddy interact in any way; and that the beacon was lit at its usual time on the night of Darcie's murder. The last was a lie. The Crown had failed. It had no eyewitnesses, no murder weapon, and no physical evidence to connect Cuddy to the murder. The bloody cotton clothing had long since returned to dust, and there was surely no motive for murder.

Cuddy, courtesy of Bryson Urquhart, was represented by one of the finest solicitors in Scotland, who, in turn, had engaged one of the leading barristers. As soon as the prosecution rested, the white-whigged barrister sprang from his seat and moved the court to dismiss all of the charges against his wrongfully-accused client. Even though there was a single piece of evidence implicating Cuddy – he was the only person on the island whose whereabouts could not be accounted for – there was simply no corroborating evidence that Cuddy had killed Darcie. Lord Judge McCallum dismissed all of the charges against Cuddy Urquhart, released him from custody, and admonished the Crown in blistering and unmistakable terms for trying to convict such a fine young man on such flimsy, and wholly uncorroborated, evidence.

Cuddy never again set foot on Ailsa Craig. Two years after the trial, he married Kirstine Tennent, with whom he would have three sons and two daughters while living in Edinburgh. Lord Judge McCallum, at the invitation of Bryson Urquhart, attended Cuddy and Kirstine's wedding. Never wanting to serve as a lighthouse keeper again, with the help of his father, Cuddy entered into a long, distinguished career at the Royal Bank of Scotland, even without the usually requisite university degree. Bryson Urquhart was thrilled that his son had come home and joined the Royal Bank at last.

Like his father, Cuddy was welcomed into Edinburgh society and enjoyed the privileges that went with being an officer at the Royal Bank of Scotland. And, like his father, he lived a long and prosperous life. In 1941, at the age of eighty-one years old, Cuthbert Urquhart passed away peacefully in the second floor bedroom of his summer home in Girvan, facing west over the Firth of Clyde and toward Ailsa Craig. It was the bedroom from which he had so frequently sat alone at night gazing upon the light from the lighthouse. His wife and children were with him when he died.

⸺◆⸺

Long before the trial, Darcie Ross's body had been taken by rail from Girvan, on the Girvan and Portpatrick Junction Railway, to Glasgow, where it was met by her parents, Beatrice and Magnus Gilday, her sister, Sally, and her brothers, Colin and Finn. Father O'Shaughnessy, consumed with guilt and grief, sat in a lonely and prayerful vigil with Darcie on the train ride. It was, after all, Father O'Shaughnessy who had sent Darcie to Ailsa Craig. As it was when Father O'Shaughnessy spoke with Darcie when they spent time walking the church grounds in Girvan or sitting in its garden, Father O'Shaughnessy could find no answer for "Why?" A beautiful and faithful young woman who had known so much loss and suffering had been killed for reasons unknown and incomprehensible, perhaps even to a supposedly all-knowing God. How did a benevolent and loving God allow, or even ordain it to happen? Father O'Shaughnessy grappled with the questions, but much more so with the lack of answers. Was it right to be angry with God, who, after all, loved each of His children?

A funeral mass was held at St. Andrew's Cathedral in Glasgow, where Darcie had been baptized and married. Her body was taken for interment to the Glasgow Necropolis, the final place of rest for 50,000 souls. Darcie was lowered into the ground on a gently sloping hillside in the Victorian cemetery. Her gravestone was inscribed with a rose above her name and with the pair of dates that bookended her brief time on earth. Two plots on Darcie's far right were reserved for her parents, who would one day take their place beside Darcie. It was not the natural order of things. To her immediate right was the tiny grave of Darcie's baby sister, Grace, who had lived for only five days. The plot to her left was reserved for Murdock Ross, should he ever be recovered from the sea.

Chapter 17

The Spiral

M y life was forever changed in a single, unimaginable instant.
When I had opened and studied Skye Brodie's family tree back in March after the Broomspiel, it had been with the intention first of modeling Molly's tree after it and, second, of learning more about Skye. She had been extraordinarily kind to me at the Broomspiel after I told her about Molly, and had even suggested the possibility of a closer relationship. I must admit that the idea held some appeal at the time, but also a sizable measure of guilt. I had been thinking about Skye a lot.

I knew, from my obsession with her photograph, about Darcie Ross, her widowhood, her savage murder, and the unjust acquittal of her murderer, Cuthbert Urquhart. I had read everything that I could find about Darcie and the trial of Cuthbert Urquhart in the digital archives of *The Scotsman*. *The Scotsman* always used Cuddy's proper name, Cuthbert. There was no doubt that Cuthbert Urquhart was Darcie's killer, and that the quarrymen knew it to be so.

Just before studying Skye's tree after the Broomspiel, I called her to thank her for being so kind, to say that I was about to delve into the family tree that she had given me, but mainly to tell her that I simply needed some time to think things through. She was just as warm and understanding as she had been in person and said that she understood. "Take whatever time you need," she said. "I know that this has to be very difficult for you." I was becoming more and more infatuated with her with every word. I was happy that I called her rather than leaving the note. It felt good to talk with her.

After the phone call, I spread Skye's family tree across the dining room table. I started to examine the names and the pictures, noting where and when her ancestors were born and died, and where they had lived. For the second time as I was standing over the dining room table – the first being when I found that picture of Darcie Ross – I was dumbstruck, unable to breathe or to move. I put my hands on the table to steady myself. Four generations back, on her father's side, I saw the name "Cuthbert Urquhart" and the dates "January 29, 1860 – August 17, 1941." It couldn't possibly be true. I looked back one more generation and saw the names of his parents – Bryson and Lottie Urquhart – names that I had seen repeatedly while reading about Darcie's murder and the ensuing trial of Cuddy Urquhart. Cuddy Urquhart, the man who had so savagely murdered Molly's great-great-grandaunt Darcie Ross with a rock, was Skye's great-great-grandfather. Everything that I felt, might have felt, or even hoped to feel about Skye Brodie changed in that instant. The Urquharts were monsters, and Skye shared their blood.

I felt betrayed, above all else. Skye was from the unrepentant tribe of Clan Urquhart. She must have known about their crime, yet still proudly wore the clan tartan; she flaunted it, even. She had told me about Bryson Urquhart, although she didn't use his name, and how he became patron of a curling club in Edinburgh, as if that made him a hero. Surely, she knew what Cuddy had done to Darcie Ross atop Ailsa Craig. If she knew about Bryson's many exploits, she surely knew of Cuddy's monstrous act, too. Perhaps she even knew that Darcie Ross was Molly's great-great-grandaunt, although I couldn't be certain about that. Had she given me her family tree just so that I could discover these things? Skye had sat right beside me, laughing, smiling – even asking me to dance with her – all while concealing the awful truth about who she – and they – were. Was she mocking me, mocking Darcie, and mocking Molly? Worst of all, the justice that they all deserved had never been brought to her clan.

I didn't devise a plan, really. It simply revealed itself to me, almost instantly and fully formed, and my only calling was to execute it. Perhaps Molly's spirit was, in fact, guiding and directing me, but I would never place responsibility for what I would do on her. It was I, and I alone, who would do what needed to be done, and I would do it both willingly and gladly. It was not my place to question what destiny had chosen for me.

It is difficult to explain, but not at all difficult to justify, what was happening inside of me. Nor did I feel as if I need to justify it, anyway. My outrage and hatred were wholly pure and righteous, and my targets were justifiably Bryson Urquhart, Cuddy Urquhart, and the duplicitous Skye Brodie. From the first moment that the truth was revealed to me on that family tree, I thought of little else. I knew that I was being called to exact justice, although some may call it vengeance. I thought of it as I lay in bed at night and upon waking up in the morning. I thought of it while grocery shopping and while walking Bozo Junior, the dog which I had recently adopted. I thought of it intentionally and unintentionally. It consumed me.

I didn't think very much about *why* I needed to exact revenge, because that was clear. It simply had to be brought down upon the evildoers, who for so long had snickered at notions of justice that applied to the rest of us, but not to them. I never questioned what I had to do.

In many ways, I concluded, Skye was the worst offender of them all. I don't pretend to know why Cuddy killed Darcie Ross, or why he did it so violently. Maybe he had his reason, although God knows what it might possibly have been. And whatever the reason might have seemed to him, it could only be indicative of a gross depravity and immorality, of a dark and long-abandoned soul. There was no reason for young Darcie Ross to die at Cuddy's hand. None. I concluded that Bryson Urquhart was also culpable, because he surely knew that his only son was a murderer. Bryson cannot, and must not, be forgiven for his role in allowing his son to escape punishment, but at least it can be understood. A father will do anything to protect his son, even at the cost of his own soul. No, I was driven to conclude, it was not Bryson, or even Cuddy who were the most egregious offenders, but Skye Brodie herself.

The more that I thought about it, the more certain I became that Skye Brodie knew everything. Not only did she not care that her beloved ancestors included a remorseless killer, she flaunted it. She wore the clan's tartan whenever she went curling. She bragged about the great and important Bryson Urquhart, patron of the Duddingston Curling Society, and about how he had secured land and constructed an artificial curling pond for the club. She even blustered about how the club championship trophy was named after Bryson Urquhart. She told these tales with ease and with pride, conveniently omitting any mention of Darcie Ross's fate at the hands of the Urquharts. She was proud to be an Urquhart and she was wholly unrepentant for their sins. I now hated Skye Brodie and was disgusted that I had allowed her to try to get close to me. If she wasn't the Devil herself, she was of the Devil's seed.

I wondered whether Skye was religious. If she was, or even if she wasn't, she must surely have heard of Moses' warning in *The Book of Numbers* that, "The Lord by no means clears the guilty, visiting the iniquity of the fathers upon the children unto the third and fourth generation."

Every time that I thought of Darcie, I saw her falling to the ground atop Ailsa Craig and being left there alone to die. And every time I thought of the young and beautiful Darcie, I thought of Molly. Molly, an innocent who had also been robbed of her life. I thought of Bryson and Cuddy, who never paid a price. Mostly, though, I thought of the revenge that must come to be exacted upon the Urquhart clan – Skye Brodie's clan.

Chapter 18

The Broilerspiel

We hosted the Broilerspiel from November 5th through 7th at our club in Belfast. I had checked the registration list in April and found that the Nae-Sayers were, indeed, coming. It had been nearly eight months since I had learned the terrible truth about Skye Brodie, Cuddy Urquhart, and their murderous clan. I had allowed my hatred, encouraged it, even, to fester, take root, and metastasize. I grew increasingly comfortable with what I had to do, and I resolved that I would do it for Molly and for Darcie.

It was surprising how easily I came to accept my calling. Every day, every time I thought about it, which was almost all of the time, it felt more and more like the only thing that I was put here to do. I had been chosen, somehow, as the one who would deliver justice, and I fully and quite comfortably embraced it.

Everything which had led me to this moment was surely not coincidental or simply random. It was all too ordered, too perfect, too manifestly aligned for that. Molly's death, Rich's invitation to try curling, my acceptance of the invitation, sorting through Molly's family pictures, that picture of Darcie Ross, discovering Darcie's relationship to Molly, learning about Darcie's murder, attending the Pumpkinspiel, playing the Nae-Sayers, sitting next to Skye after the game, discussing genealogy with Skye, seeing her family tree, recognizing Cuthbert Urquhart in Skye's tree, Skye bragging about Bryson Urquhart, the Nae-Sayers coming to the Broilerspiel. It was all obviously ordained for the truth to be revealed to me, because without even any one of those events, I would never have been led to this place. There are no coincidences, some would say. Count me amongst those who believe it.

I was still living in the house which Molly and I had shared on Saddle Road, no more than a ten-minute drive from the curling club. Shortly after learning that the Nae-Sayers were coming to the November Broilerspiel, I had adopted another dog, a golden retriever mix like Bozo. He even looked a little bit like Bozo, although he wasn't nearly as smart. Adopting a dog was an important part of the plan from the very beginning. Not feeling very creative, being completely preoccupied with my preparations, and not having the creative energy to think of a good name, I named him Bozo Junior, although I mostly just called him Bozo. If I wanted to be stern with him, I used his full name or just "Junior."

Owning a dog afforded me a reason and lots of opportunities to walk the neighborhoods and the waterfront around my house multiple times, day and night. Even though I had lived in Belfast for more than two decades, I had never really taken that much notice of the individual houses. Walking Bozo Junior gave me the chance to do just that. Over the course of the summer and fall, I walked just about every street within a mile of my house dozens of times. I took note of whether a house had a paved or unpaved driveway, of how close it was to its neighbors, of how far back from the street it was set, of whether it had security cameras and motion detectors, and of whether it had a video doorbell. At night, I made note of how much traffic was on each street. There were no traffic cameras in any of the residential neighborhoods. After each walk, I went into my home office and immediately wrote down my notes in a loose-leaf binder. I dared not put them on my computer.

I finally had to start making small, handwritten maps of each street, with house numbers and codes. "P" meant a paved driveway, "SC" meant security camera, "MD" meant motion detector, "VD" meant video doorbell, and so on. I even developed a numeric system to chart how much traffic was on each street. It would have been easier to print street maps off of my computer, I know, but that would not have been wise and could have possibly been fatal. I could not allow anything to be found on my computer.

By the fall, I had narrowed my options down from dozens of houses to four houses on four different streets. I began to walk Bozo Junior more frequently on those particular streets, especially at night, although I continued to vary my routes. By the week of the Broilerspiel, it was down to one particular house on Eagle Road. My notes and maps for all of the other streets were burned in my fire pit, but only once the evenings had gotten cold enough so that other people in my neighborhood were using their pits as well. I couldn't be the only person in the area who had a fire going. I made sure to sit outside by the fire for an hour or so, just in case anyone happened to notice.

What had once been nothing but warmth and affection for Skye Brodie had long since devolved into a deep, primal, and abiding hatred. When I had last seen her at the Broomspiel in March, there had been thoughts of maybe visiting her in Canada and the possibility of a relationship. How could I have been so stupid? Two days later, when I had learned who she really was and that Cuddy Urquhart's venomous blood was coursing through her veins, I felt little but disgust, deception, and betrayal. In fact, it was all that I felt. Cuddy Urquhart had murdered Darcie Ross and walked away a free man, living the privileged life of a Royal Bank of Scotland officer, with a summer home in Girvan, looking straight across the Firth of Clyde to Ailsa Craig and the lighthouse he had once kept.

On Friday night, the Broilerspiel began. I had spent much of the day at the club, helping to set up tables, clean, stock the bar, and prepare the ice. I volunteered to help with all of the preparations mostly just to keep myself busy. By three o'clock, everything was ready. Rich and I, along with a few other club members, poured beers from the bar and sat and chatted, relaxing before twenty-four curling teams started to arrive. I tried to act as normal and calm as possible, but it was quite a challenge. Everything that had happened since Molly's death had led me to this moment. Perhaps my entire life had led me to this moment. When we had finished our beers, I went home to feed and walk Bozo Junior and to try to take a quick nap, which proved impossible, before the bonspiel got underway. I had to be ready.

I arrived back at the club at five-thirty to prepare for our first draw of the Broilerspiel against a team from Petersham Curling Club in Massachusetts. I went downstairs to retrieve my curling shoes and broom from my locker, and we took to the ice to get the weekend started. My team played terribly, and by the time the third end was over, we were trailing 7-0. I was the skip for our team in the first game and felt personally responsible for our predicament. It was so, so hard to focus on the game. Most serious teams have set positions for each player, so that the lead, second, vice, and skip never change. We were much less serious and less structured than those teams, choosing to rotate positions, so that each of us got to experience playing at each position. I got to be the skip in this game.

As the skip for our first game, I stood in the house at the far end of the ice, facing back toward the viewing area in the warm room, for the fifth end of our match. It afforded me a good view of the warm room, and I thought that I saw Skye Brodie standing with the Nae-Sayers. I got a chill. I wasn't completely sure that it was her, though, since they were nearly 200 feet away and behind glass, but I'm pretty sure that I saw the kilts. I continued with our game as if I hadn't noticed the people in the warm room, but my full attention wasn't on curling. Our Petersham opponents lost some of their enthusiasm and concentration after surging out to an all but insurmountable lead, and the game ended with Petersham winning 11-6. In the scheme of things, that was not too bad a result for us.

As we exited the ice and climbed the stairs to the warm room, we passed the other teams which were now heading down for their seven-twenty draws, including the Nae-Sayers. I had to grudgingly admit to myself that Skye looked as great as ever in her Scottish get-up. "Good luck," I said, summoning all of my resolve to feign a smile and pat her on the shoulder as she passed. "It's great to see you," she replied, with the warmth that I so clearly remembered from the last time that I had seen her. A lesser man might have lost his resolve then and there. I did not. Luckily, there was no time for anything else as we passed each other on the stairs.

Knowing what I now knew about Skye, actually seeing her for the first time since discovering her relationship to Cuddy Urquhart left me shaken. My heart was pounding, and I felt a revulsion and repulsion which I dared not let anyone see. Cuddy Urquhart was the Devil and all who shared his blood were likewise, particularly Skye Brodie. I was more certain than ever that justice had to be done.

We sat with our Petersham opponents and recounted the match, re-living the good and bad, lucky and unlucky, shots. Of course, we each drank a Maine craft beer, since the club had long-since decided that it would be silly to serve anything other than the best beer in the world. We watched a little of the play on the ice below, but mostly we just sat and chatted. I quite intentionally didn't watch much of the Nae-Sayers' match or comment on it, unless someone else mentioned it. Rich, among all of us, seemed the most interested in how the Nae-Sayers were doing. I made sure to say hello to everyone at the club on Friday night and to have at least a couple of words with each and every one of them. As one of the hosts, I felt like I should. As part of my larger plan, I knew that I must.

It was after nine o'clock when the Nae-Sayers wrapped up their match and entered the warm room. They sat with their humbled opponents a couple of tables away from us. Eventually, I made my way over and said hello to each of them, including Skye, paying her neither more nor less attention than the others. I wanted nothing more than to just go home, but I also needed to find just a moment alone with Skye. I continued chatting up some of the other teams in the warm room, continuing my responsibility as a member of the host club. Finally, Skye got up to check the day's results and the next day's schedule and draws, which were posted on the bulletin board on one of the walls. I walked over and pretended to study the schedule while standing next to her.

"Hello, Skye. Thanks for giving me time to think about things. And thank you for the family tree, it was a really big help. I'd love to talk, but not tonight, not here. Belfast's a small town, you know. Do you think that we could sneak away tomorrow night, hopefully alone?" I couldn't really have cared less what people in town might have said about me seeing someone. I was still relatively young and had been alone for a year. If people talked, so be it. But it was a good excuse to keep Skye from saying anything to anyone.

"I'd like that," she smiled, "I thought you'd never ask. I've really been looking forward to seeing you."

"Me, too," I answered. Our reasons were no doubt quite different. I couldn't know for certain just what Skye was thinking about my offer, but I could guess. She had agreed quite quickly to sneak away with me the next night and seemed excited that I had even asked. Deep down inside, I had suspected that she was hoping that we would get to spend some time alone together.

I knew that I had to excuse myself before people took note of our private conversation, but more so to make sure that Skye didn't notice me quaking or detect the tremor in my voice. "I'm heading home. I've been here all day and I'm pretty beat." I gave her the best smile that I could muster and hoped that my eyes didn't betray me. I made a beeline for the exit and a much-needed night's sleep, while Skye went back to her table. I needed to be well-rested for the next day.

Our paths didn't cross much on Saturday, fortunately, with the Nae-Sayers playing in the winners' bracket and with us in our customary position in the losers' bracket. When I was at the club on Saturday, I made sure that I always had something to keep me occupied, like a game, or helping to tend the bar, or re-pebbling the ice. As I had carefully done on Friday, I went out of my way to once again speak to everyone for at least a moment. I needed to have as little interaction with Skye as possible without seeming to ignore her. She seemed to get it.

I finally caught up with her later in the afternoon, again as she checked the schedule and the remaining draws. "You wanna stop over at my place tonight after your last draw? We can finally get some alone time."

"Sure," she answered, "Sounds like fun." There was definitely a tone of anticipation in her voice.

"Two Eagle Road. It's just a couple of minutes from here. Eight o'clock?" I asked.

"Sounds good," she said. "It's a date. Two Eagle Road."

"And don't be late," I added, winking. Conspiratorially, I added, "Mum's the word, remember. Belfast is a really small town. People love to talk." And with that I returned to my table. Even though I didn't know very much about Skye's personality, I suspected that promptness was one of her stronger traits. It was important that I was correct about that. More importantly, I had to trust her not to tell anyone about our little rendezvous.

I had some food from the buffet which the club had put out, despite not having much of an appetite. I drank water rather than beer, even though I could have really used a beer. At around quarter to seven, I announced to everyone who was at my table, including Rich, that I was heading home for the night, having spent nearly the entire day on my feet at the club. I also told some folks on my way out that I was headed home. On the ice below, the Nae-Sayers were in the sixth end of their match. I didn't take any notice of the score or who they were playing. I headed straight home to Saddle Road, where I would make my final preparations.

It was pitch dark and overcast, with rain in the forecast, when Skye pulled into Bill and Elizabeth Green's driveway at 2 Eagle Road. It was precisely eight o'clock. Some lights were on in the house, controlled by timers, as I knew they would be. Bill and Elizabeth had fled for Florida ten days earlier, as they always did, at the first hint of frost. I had been waiting in the driveway for only four minutes, although it seemed much longer. I silently congratulated myself for being right about Skye's punctuality. Skye got out of her car and approached me as I stood in the driveway. She smiled and said, "Alone at last." Those were the last words that Skye Brodie ever spoke.

I had played this moment out in my head hundreds of times. I knew that I could not dare to speak a word to her or engage in any conversation, lest I lose my resolve. In that brief instant, I wondered if she found it strange that I didn't speak.

It was over in a swift and brutal instant. I didn't really know what I was capable of until I actually did it. It takes courage and a true commitment to the task to strike someone hard enough to kill them. Seeing Urquhart blood on the driveway made everything worthwhile, though. I hurried, but didn't run, back to my home on Saddle Road, taking the route that I had painstakingly planned for some time. On the walk home, I was hoping that she didn't suffer. It was not my place to cause suffering, only to deliver justice.

Chapter 19

The Investigation

S kye's body was found mid-morning on Sunday. One of the Nae-Sayers had called the Belfast police when Skye didn't show up at the club for their nine o'clock draw. She hadn't answered her cell or motel room phone, either. Absent an extreme emergency, there was simply no way that Skye would ever be late for a curling match. Two officers arrived at the club just before ten o'clock, as two matches were already underway. One sheet sat empty. I was not yet at the club, since my final draw in the Broilerspiel was not scheduled to start for another hour.

One of the Nae-Sayers had already driven back to the motel to see if there was any sign of Skye or her car. Her car was not in the parking lot. It took a few minutes and a raised voice to convince the motel manager to go to Skye's room to check on her. She was not in her room, nor did anything appear to be out of the ordinary.

The Nae-Sayers told the police what kind of car Skye was driving, gave them a physical description, and texted them a group photo of their team. Shortly after ten-thirty, I pulled into the club's parking lot, not at all surprised to see a police cruiser parked near the door. Frankly, I was a little surprised that there was only one.

There was a good chance that I would know the officer or officers inside from my years of practicing law in Belfast, a city of fewer than 7,000 people and a police force of just twenty officers. I was on fairly good terms with most of them, despite occasionally cross-examining a few of them a little aggressively, but never impolitely. It was understood that we were all just doing our jobs. Truth be told, most of the officers much preferred Molly to me, which was entirely understandable. The police genuinely appreciated Molly's commitment to safe biking and her efforts to educate riders about bicycling laws. Most officers had long ago concluded, based on experience, that they would rather not be called to respond to any more scenes of an accident between a car or truck and a bicyclist.

The atmosphere in the warm room was subdued when I walked in. People were milling around, not paying much attention to the two games still being played on the ice below. Not everyone playing in the bonspiel was at the club yet, just some of the people on the teams with eleven o'clock draws. People continued to filter in. Officers Danny Cutts and Susan Wells were there, talking with the curlers and jotting down notes. Before I had arrived, the officers had asked that no one leave until they had spoken with everyone.

I saw Rich and walked over to him. "What's going on?" I asked, as if I didn't know.

"One of the Nae-Sayers hasn't shown up for their nine o'clock draw – Skye," Rich said. He seemed genuinely concerned. Before I could say anything, Officers Cutts and Wells approached. I knew both of them professionally, Cutts more so than Wells, since he had been on the force for quite a bit longer than she had been. Officer Wells was a bit more stand-offish. I sensed that she remembered that I had gotten one of her early cases tossed out over a chain-of-custody technicality. The officers were holding notepads and printouts with the names of everyone who was participating in the bonspiel.

"Hi, Danny. Hi, Susan," I greeted them.

"So, you know why we're here, I guess," offered Officer Cutts.

"I just heard from Rich," I said, gesturing toward my friend. I wasn't sure whether either of the officers knew him or had spoken with him yet.

"Do you know a Skye Brodie?" Cutts asked me, keeping his reference to her in the present tense. I immediately took notice of that detail.

"Sure," I answered, "I'm guessing that just about everyone here knows Skye," also quite deliberately answering in the present tense.

"When was the last time that you saw her?"

"Umm, maybe quarter to seven or so last night," I answered, taking just a moment to appear reflective, even though I had rehearsed my answer. "She was on the ice finishing up a game. I was up here watching until I decided to head home." It was the first of several lies and omissions that I would have to tell, or, in the case of omissions, not tell. The fewer the lies, the fewer that I would have to remember. I had prepared myself for the anticipated questions, although I had assumed that by now they would be speaking of Skye in the past tense.

The officers asked me a few more questions, and I answered every one of them as truthfully as I could. No, Skye hadn't said anything about any plans in Belfast. No, I hadn't heard any arguments or disagreements. No, I didn't know if she had any friends in the area. They didn't really need to ask anything else at this point. After all, she was a healthy adult woman who had only been reported missing this morning. And the police already knew what kind of car she was driving, what motel she was staying at, what she looked like, and what her cell phone number was. They asked Rich all of the same questions and got all the same answers, except that he had stayed at the club a little longer on Saturday, until around seven-thirty. He thought that Skye might have still been at the club when he left, but couldn't be completely sure. Rich's recollection about when he had last seen Skye didn't much matter, though, since the Nae-Sayers and the team they were sitting with after their match had all said that Skye stayed at the club until around seven forty-five, when she said that she was tired and ready to call it a night. No one had seen her that morning.

Officer Wells was the one who got the call. A woman's body was found on Eagle Road after a patrol officer spotted Skye's car with the Canadian plates in the driveway. The Belfast Police Department was about to begin only its third murder investigation in twenty years.

I had chosen 2 Eagle Road as the location based on a number of things that I had learned during my months of reconnaissance walks with Bozo Junior. First, it was at the end of a dead-end street, meaning that there would likely be very little vehicular or pedestrian traffic. Second, as far as I could ascertain, none of the eight houses on the street had security lights, cameras, or video doorbells. Belfast, after all, had a very low crime rate, especially for violent crime, and most people just didn't feel the need. Third, it had a paved street and stone driveway, reducing the risk of leaving footprints in the dirt or mud. Fourth, it was only a brisk six-minute walk from my house. Fifth, I knew the owners, Bill and Elizabeth Green, were snowbirds and fled south each year around the first of November, before the Maine winter weather settled in. My handwritten notes and street drawings with this information had long since been shredded and burned in my fire pit on a brisk October evening when lots of locals were sitting around their backyard fires and the whole town smelled of burning pine. It was through my sheer good fortune that it had rained in the early Sunday morning hours. I couldn't have planned on that, but it was a welcome bonus.

During my career as a lawyer, I had never handled any violent crime cases, much less a murder case, but I nevertheless had a pretty good idea of how the police investigation would play out. Detectives from the Belfast Police Department would notify the Maine Attorney General's office, which would lead the investigation. Detectives would secure the crime scene and await the arrival of the Maine State Police, who would process the scene. A medical examiner would inspect the body on-site, examining the eyes; state of rigor mortis; and would take body, air, and ground temperature readings in order to determine a preliminary estimated time of death. The body would then be taken to the medical examiner's office in Augusta for a complete forensic examination and autopsy.

Under ideal circumstances, a body loses about 1.5 degrees Fahrenheit per hour after death, although many factors can affect the rate of cooling, including the size of the body, ambient temperatures, and the kind of clothing the victim is wearing. Skye's body temperature was 76.2 degrees on initial examination, suggesting that she had died at around 8:00 p.m. on Saturday night, assuming that she had a normal temperature of 98.6 degrees at the time of death. Since it is impossible to pinpoint a time of death with that degree of specificity, the medical examiner's best preliminary estimate of the time of death was between 6:30 and 9:30 p.m., a small enough window to eliminate anyone who had an alibi for those three hours, yet large enough to account for unknown variables. At the scene, the medical examiner also reached the preliminary conclusions that the cause of death was a severe blow to the head, above the left ear, and that the manner of death was, in fact, homicide.

It didn't take long after Officer Wells got the call for word to spread throughout the club. Nearly everyone participating in the Broilerspiel was now there, either having finished their morning match, currently playing a match, or preparing for their next one. Officers Cutts and Wells were still there, as well, and they adopted a much more serious tone. Those of us who were members of the club and hosts for the Broilerspiel huddled together and immediately cancelled the rest of the bonspiel. The curlers who were currently playing were summoned from the ice. The officers addressed everyone in the warm room and asked that no one leave until further notice. They couldn't force anyone to stay, but everyone did. Only one team had left already, having been eliminated early that morning and having headed for home just before the officers arrived. Each of those people would get a phone call from the police later in the day. Everyone else playing in the Broilerspiel was in the warm room, except, of course, the late Skye Brodie.

One-by-one, the officers interviewed everyone again, trying to find any inconsistencies with what they had been told earlier, but also asking what each person was doing between six-thirty and nine-thirty the night before and whether anyone else could confirm their whereabouts. They seemed to spend the most time with Skye's Nae-Sayer teammates, since they were the ones who knew Skye the best and who had the most interaction with her. Some of the people had airtight alibis, such as being at the club the entire time or having gone out for drinks and dinner with a group. Others had alibis for part of the time, like me, when they were at the club before heading for home or their motel. One-by-one, after the second interviews, the officers told the people that they were free to leave, but not before handing each one a business card and asking them to call if they thought of anything else that might possibly be helpful.

Since the officers knew me and knew that I lived in town and wouldn't have to travel to get home, I was one of the last people to be questioned for a second time. I told them precisely what I had told them earlier – that I had last seen Skye when she was on the ice playing her match at around quarter to seven, when I had decided to head home for the evening; that I hadn't heard Skye mention any plans for the night; that I had not heard any arguments or disagreements; and that I didn't know whether Skye had any friends in the area. When asked what I did after leaving the club on Saturday, which was a question that I hadn't been asked earlier, I told them that I had gotten home around seven, taken Bozo Junior for a walk, which I thought took about half-an-hour, re-watched the final two episodes of *Breaking Bad* on Netflix, checked my emails, put out some recycling, and tried to go to sleep. When asked if I knew Bill and Elizabeth Green, the owners of the property where Skye was killed, another new question, I told them that I did, although not well, and that I thought that they usually headed south for the winter. If it were ever to come to that, all of those things could be easily verified. The only lie was telling them that I had no idea what would lead Skye to the Greens' house on Eagle Road. When asked if I would be around in case they had other questions, I told them that I was leaving on Tuesday evening for a long-planned trip to Scotland to do some curling research, but would be back later in the following week. Officers Cutts and Wells didn't seem at all concerned.

I knew for certain that I had done the right thing in killing Skye to avenge Darcie Ross's murder. For nearly a century-and-a-half, Cuddy Urquhart's bloodline had lived their lives unencumbered, unpunished, and unrepentant for what he had done. Cuddy himself had died at a generously old age within eyesight of Ailsa Craig. I had finally brought justice for Darcie Ross's murder, and by extension, for Molly. I had absolutely no regrets.

Not much happened regarding the murder investigation over the two days before I left for Scotland, at least that I knew of, although I am quite sure the investigators were hard at work and that the Facebookers were churning out a lot of helpful theories. There were a few phone calls from people that I knew, most of them only casually, spreading rumors and fishing for any bit of dirt, but I fended them off by saying that I didn't really know anything and then finding an excuse for why I had to hang up. The police made no attempt to contact me, which was a very hopeful sign. The *Kennebec Journal* in Augusta and the *Portland Press Herald* left voicemails, which I ignored. I was more than happy to be leaving town.

There remained the not insignificant matter of the murder weapon – the rock. I didn't know whether there was blood or DNA on it, or even fingerprints, but I wasn't about to take that chance. While Cuddy Urquhart didn't have to concern himself too much with such things in 1889, I did. Around dusk on Sunday, less than twenty-four hours after the murder, I took Bozo Junior for his walk along the waterfront, as I had been increasingly doing over recent weeks. While strolling along the water's edge with Bozo Junior, and with no one within eyesight, I quietly tossed the rock into the sea, just as Cuddy Urquhart had done with his.

All of the forensic analysis took place at the Maine State Police Crime Lab in Augusta. Skye's car had been taken there on Sunday after it was inexplicably found at 2 Eagle Road. Skye's body was taken to the Office of the Chief Medical Examiner, also in Augusta. The Medical Examiner confirmed the preliminary analysis which had been done at the crime scene. Skye was killed by a blunt force trauma to the head, above and behind the left ear, causing swelling of the brain, subdural hematoma, and loss of blood, followed by a second trauma when her forehead hit the ground. Judging by the irregular shape of the wound to the skull and trace material in Skye's scalp, the first trauma was most likely caused by a rock. Darcie Ross had died 133 years earlier in precisely the same way, which was no mere coincidence. Otherwise, Skye had been perfectly healthy, with no signs of other injury or illness. The preliminary estimated time of death, calculated at the scene, of 6:30 – 9:30 p.m., was confirmed.

There was one autopsy result that held some significant promise for the investigators. There was no sign of violence, but semen was recovered from Skye's body. The semen was analyzed through the Combined DNA Index System maintained by the FBI and also through Maine's own state database. Although the combined databases contained fifteen million unique samples, none of them matched the seminal fluid recovered from Skye Brodie. Accessing the Canadian database for comparison to the Canadians at the Broilerspiel would take longer, but would ultimately yield no matches, either.

The search and forensic analysis of Skye's car focused the investigation much more narrowly. It was clear that the attack had taken place in the driveway, not in the car, and there was nothing found in the car to refute that. There were no signs of a struggle, nor was any blood found in the car. The interior was immaculate. The crime lab did retrieve a fresh set of fingerprints on the passenger side, though. Fingerprints which were quickly matched to my good friend and teammate, Rich Scamman.

Rich's fingerprints were on file with the State Police because he had been arrested twelve years earlier on a DUI charge, one for which I had represented him. After a lot of negotiating with the assistant district attorney, I managed to get Rich off from that charge, having him plead guilty to the far less serious charge of reckless driving instead. At that time, there were a lot of questions about the field sobriety test administered to Rich and about the calibration and accuracy of the breathalyzer being used by the Belfast Police Department, which I was prepared to exploit, and the district attorney preferred that those not become public knowledge at a trial, which could have caused an embarrassing number of convictions to be tossed out. The district attorney, who would have to stand for re-election, and the police chief, preferred to plea bargain the case quickly and quietly, which we did.

The detectives called Rich on Thursday, while I was in Stirling, Scotland, looking at the world's oldest curling stone and football. He arrived at the police station an hour later. They asked him all of the same questions that they had already asked twice on Sunday and his answers were all the same. "Is there anything that you're not telling us?" one of the detectives asked, seemingly wrapping up the interview.

"Not that I can think of," Rich answered, quite nervously. The officers looked Rich straight in the eyes and waited a beat to see if he was going to elaborate. He didn't.

One of them finally asked, "Do you have any idea why your fingerprints were found in Skye Brodie's car?"

"Shit," Rich thought to himself.

Rich knew that he hadn't done anything wrong. A couple of hours in a motel with an attractive and charming woman on a Friday night wasn't against the law. The detectives asked Rich if he would be willing to provide a DNA swab, which he willingly did. He knew that it would be a match for the seminal fluid which, Rich surmised, the investigators had certainly recovered from Skye's body or motel room.

At this point, Rich rightly concluded that it was time to tell the whole truth, so he did. He and Skye had met at the Pumpkinspiel and again at the Broomspiel and seemed to hit it off. Not like lightning and thunderbolts hitting it off, but a bit more than just passing fancy. When their eyes met on Friday night at the Broilerspiel, they knew that something good was going to happen. On Friday evening, when he caught her alone for a moment, Rich asked Skye if she wanted to take off later, to which she readily agreed. Since Rich was in the midst of a separation and a somewhat contentious divorce, he asked Skye not to tell anyone. He really didn't want to add an affair to his wife's list of grievances and bargaining chips. They left the curling club together in Skye's car on Friday night, since Rich didn't especially want his car spotted at a local motel. They spent a couple of hours in Skye's motel room, from which the crime lab had also collected fingerprints and DNA, and Skye then drove him back to the club, where, by that time, Rich's was the only car left in the parking lot. On Saturday, Rich had asked Skye if she wanted to escape again that night, to which she replied that she couldn't. And that, he told the detective, was his last interaction with Skye Brodie. I wonder if Skye found it odd that Belfast men wanted everything to be a secret.

"So, you wanted to see her again on Saturday and she refused?" the detective asked. Rich wasn't crazy about the phrasing of the question, or about its implication.

"She didn't refuse,'" Rich said. "She said that she couldn't, and we left it at that. I just assumed that she had other plans."

The detective probed into the details of Rich's story about his Friday night with Skye. There wasn't much else to tell or to clarify, since Rich had told them everything about what had happened. The detective asked whether Rich had told anyone else about his relationship with Skye, which he told the detective he had not. The final questions were about Rich's whereabouts from Saturday night into Sunday morning. For the third time, Rich explained that he had left the club at around seven-thirty on Saturday evening and gone directly home, where he remained until he drove back to the club between ten and ten-thirty on Sunday morning. Unfortunately, Rich told the detective, he couldn't think of anyone who could confirm those things.

With the interview complete, the detective escorted Rich out of the station. On the way out, he made sure to ask Rich if he was going to be around for the next few weeks.

"Yes, I'll be around," Rich said. "I don't have any plans."

"Good," the detective said nonchalantly, "We'll be back in touch." Rich was certain that they would be.

———◆———

My cell phone rang when I was in my hotel room in Scotland on Thursday night. I could see that it was Rich calling, which was very strange, since he knew that I was in Scotland. I assumed that he was calling to see how my trip was going. "They think that I did it," he said. I had no idea what he meant.

"Did what?" I asked.

"They think that I killed Skye."

"Who thinks that?" I asked.

"The police."

I, alone, knew that he hadn't, but I obviously couldn't say that. I paused for a moment, never having considered this development. All that I could say was, "Rich, stop talking now. I'm not your attorney and it's possible that none of this conversation is privileged. They might even be listening to us. You can't take that chance. Here's what you do – call Steve Alexander. He's the best criminal defense attorney in Belfast. Tell him that I referred you. He'll know what to do." Rich started to say something, but I cut him off. "I'm serious, Rich, shut up. Don't say another word to me or anyone else before you talk to Steve. Call him right now. Now!" I hung up. Was it a trap? Did the police know that it was me and had put Rich up to calling me to see if I would say something stupid? No, it couldn't be that. Rich would never do that to me.

Steve Alexander was actually only the second-best criminal defense attorney in Belfast, although he was very, very good. I was saving the best one for myself, in case I should ever need her.

Chapter 20

Scotland

It was not at all coincidental that my trip to Scotland was scheduled to begin just two days after the Broilerspiel. In the late spring, I was simultaneously following the planning for the granite harvesting on Ailsa Craig and the registrations for the Broilerspiel. I learned at nearly the same time that the Nae-Sayers were coming to the Broilerspiel in Belfast in early November and that the granite harvesting would begin on Ailsa Craig on Monday, November 15th, after the birds' breeding season. It takes considerable time, meticulous planning, and extensive paperwork for the harvesting to proceed. Kays Curling, the Royal Society for the Protection of Birds, the Commissioners of the Northern Lighthouse Board, and the various environmental and governmental groups all want their say as to exactly where, when, and how the granite will be harvested. The timing of the harvesting was most fortuitous for me.

I had become completely obsessed with curling and its history, but even more so with the tiny island that was home to the world's only blue hone granite. I simply had to see it for myself, especially after learning the names and fates of Darcie Ross and Cuddy Urquhart. I had begun my planning immediately after learning who Skye Brodie *truly* was, seven months earlier following the March Broomspiel. I had put the picture of Darcie Ross in a frame and stood it next to one of Molly on my dresser, where I saw Darcie every single day, and every time that I saw her, I pictured Skye's own great-great-grandfather felling her atop Ailsa Craig.

All of my warm feelings toward Skye Brodie at the Broomspiel in March had dissolved into a hatred that I nurtured and cultivated after I learned the truth about what she had done to Darcie Ross – or, rather, what Cuddy Urquhart had done to her. Hatred, though, is a wholly inadequate word to describe the feeling. It was a malevolence such as I had never felt, or even imagined that I could feel. Anyway, the chore was now done.

It took a lot of work, and some begging even, to convince Kays Curling to let me witness the granite harvesting in November. Months earlier, I had contacted them and told them who I was and where I was from. I let them know that I was trying to compile the most detailed history of curling ever attempted and that Ailsa Craig and Kays Curling were essential parts of that history. I showed them that I was serious by confirming that I had made arrangements with Nicole Taylor, manager of the Stirling Smith Art Gallery and Museum in Stirling, to see the oldest known curling stone, inscribed with the date 1511. I told them that I had made arrangements to meet with some of the most historic clubs in Scotland, and, if offered the chance, to throw a stone or two. I also managed to finagle references from the Grand National Curling Club, the regional United States association which included Maine, and from USA Curling, the national governing body for curling in the United States. My persistence ultimately paid off, and Kays Curling grudgingly agreed to allow me to accompany them to Ailsa Craig for one day, Tuesday, November 16, 2022. I was to report to Kays Curling at 6:00 a.m. sharp on November 16th. Although I truly did want to witness the granite harvesting as part of my research, there were lots of other things that I was far more interested in doing in Scotland.

My plane from Boston landed in Glasgow at 7:30 a.m. on Wednesday, November 10th, after a seven-hour flight. I checked into the Clayton Hotel overlooking the River Clyde, which was less than two blocks from my first destination. I plopped down on the bed for a nap, but I was far too hyped-up for sleep. After a fitful hour, I put on some fresh clothes, got a large coffee from the lobby of the hotel, and stepped out onto the sidewalk on a mild, fifty-degree morning. I turned left, walking eastward on Clyde Street.

Within five minutes, I was standing in front of St. Andrew's Cathedral, a magnificent, although fairly small, Roman Catholic cathedral built in 1816 in the Scottish Gothic style. The cathedral is relatively modest, constructed without a steeple or bell tower, because of the historic persecution of Catholics in Scotland prior to the enactment of the Roman Catholic Relief Act of 1791. The Relief Act granted Catholics the right to worship openly, but only so long as the church doors remained unlocked; permitted them to run schools, provided that no Protestant children were enrolled; banned steeples and bells from their churches; and allowed Catholics to practice law and to be notaries. Like I said, neither Molly nor I really understood or were terribly fond of organized religion. I finally stepped inside, taken by the majesty and the history. I tried to imagine Darcie and Murdock Ross on their wedding day 135 years earlier, not Darcie's funeral mass, both of which took place at St. Andrew's. Agnostic or not, I lit a candle for Darcie and another one for Murdock. I sat alone with my thoughts for some time before finally leaving.

Once outside, I made my way north to the Glasgow Necropolis, a walk of nearly a mile. The Glasgow Necropolis is an enormous cemetery, located on the eastern end of the city. It is the final resting place for more than 50,000 souls, including Darcie Ross and her family. Despite months of planning, I still wasn't sure what I was going to do if I actually found her grave. It became quickly apparent that I would never find her by simply walking around looking for her gravestone. I walked back to the main building and told one of the women working there that I was looking for the grave of Darcie Ross. She asked me if there was a maiden name and for a date of death. I told her that the maiden name was Gilday and that the date of death was August 7, 1889, a date which I had long-since memorized. The woman searched her database and found Darcie Gilday Ross. She handed me a map of the cemetery, told me which section the grave was located in, and circled the spot. She walked me to the door, pointed out the path, and told me that it was about a 500 meter walk. I started walking, bracing myself for my first encounter with Darcie.

My walk unconsciously slowed as I neared the section of the cemetery where I would find her. What would I say to her? Would I tell her about Cuddy Urquhart and Skye Brodie and what I had done to secure justice and retribution for her? Would I say anything at all? I was struck by how ill-prepared I was to talk to her, even though I had been planning to visit her for months. At the very least, I would surely tell her about her great-great-grandniece, Molly.

I began walking down the rows of gravestones, looking at each one. There were some long lives and some short ones, the longer ones having not been cut short by a plague or a war or an accident, or even by a murder. Generations of families were buried together and interspersed amongst those who were spending their eternity alone. And then I saw them. The gravestones of Magnus and Beatrice Gilday. To their left were three more gravestones, one smaller than the other. The small one was for Darcie's baby sister, Grace, who only lived for five days. Next to Grace lay Darcie. Next to Darcie was the headstone atop the empty grave of Murdock Ross, engraved only with his name, date of birth, and the words "Beloved Husband of Darcie Gilday Ross."

The afternoon air had turned chilly and the wind was brisk. I sat down on the ground at Darcie's feet. For a long time, I simply sat in silence, alternately staring at the headstone and at the ground. Maybe there were other people walking nearby, maybe not. I simply didn't notice, nor did I care if there were.

It seems silly, I know, talking aloud to a stranger's gravestone and to the body lying beneath it, yet I did it anyway. In a hushed voice, with my head bowed, I explained to Darcie who I was and how I had come to learn about her and about Murdock. I first told her how sorry I was about Murdock and that I had lit a candle for him at St. Andrew's. I thought that Darcie would like hearing that. I told her a lot about Molly and about how their pictures stood next to each other on my dresser. I told her about Cuddy Urquhart and how he had walked away a free man, despite what he had done to her. Lastly, I told her about Skye Brodie and about how I had finally secured justice for what Cuddy had done. I stopped speaking and looked up at Darcie's gravestone, as if expecting a response. I got none. I reached into my pocket and pulled out a picture of Molly. Finally checking to see that no one was around, I took my index finger and dug some dirt from in front of Darcie's headstone. I placed the picture of Molly in the hole and covered it. "You two would have loved each other," I told them both, even managing a slight smile. I stood up, placed my hand on her gravestone, said goodbye to Darcie, and headed out of the Glasgow Necropolis.

I stopped for supper, having long-ago decided that my first supper in Scotland was going to be cullen skink, a thick Scottish soup of cold-smoked haddock, potatoes, and onion, which was better than I ever could have dreamed. I walked back to my hotel, lay down on my bed, and fell into a deep sleep. Just twenty-four hours earlier, I had been in Maine. Tomorrow, Thursday, I would start my research into the history of curling in Scotland, which was, after all, supposed to be my reason for being here. I had actually started writing about curling months before, as part of my planning for the Broilerspiel and my trip to Scotland. Those little details are important.

Morning came way too quickly. I showered, grabbed a large cup of coffee, and set off for Glasgow Queen Street to take the express train to Stirling, a quick thirty-five minute train ride to the northeast. My appointment with Nicole Taylor at the Stirling Smith Art Gallery and Museum was set for ten o'clock, and I had deduced from her manner when we had spoken that it was probably best that I arrive on time. The museum was only a few blocks from the train station, and I had plenty of time, so I stopped in a small bakery, ordering a cup of tea and a scone. I was actually getting a little excited to be seeing the oldest known curling stone in the world, allegedly 510 years old.

I entered the museum at nine-fifty and informed the receptionist that I had a ten o'clock appointment with Ms. Taylor, and I was directed to take a seat. At precisely ten o'clock, she appeared. She was much less stern and proper, and also much younger than I expected a director of a contemporary art gallery and museum to be, looking more like an art history grad student than a museum director. As we started walking toward the archives, she emphatically warned me not to touch *anything* without first asking. She actually seemed pleased, though, that an American was taking such an interest in "the manly Scottish exercise." Putting on gloves, Nicole unlocked a large cabinet and removed the stone and placed it on a table on top of a soft cloth. Even though I had seen dozens of pictures of it, it was still a little less imposing than I imagined it might be.

Nicole Taylor explained that the stone was found many years earlier at the bottom of what was believed to be an old curling pond in Dunblane, just north of Stirling, when the pond had been drained. She told me that the stone was made of blue whinstone and that it measured 9 inches by 7 1/2 inches by 4 5/8 inches and weighed twenty-six pounds. It wasn't round, like a modern curling stone, nor did it have a handle, but rather it was more rectangular, with the short sides slightly rounded. She carefully showed me the two inscriptions on the stone, the first being, "A GIFT." Naturally, I asked her what that meant. "As far as we know, it means simply that. It was a gift. To whom and from whom, we have no idea." The second inscription read, "St. Js B Stirling." Nicole seemed fairly confident that "St. Js" referred to Saint James. Saint James has dozens of locales, buildings, and streets named after him in the Stirling area and was a very influential and popular saint in 16th century Scotland. As to what the "B" stood for, Nicole was far less confident. Her most educated guess was "Brotherhood." Lastly, she pointed out the finger holes which had been cut into the stone. I took feverish notes and seemed to hang on her every word, although I already knew everything that she was telling me from my research. I took some pictures.

Finally, she returned the stone to its cabinet. "Do you have any other curling artifacts here at the Smith?" I asked.

"No," she answered, "we only have the stone because it was found nearby and they decided to bring it here simply because we were the closest museum. Decades ago, we actually lost track of it until someone found it stashed away down here. We do have the world's oldest football, though. Would you care to see it?" By "football," she meant, of course, soccer.

"Sure," I answered, not wanting to be rude, and she went to another cabinet to retrieve it. Nicole returned with a round, gray object about the size of a grapefruit. She explained that the ball had been discovered behind some wood paneling in the chambers of

Mary, Queen of Scots, when renovations were made to the Stirling Castle in 1981. The ball was constructed of leather, probably from a cow or horse, stitched together around a pig's bladder. It may have belonged to Mary, Queen of Scots, when she was a young girl, since she spent the first five years of her life, until 1548, at Stirling Castle, although no one knows for certain that it actually belonged to her.

"How did it end up behind paneling?" I asked.

"No one really knows," Nicole replied, "but one theory is that it might have been put there intentionally to ward off evil spirits. Quite a common practice in those days." With that, Nicole returned the football to its home and my private visit to the archives was over. As she escorted me out, I asked her where else I might find any curling artifacts. She suggested that I visit Scottish Curling, in Edinburgh, or perhaps even the McKechnie Institute in Girvan. I didn't tell her that both of those places were already on my agenda. I thanked her profusely as we reached the reception area, shook hands, and I stepped outside for the next stop on my odyssey.

Since I knew that I would be at the museum in Stirling on Thursday morning, I thought that I might try my hand at curling at a real Scottish venue. Some months earlier, I had emailed The Peak, a curling arena within the Stirling Sports Village, to see if there would be play taking place on Thursday, and to ask if I could stop by, simply to watch. To my fortunate surprise, I was told that there were "open" games on Thursdays at 2:00 p.m., meaning that any experienced curler who was a member of a club could come and play. Teams, or "rinks," were constituted on the spot, based on how many people showed up. Luckily for me, at two o'clock in the afternoon, it was mostly seniors. I signed my liability waiver, retrieved my curling shoes from my backpack, and stepped onto genuine Scottish curling ice. I felt what I imagine religious pilgrims feel when standing on holy ground. I felt like I was part of history, in kinship with the curlers who had invented and perfected the game.

Playing with the Scots was exhilarating, even if I didn't understand everything they said. In the back of my mind, though, was the thought, "What kind of person commits a murder on Saturday and by Thursday is out on the ice, laughing and joking, playing a game?" I tried not to dwell on that thought, nor on the thought that in St. Andrews by-the-Sea, Canada, funeral arrangements were probably being made for Skye Brodie. I enjoyed a *Dark Island Ale*, a chocolatey, malty brew from The Orkney Brewery, after the game. I had never tasted anything like it in the States. I chatted with my new Scottish curling friends in the warm room, still trying not to think about what must be happening in Maine and Canada. It was finally time to take the train back to Glasgow. On the train ride, I organized my notes from my day in Stirling. Not long after arriving back at my hotel, I got the phone call from Rich.

On Friday, I had an appointment to meet with the historian at the Royal Caledonian Curling Club, now known as Scottish Curling, the national governing body for curling in Scotland. Scottish Curling is located just outside of Edinburgh, in the Cairnie House at the Ingliston Showground. It was a longer train ride than the one to Stirling the day before, taking an hour-and-a-half. I again bought a large coffee and settled in for the ride. I added more details about curling at The Peak and about the world's oldest curling stone to my notebook, and jotted down a few questions for Scottish Curling.

When I arrived at the Cairnie House, I was greeted by a receptionist who escorted me to the office of Mr. Bruce Andrews, an imposing, yet jovial man with an amazing salt-and-pepper beard, whom I suspected was in his early fifties, like me. Mr. Andrews knew from my emails that I was in Scotland conducting research into curling's history, and he assured me that Scotland was, without a doubt, the best place in the world in which to be doing that. I told him about my trip to Stirling and about curling at The Peak. I also told him that I would be heading to Ayr on Sunday to watch the Scottish Senior Men's Championship qualifiers and maybe hear some curling tales from the old-timers. Mr. Andrews assured me that it would probably not be difficult to coax stories out of them, since the old-timers loved nothing more than sharing their curling tales, some of which might actually contain a kernel of truth. Lastly, I told him that I would be going to Ailsa Craig on Tuesday with Kays Curling to witness the start of the granite harvesting. He was duly impressed by that, jokingly adding, "How'd ya get those scabby bassas to agree to that?" I had no idea what that actually meant, but I had a decent guess.

Rather than start off with a bunch of specific questions, I thought it might be best to ask some general, open-ended questions and see what Mr. Andrews wanted to talk about. I had already deduced that getting him to talk about curling would not be difficult. "So, what can you tell me about the history of curling?" I led with. That was more than enough to get him started. In no uncertain terms, he told me that curling originated in *Scotland*, not The Netherlands, as some less-knowledgeable and wholly uninformed people tried to claim. Of that fact, there could be no debate. There could also be no debate that the Scots developed a far superior game to that played on the continent. He opened a book and read to me a portion of a letter written by a Scotsman, Thomas Purdie, in the 19th century about studying curling in Germany:

You will see . . . that it has little in common with our roaring game – no wicking, guarding or running a port; and, famed as Bavaria is for its brooms and broom girls, there is even no sweeping, so that their game is but child's play compared to our noble science. In fact, we may consider the Bavarians to be in a state of heathenish ignorance on the subject of Curling – most degenerate sons of worthy sires, if the game has descended to them, as to us, from our common Gothic ancestors; and I conceive this to be a fair field for the missionary exertions of the Royal Caledonian Curling Club, – the manifold corruptions which have crept into their game rendering reformation of the utmost consequence . . .

Andrews then launched into a stream-of-consciousness monologue about the 1511 curling stone, which I had just seen the day before; Rabbie Burns and "the manly Scottish exercise;" the 1541 challenge match at Paisley Abbey between the monk and the abbot; the first curling club formed in Kilsyth in 1716; the Royal Caledonian Curling Club; and about how the Scots took the game with them to North America. It was like hearing a college lecture, and a damn good one at that. Andrews was so entertaining, so passionate, and so proud of the Scots for inventing and perfecting the game, that I didn't have the heart to tell him that I already knew most of what he was telling me, so I constantly scribbled notes into my notebook.

I asked him a question about how the rules of the game had changed, which inspired another lengthy soliloquy. At first, when the game was played outdoors on ponds, rivers, and lochs, there basically were no rules, just a bunch of men trying to slide their rocks closest to the mark. The game might have had only one or two players on each side, or it might have had upwards of fifteen or twenty. Not until a little later was the element of sweeping in front of the sliding stone introduced. Before then, brooms or "besoms," were only used to clear snow and prepare a curling surface. He then told me of how, in the beginning, some curlers would meticulously fashion their own stones, cutting fingerholds at whatever depth and location that they pleased. Handles didn't exist until someone, somewhere in Scotland, attached one to his stone, prompting others to do the same. Stones might weigh fifteen pounds or they might weigh eighty pounds, whatever the owner preferred. When matches were played, particularly in what were early versions of bonspiels between teams from different towns or parishes, agreeing on the rules might take weeks of correspondence and negotiation, and even then they were subject to the whim of old John Frost. It took the formation of the Royal Caledonian Curling Club in 1838, with its adoption of a standard set of rules, to create order out of the chaos.

I was curious about outdoor curling and asked my mentor about it. He smiled. "Many a wife nearly became a widow," he started. "Curlers were always at the mercy of the weather." He went on to explain that ponds, rivers, and lochs don't generally freeze into a flat surface. The wind, currents, springs, and tides leave most surfaces uneven. Nor does outdoor ice freeze to a consistent thickness. Shallower spots and deeper spots have differing water temperatures and freeze at different rates. It usually took a good deal of scouting to find a proper surface that could support several dozen curlers and stones. There are tales of outdoor curlers taking an unexpected dip into the water when the ice gave. "I've not heard of any curlers being lost, though, thank the Lord. A good slug of whiskey probably warmed them back up after they were pulled out,"

Andrews chuckled. Tragically, though, he did know of two boys who went to watch a match on Lochleggan and drowned after the ice gave way. Ice giving way probably explains the 1511 curling stone being found at the bottom of a pond.

It wasn't until later, but certainly by the 1800s, that clubs started to build artificial outdoor curling ponds. They would find an appropriate piece of land, buy it or lease it, level it, and construct a concrete or tar and macadam floor which could be flooded with water. That way, they could construct curling rinks at consistent, shallow depths and in locations which were accessible to their members and to teams coming to bonspiels. Finding a spot along a rail line was coveted, because trains could make unscheduled stops at the ponds to allow curlers and spectators coming to a bonspiel to climb off. Most clubs also built a small building next to the rink to store stones and supplies. Some of those rinks and buildings are still standing. The intentional construction of artificial outdoor curling rinks eventually led to the introduction of indoor rinks.

After nearly forty-five minutes, Mr. Andrews showed me to a computer on a small table in his office. "This thing will teach you more about curling in Scotland than I ever could," he said. He logged me on to the Historic Scottish Curling Places database, which has painstakingly cataloged every known site in Scotland related, even in some remote way, to curling. There were more than 2,700 places in the database, complete with source documents, maps, surveys, newspaper accounts, photographs, and notes. Each and every place was pinned on a map of the country. "Look around for as long as you like," he told me. I started scanning the list of places, most of which were identified as historic outdoor curling locations, although there were some quarries and curling stone manufacturers in the list as well. I was enthralled by the database, and in particular by the source documents, many of which recounted games played nearly two centuries earlier by hearty curling pioneers long since gone. For example, *Bell's Life in London and Sporting Life*, a weekly newspaper, reported on the discovery that players could make a stone turn, or curl, by turning the handle:

> *A correspondent, who signs himself 'A Keen Curler,'*
> *says – This great national and truly scientific game*
> *may be said to be yet in its cradle, and till very lately its*
> *perfections were little known. The point we principally*
> *allude to is what is called the twist or turning the hand;*
> *that is, making the stone, by the delivery, come in either*
> *from the right or left at pleasure; or in making it, like*
> *a biassed bowl, describe, when played, a segment of a ci*
> *rcle.*

The *Fife Herald* reported on curling in Kirkaldy in 1855:

> *The 'roaring game,' as it has been called has been,*
> *during the past week, the absorbing subject of interest*
> *in this quarter . . . [A] variety of matches, of less or*
> *more interest and importance, have been played. The*
> *chief of these matches was between the bachelors and the*
> *married men; and we regret to state that the bachelors*
> *gained the day – the result being, married men 21*
> *shots, bachelors, 53.*

I was unable to deduce exactly why the reporter was rooting for the married men over the bachelors, but he clearly had his preference. Later, upon reading John Kerr's 1890 book, *History of Curling: Scotland's Ain Game*, I learned the answer. Kerr wrote:

> *[N]early all of our curling clubs... have an annual*
> *match, The Married v. The Unmarried, the purpose*
> *of which is the same as that of our young patronesses,*
> *viz., to exterminate the race of bachelors and send*
> *them over to 'the great majority.' In this match,*
> *the married are generally successful, and the poor*
> *bachelors who chance to escape with their lives very*
> *soon put the chain of Hymen round their necks in*
> *despair, and commit the 'happy despatch.'*

I learned that curlers back in the day would sometimes go to extraordinary lengths to play their beloved game. The January 17, 1856, *Fife Herald* reported on one ill-fated attempt to curl on Haining Loch:

> *On Saturday morning last, the members of the*
> *Selkirk Curling Club sallied forth to play a game*
> *... but came home again sooner than was expected.*
> *Finding the stones clogged with ice... the happy idea*
> *was unhappily hit upon by some of the more eager*
> *and less scientific members to put matters to rights*
> *by kindling a fire and throwing the stones in it to*
> *thaw. The result was, that in a few seconds the club*
> *was reduced to utter destitution, the stones splitting*
> *up into fragments.*

I continued to pour through hundreds of accounts of 19th century curling. In 1869, a match was played between the King's Inch club and the Blythswood club at the King's Inch pond.

The *Paisley Herald and Renfrewshire Advertiser* reported on the competition:

> *A beef and greens match took place between the above clubs . . . on Saturday last. The ice was in bad condition for play owing to the thaw which set in about midday. Notwithstanding this disadvantage, the contest between the scion and parent-stock was so keen, and the anticipation of the beef and greens so invigorating, that, rather than leave victory undecided, the game was carried on until the stones were nearly swimming round the ice. The Blythswood Club most undutifully vanquished its parent – this being the second offence of a like nature out of three matches . . .*

Beef and greens was the traditional meal which a losing club was expected to provide to the victors after a match. The February 4, 1871, *Hamilton Advertiser* reported on a match in Douglas, Lanarkshire:

> *On Monday the tailors and shoemakers met on Boncastle Pond, for the second time, to test their skill at the roaring game. The knights of the needle, for some years past, have had to confess themselves second best, but they have this year shown their superior skill by beating their opponents twice . . .*

I assumed that the "knights of the needle" were the tailors. I was a bit surprised to discover that 19th century curling in Scotland may have provided an excellent opportunity for a gentleman to catch a young lass's eye. Even the reporters who covered the matches took note of the many women spectators. The February 19, 1838, *Caledonian Mercury* reported on the outcome of a match between Dunoon and Bute, then added, "The day was most propitious for the curlers, and such a display of ladies was never seen on Lochloskin." For a moment, I wondered whether I would have caught Molly's eye had I been out there curling on the loch 200 years ago. The February 1, 1879, edition of the *Oban Times and Argyllshire Advertiser* reported on a match in Lochlomond:

> *104 players took part in the contest, and after a keen and spirited competition the Helensburgh Club took the prize. Dumbarton and Duntocher being next and equal . . . About 1,000 spectators witnessed the game, amongst whom there was a sprinkling of ladies.*

Before I realized it, I had been pouring through the database, reading everything and scribbling notes, for three hours. Andrews stopped by. "Finding anything interesting?" Andrews asked, with a sly smile. He had apparently observed me clicking away and writing down page after page of notes.

"This is amazing. It must have taken years to put this together," I answered.

"Decades, and still a work in progress," he told me. "A real labor of love. It seems as though someone discovers a new place every day. Once we confirm the veracity of the new information and source material, we add it in." I hadn't looked at even ten percent of the information, but it was time to head back to Glasgow, since I would be leaving for a long, important trip to Fraserburgh early the next morning.

"Email me when you get back to America. I think that I can arrange for you to access the database from there, if you'd like."

"Absolutely," I answered, and then bid Mr. Andrews farewell, but not before he reached into a cabinet, producing a bottle of Drambuie and two shot glasses, which he filled. We raised our glasses and offered a "Good Curling" toast to *The Roarin' Game* we both loved. On the train ride back to Glasgow, I realized that I had not thought of either Darcie Ross or Skye Brodie for hours.

Saturday brought the long trip north to Fraserburgh, in the far northeastern corner of Scotland. Despite the long distance, it was a train ride that I had no choice but to make. I began the five-hour ride from Glasgow very early in the morning, in the darkness. I took all of my curling research with me and tried to organize it and convert the notes into some kind of prose to pass the time. If I were to actually write a book about curling history, I might as well start to actually write it while in Scotland. My trip to Fraserburgh was entirely unrelated to curling, however. I needed to speak to Cuddy Urquhart.

Fraserburgh is home to the Museum of Scottish Lighthouses and is located on the grounds of Kinnaird Head Lighthouse, the first lighthouse built by the Commissioners of Northern Lights and one of the first lighthouses at which Cuddy Urquhart had apprenticed. The lighthouse was constructed through the center of the haunted Kinnaird Head Castle, which itself had been built by the Frasers of Philorth as a symbol of their great wealth and power.

I took the tour of the lighthouse with a small group of people and a funny and thoroughly entertaining docent, who delighted in telling the story of how the castle is haunted by the piper who was imprisoned and drowned there. The docent implored us to listen closely during the tour for the sound of the piper playing and to immediately report upon hearing him. She showed us where the piper's lover had jumped to her death from atop the castle. I climbed the stairs which Cuddy had climbed, walked the gallery which he had walked, and took in the view of the North Sea which he had no doubt taken in. There were the clockworks which he had wound and the kitchen in which he had eaten. My blood ran cold picturing him going about his work. I would have spoken to him then and there, but I was with the group and had to remain silent and await another chance, which I knew would come.

After the lighthouse tour, I went inside the museum, which holds thousands upon thousands of Scottish lighthouse artifacts. I was only truly interested in one of them, though – the original Fresnel lens from the Ailsa Craig lighthouse. The lens stood on the floor along one wall of the museum with a plaque explaining its history at Ailsa Craig. The lens was nearly as tall as me. It was the lens which Cuddy had cleaned and polished every day while serving alone on Ailsa Craig. It was the lens which he had sat beside while deconstructing his bloody clothes. It was the very lens which he had set spinning on the night that he murdered Darcie Ross.

It was only a week ago that I had brought Skye Brodie to justice. Three days ago, I had visited Darcie's grave and told her that I had brought vengeance to the Urquharts, and now I would tell Cuddy, too, what I had done. The museum was mostly empty on a November afternoon. With no one nearby, I spoke softly to Cuddy's lens. "You didn't get away with it, Cuddy," I assured him. "I saw to that. I did to your blood what you did to Darcie's." I stood there staring at that lens. I wanted Cuddy to feel the pain, to suffer in it, to know that an Urquhart had suffered the same awful fate as Darcie Ross. I took enormous pleasure in telling Cuddy what I had done and in knowing that I had brought upon him the pain that he, and the rest of his clan, needed and deserved. It made my ten-hour journey on a train more than worth the time.

On Sunday morning, I checked out of my hotel in Glasgow and boarded the train heading south to Lockerbie. I wasn't going to visit Scotland without stopping at the Garden of Remembrance and Lockerbie Air Disaster Memorial. The garden is beautiful, peaceful, and exquisitely maintained, a stunning contrast to the violence and brutality of Pan Am 103's downing. I stood and stared at the granite memorial, reading the names of the 259 people on board and eleven on the ground who were so suddenly and pointlessly taken. I simply could not understand what could drive someone to decide that the only outlet for their hatred was to kill people who had done nothing to them. The terrorists could rot in hell, for all that I cared. I hoped that there actually was an Old Testament, vengeful God, for punishment on earth was nowhere near sufficient for them.

Sunday afternoon found me in Ayr, on the west coast of the Scottish mainland, with the Isle of Arran faintly visible on the horizon twenty-four miles across the Firth of Clyde. I wanted to just sit and enjoy watching some real, high-level curling, and maybe even hear some yarns from the old-timers. The happenstance of the Scottish Curling Senior Qualifiers being held in Ayr, at the Ayr Ice Rink, the weekend that I was there was another stroke of pure luck. I arrived at the rink and was immediately treated to a fantastic game, won by Peter Wilson's team from Stranraer, which had been trailing 8-6 entering the tenth end, only to score four in the tenth for a 10-8 victory. Wilson's team qualified for the national championships and eventually earned the silver medal two months later.

I went out of my way to talk to some of the old-timers who were not only watching the qualifiers, but also opining on each and every shot. I introduced myself and asked them if they had any old curling tales they could share with me. As Bruce Andrews had suggested, they all had tales to tell – some of them maybe true, even. Sometimes, they seemed to be competing with each other over who had more, and the most dedicated, curlers in their families. One told the story of a bonspiel at Johnston Loch in Lanarkshire in the late 1800s which drew more than 400 curlers, including his great-great-grandfather. Another told of a match on Airthrey Loch at the Bridge of Allan in Stirling, at which the castle cook made a very large pot of Irish stew for the curlers and proudly brought it down to the loch. The curlers weren't quite done with their match and asked the cook to put the steaming pot of stew down so that they could feast on it when the match ended. Some of the curlers even covered the pot with their coats to keep the stew warm. When the match ended, and the curlers were ready to eat, they found nothing but a pile of coats and a perfectly round hole in the ice. A third told of an important annual match between the bearded and clean-shaven men at his grandfather's club. For years, the bearded men had taken the medal, largely on the strength of the most accomplished player in the club. On the day of the match, the man arrived clean-shaven for the first time in his life, abandoning his bearded mates, and led his new team, the clean-shaven, to victory. It sounded a little bit like an O. Henry story.

The curling tales just kept coming and coming, especially after the ale started flowing more freely, and I feverishly wrote them all down. I heard the legend of "Whirlie," an early 1800s curling stone, before curling stones became round and standardized, emasculated of individual personality. Whirlie was a triangular stone, which gave it a unique advantage. When an opponent's stone would strike Whirlie on one of its corners, rather than move, Whirlie would simply spin around in place, while the other stone would ricochet off at a right angle. Opposing players, teams, and clubs became so annoyed by Whirlie that they got together and forever banned it. After I returned home, I tried to find out whether the legend of Whirlie was true, and came across this sad account from the

Penicuick Curling Club, written in 1847, by a man who had actually played with Whirlie. It reads a little like a love letter:

> *It was the first stone which the writer of this ever played with. It being our first attempt at curling, we were appointed to lead, which we happened to do in such a manner that Whirlie was uniformly laid on or near the Tee; to remove it from the position on which it had taken rest was no easy matter; because, should the stone which was destined to remove it strike any one of the angled corners, round went Whirlie, round and round, without ever shifting from its position. Stimulated with the success of our first attempt at curling, we went early next day on the field of action with Whirlie in our hand. But to our utter disappointment, dear fellow, a Curling Court was held upon him, and he was unanimously condemned to perpetual banishment. This, however, we could not stand. We got him mounted in a more modern and fashionable uniform, by rounding his more acute angles, and in this capacity we introduced him as a stranger on his ancient domain. A bad character and bad habits, however, have a mark put upon them, and are not easily surmounted. The rogue, in spite of our endeavours, was still seen in his new shape and in his habits likewise, for his roundabout way of going to work never forsook him, and again and again has he been banished from, and restored to the society of his fellows; until at last we had the galling mortification to hear his final doom decreed by the present Baronet that this*

favourite stone should be played with no more. Since then, the Ice, and all the curlers, except ourselves, who well knew him once, know him no more, and perhaps forever. But many are the lingering emotions and fond affection with which we have sought after him; nor will we desist from the search until we in our turn shall be consigned to oblivion.

That tale inspired another old-timer to tell of how people used to name their curling stones, mainly based on their size or appearance. There was "Rockie," "The Goose," "The Horse," "Cockit-Hat," "President," "Black Meg," "Bluebeard," "The Egg," "Town Clerk," "The Girdle," "The Bible," "The Doctor," "The Grey Mare," "The Soo," "The Baron," "The Fluke," "Robbie Dow," and "The Ego," which was a massive beast of a stone weighing in at 115 pounds. I heard the no-doubt embellished story of a player in Lochmaben who was challenged by a player from Tinwald to a test of strength. The Lochmaben man took a seventy-pound stone and threw it across the length of the pond, which was nearly a mile long. He then said to the Tinwald man, "Now, sir, go and throw it back again, and we'll then confess that you are too strong for us." Yet another told of a match attended by his great-great grandfather in Wigan. The curlers had brought with them a barrel of beer which they planned to tap during a break between games. Unfortunately, by the time that there was a break, the beer had frozen into a solid block in the barrel, leaving the poor men with an unquenched thirst.

At the Senior Qualifiers, I got to see the legendary Gordon Muirhead play. As a younger man, Muirhead was an Olympic curler who had won gold medals in both the World and European championships. Muirhead's daughter, Eve, was in the crowd, as she had been hundreds of times before to watch her father play, fresh off of winning the Olympic gold medal with the Great Britain women's curling team in Beijing in February.

By Sunday afternoon, I was ready for some time alone and decided to take in some of the tourist sites in Ayr. I visited the haunted Culzean Castle and the Robert Burns Birthplace Museum, then finished the day with a leisurely walk on the Lang Scot's Mile along the waterfront on the firth.

On Monday morning, I checked out of my hotel in Ayr and boarded the train for the quick 25-minute ride south to Girvan, where on Tuesday I would be traveling with Kays Curling to Ailsa Craig for the granite harvesting. I spent most of the morning at the McKechnie Institute, a rather small museum focusing on local history and artifacts. Their collection includes specimens of the various kinds of Ailsa Craig granite, old Ailsa Craig curling stones, and offers a lot of Ailsa Craig history. Again, I took extensive notes and lots of pictures. In the afternoon, I walked around Girvan, trying to imagine what it must have been like during Darcie Ross's brief time there. I stopped into the Sacred Hearts of Jesus and Mary Catholic Church. The church is the oldest Catholic Church in Girvan, dating to 1860. I didn't know for a fact that Darcie Ross attended mass there, but I suspected that she did. I located a plaque inside of the church listing the priests who had served there, and Father William O'Shaughnessy's name was on it. Father O'Shaughnessy was mentioned briefly in the reporting on Darcie's death and Cuddy Urquhart's trial, and he had been the church's priest when Darcie lived in Girvan. Once again, I lit a candle for Darcie, on the off-chance that such things matter.

On Tuesday, November 16th, I was awakened at 4:30 a.m. by my alarm. I would be spending most of the day on Ailsa Craig with the crew that would begin the harvesting of granite for Kays Curling, unless I was late in arriving at the docks for the boat trip across the firth. I arrived at the dock at 5:45 a.m., fifteen minutes early. Most of the crew were already there, loading supplies and prepping the boat for the journey across the firth to Ailsa Craig. I was introduced to James Gordon, the foreman, who, quite frankly, didn't seem terribly excited to have a visitor tagging along. The quarrying would be a lot of work, and it had to be completed on a strict time schedule. Nonetheless, Gordon gave me the overview of what they would be doing that day, including the first blasting, but spent most of the time going over safety protocols and reminding me to obey anything and everything that I was told and to stay out of the quarries. I was to observe only from a distance. If I was within eyesight of the quarry, I was to wear my hardhat.

I assured Gordon that I was interested in watching some of the granite harvesting, but that I would spend most of the day exploring Ailsa Craig on my own. He seemed pleased by that. I also assured him that I had my own lunch and water in my backpack and would stay out of the way. I had my map of the island and a notebook full of pictures which I had studied, and I felt like I would know my way around fairly well. It would be nearly impossible to get lost on such a small island, anyway.

Kays Curling would begin harvesting blue hone granite from the North Quarry today. The crew had been to the quarry the day before and had surveyed, identified, and marked the areas where they would be blasting and harvesting. Today, they would be placing the charges, running the wires, and setting off the first deflagrations. I watched from a distance for about an hour as the men meticulously went about their work. Gordon, at one point, told me that it would likely be mid-afternoon before any blasting happened. I understood that to be a suggestion that I stop watching and head off to roam the island.

I decided that I would walk the island clockwise, initially walking south from the quarry. I was using Reverend Lawson's map of Ailsa Craig from 1888, since I wanted to know the place names as they were known in the late 19th century, when Darcie Ross briefly lived there, but also because not much about the island had changed over the past 134 years. I walked past the now-modernized lighthouse from which Cuddy Urquhart had studied and obsessed over Darcie Ross. I stopped and stared at it. My heart pounded. I walked past the remnants of the castle tower, the lower chapel ruins, the abandoned railroad tracks, and the wells. I continued around the island's perimeter, past one of the giant, rusting foghorns, MacNall's Cave, Swine Cave, and Water Cave. I peeked into the caves, but didn't go in, not out of fear, but thinking that it just wouldn't be the smartest thing to do with no one accompanying me, and with nagging doubts about whether James Gordon would even send anyone to look for me if I didn't return. If something bad were to happen, perhaps someone would find *my* skull a hundred years later while shoveling guano from one of the caves. It took more than two hours for me to nearly circumnavigate the island while making notes and taking pictures. I could now see the North Quarry again, but this time from the west. It was still morning.

At last, I began the steep walk up to the summit. To the southwest, on this sparkling clear day, I could see all the way to Northern Ireland on the horizon. I had been thinking about this walk for months, yet I was woefully unprepared. My heart was once again beating fast, partly from the climb, but mostly from the anticipation. I had no idea how I would react upon reaching the chapel ruins at the top, the place where Darcie Ross had been viciously murdered and left on the ground by Cuddy Urquhart. Finally, I found myself standing at the spot where I surmised that Cuddy had dealt the fateful blow. I began to imagine it happening, but quickly tried to think of anything else. It was an absolutely beautiful place, and I understood why Darcie came here to pray. It was certainly not a place for a young woman to die.

The week before, I had been at Darcie's grave in Glasgow and had told her almost everything that I needed to tell, including a lot about Molly. There was still one more thing to tell her, though. I reached into my pocket and pulled out a silver necklace and cross. It was Molly's favorite piece of jewelry, despite the fact that she was not very religious, and she had worn it almost all of the time. I explained that to Darcie as if she were right there with me. I told her that Molly and I wanted her to have it. I took the necklace and placed it in a crevice under a slab of granite, perhaps the last one that Darcie had sat upon.

A strange thing happened as I sat and thought of Darcie. A feather drifted slowly down from the sky and landed not far from my feet. I had no idea at the time that a feather landing nearby had any particular meaning or significance, and I shrugged it off as merely coming from one of the thousands of birds on Ailsa Craig. When I later learned what a falling feather actually means, it confirmed that everything that I had done was right and just, although I didn't need confirmation.

By the time that I was finished with my visit to Ailsa Craig, after returning from the top of the island and watching the quarrymen do their work, I was ready to get back home to Maine and whatever might await me there. More than anything, I was exhausted and ready to leave Scotland. I had done everything that needed to be done.

Chapter 21

The Bell Man

The Bell Man stood outside of the Heather Curling Club in St. Andrews by-the-Sea in New Brunswick, Canada, ringing a small bell and inviting people to enter. In old Scotland, it was the Bell Man who walked through the town ringing his bell to announce a death. This morning, the Bell Man announced a funeral. Inside of the club where she had spent so much of her life, lay Skye Brodie.

Skye was clothed in her kilt and the rest of her curling attire, which she would be buried in, just as she would have wanted. She also wore sixty-eight pins from various curling clubs where she had played. The collection and trading of club pins is a common occurrence at bonspiels, and Skye was always on the lookout for new pins wherever she played. Each one commemorated Skye's love for *The Roarin' Game* and had a story behind it.

Everything about the service and the funeral spoke of Scotland. For twenty-four hours before the service, club members had taken turns sitting with Skye, a Scottish tradition harkening back centuries to a time when people kept constant watch over the body just to make sure that the person was actually dead before being buried. Just as importantly, they also maintained their vigil to prevent the Devil from making off with the body.

The service was meant to be a celebration of Skye's life, but it was hard for anyone present to feel celebratory, given the tragic circumstances. The three remaining members of the Nae-Sayers spoke at the service. They spoke of Skye's love for curling, of the glorious times that they had attending hundreds of bonspiels, and about her warmth and caring. Not a word was spoken about how she had died, nor about Belfast, Maine, and the Broilerspiel. This was supposed to be a celebration of Skye's life, not a recounting of her death. Dozens of others rose to share their recollections of Skye. Some were funny, others awkward, but all were from the heart. The last person to speak was Eden Payne.

Eden Payne was sixteen years old. At the age of seven, she had been removed from her mother's care following years of abuse and neglect. Her mother was both an alcoholic and addicted to opioids, and was wholly incapable of safely raising a child while caroming from shelters to relatives' homes to the streets, in an unending cycle. For four years, Eden's birth mother was provided with a series of interventions ordered by the Family Court in New Brunswick, in the hope that she would overcome her addictions, find a measure of stability, and be reunited with Eden. There were hopeful times, but more often very dark times. When Eden's mother was finally unable to break free from her cycle of dependency and homelessness, her parental rights were terminated by the court. As a result, Eden lived in thirteen different foster homes between the ages of seven and fourteen. During those seven years, Skye Brodie served as Eden's volunteer guardian *ad litem*, charged by the court with representing and advocating for Eden's best interests, which she did fiercely. Two years before her death, Skye had finally been able to help facilitate Eden's adoption into a forever home.

"Miss Skye was my best friend. She never gave up on me," Eden began. "Even when my mom was doing bad things and I was doing bad things, Miss Skye was always there for me. No matter where I was living, no matter who my foster family was, she always came to see me. Even though she wasn't really supposed to, sometimes she even brought me little presents like these bracelets that I'm wearing. She called me every year on my birthday and at Christmas. I wished that she was my mom and that I could go to live with her." No one made a sound as Eden spoke.

"Two years ago, Miss Skye came to visit me and told me that I would finally have a forever home. It was the happiest day of my life. My new mom and dad and little sister are the best family anybody could ever have, and I have them because Miss Skye always believed in me and always looked out for me. My social workers came and went, foster parents came and went, teachers came and went, I never really had any friends, but Miss Skye never left me. Even after I was adopted, Miss Skye still called me and did things with me, even though she didn't have to. She even brought me here one time and tried to show me how to curl. I wasn't very good at it, though." There were smiles and laughter. Most of the people could clearly picture how that scene would have looked. Of *course*, Skye took Eden curling.

"I wish that every kid had someone like Miss Skye to look out for them like she looked out for me. I never told her that I loved her when she was alive, but at least I can tell her now. I love you, Miss Skye." With that, Eden returned to her seat with her new family. If only everyone left that kind of legacy.

When the service ended, Skye was carried the six blocks from the curling club to the Greenock Presbyterian Church Cemetery. She was taken on foot, the honor of carrying the coffin shared among her friends. They first went onto Harriet Street, and then turned left onto Montague Street. The Bell Man and bagpipers led the procession of nearly two-hundred people, many in kilts, hose, tams, and sporrans. Skye finally arrived at her final place of rest. Slowly, and with gentle care, she was lowered into the ground in front of her gravestone as her friends recited the 23rd Psalm, "*The Lord is my shepherd; I shall not want. He maketh me to lie down in green pastures; He leadeth me beside the still waters. He restoreth my soul; He leadeth me in the paths of righteousness for His name's sake. Yea, though I walk through the valley of the shadow of death, I will fear no evil; for Thou art with me; Thy rod and Thy staff they comfort me. Thou preparest a table before me in the presence of mine enemies; Thou anointest my head with oil; my cup runneth over. Surely goodness and mercy shall follow me all the days of my life; and I will dwell in the house of the Lord forever. Amen."* The pipers played "Amazing Grace," and Skye came to rest.

Chapter 22

Further Investigation

I arrived in Boston late on Wednesday afternoon, and four hours later I was back home in Maine. It was only mid-November, but there was already a little bit of snow on the ground. Exhausted from my visit to Ailsa Craig the day before, as well as from a full day of flying and driving, I passed out on my bed.

I was awakened at nine-fifteen the next morning by my phone. It was Mark Cunningham, the lead Maine State Police detective, asking if I could stop by the Belfast police station that morning. I knew that a call would be coming eventually and had been expecting it, just not barely twelve hours after arriving home from Scotland. "I just flew in from Scotland last night. Eleven-thirty OK?" I asked.

"Fine," Detective Cunningham answered. After a brief pause, he asked, "Aren't you curious what this is about?" The cat and mouse game was underway.

"I know what this is about," I replied. "I'll see you at eleven-thirty." I was still not fully awake, but my mind was racing. I put on a pot of coffee, suddenly wishing that I was back in Ayr listening to the old-timers telling their curling tales. I sat down with my coffee and tried to think about why the police would be summoning me on the very first morning that I was back. During the initial questioning at the club, I had told them about my trip when they asked if I would be around in case they had any other questions. I surmised that they had made a note of when I would be returning.

I sat at the kitchen table that Molly and I had once shared and tried to figure out exactly what questions the detective might have in mind for me. I concluded that there were two different – very different – possibilities. The first, which I determined was the "doomsday" scenario, was that the police had discovered one of the many ways that I had no doubt screwed up my crime and given myself away. If that were to be the case, things would be getting awfully bad for me very quickly. The problem was, I didn't know what kind of evidence they might have found, or what kinds of mistakes I may have made. The second, more benign possibility, was that they were going to grill me about Rich. That would be no problem, because simply telling the truth about anything that they asked me about him would not be bad for Rich, or for me. I wrote down the phone number for Denise Strong, the best criminal defense attorney in Waldo County, and put it in my wallet, just in case.

I arrived at the station at precisely eleven-thirty and was escorted to an interview room by the detective. "Would you like a coffee?" he asked before we sat down. I didn't know if he was simply being cordial or wanted to trick me into leaving a DNA sample behind. "No, thanks," I answered, "I just had some." Besides, I had choked down police station coffee before, and it was usually even worse than gas station coffee. We sat.

"Thanks for coming down on such short notice," Detective Cunningham began. "So, you know why I asked you to come down this morning?" he asked, although it was more of a statement than a question. He had probably asked the same question thousands of times to thousands of people. It's a deceptively simple question that has gotten a lot of people into a lot of trouble because they nervously blurt out stupid answers.

"I assume that it's about the Skye Brodie murder," I replied.

"It is," he answered. "And we're hoping that you can help us."

"I'd be happy to, if I can. What do you want to know?" The answer to this question was going to tell me a lot about whether the police had anything on me or not. I braced myself for the question that might determine the course of the rest of my life.

"How do you know Richard Scamman?" he asked. I seemed safe – for the moment, at least.

"I've known him for quite a few years. I did some legal work for him years ago. The last couple of years he's been my teammate at the curling club," I answered. My biggest fear was somewhat alleviated when I was asked about Rich. Maybe the detective was trying to misdirect and was going to spring something else on me later. Or maybe he was the good cop biding time until the bad cop popped in. I was still wary.

"When was the last time that you saw him on the night that Skye Brodie was murdered?" he asked.

I paused for a moment, trying to appear pensive, although the answer was honest and simple and required no reflection. "I left the club around six forty-five or so. Rich was still there when I left. I didn't see him again until Sunday morning at the club." I hadn't been asked when I next saw him, only the last time that I had seen him on Saturday night, but the police like it when you volunteer a little extra information, and it was a truthful and harmless answer anyway. "Why are you asking about Rich?" I asked the detective. "Is he in trouble?" I knew that the detective wasn't going to answer my question, but I asked him anyway. It was time to show a little bit of indignation, which all attorneys put on display at some point in their careers, mostly just for effect.

"We're just following up with everyone," Cunningham replied rotely and predictably. It was precisely the answer which I expected.

I'm quite sure that he always gave that same non-answer to that question. "How well do you know Mr. Scamman?" he asked.

"Well enough that he called me in Scotland and said that you guys thought that he did it." I was starting to run a little hot, knowing that Rich had absolutely nothing to do with Skye's death. I still didn't know about the fingerprints, the DNA, or Rich's Friday night spent in *flagrante dilecto* with Skye.

"What else did he tell you when he called you in Scotland?" The detective hoped that he was onto something. He wasn't.

"Not a damn thing. I didn't let him. As soon as he said that you thought that he killed Skye, I told him to shut up and not say another word. I told him to call Steve Alexander immediately and to say that I referred him. Then I hung up. If you've seen his phone records, which I'm guessing you have, you know that the entire call lasted maybe a minute." As I had surmised, the investigators already knew about the call, if not its contents.

"Have you talked to Mr. Scamman since that call?"

"No."

"Other than that phone call while you were in Scotland, have you spoken to Mr. Scamman?" the detective asked.

"Other than that one phone call, I haven't spoken to Rich since we were all at the club on the Sunday morning that Skye's body was found. And we haven't texted or emailed, either," I added, even though I hadn't been asked. I was sure that the detective already knew that, anyway. I had to fight my instinct to want to spar with the detective, to be cute. The police hold all the cards during questioning, since they know what evidence has been discovered, what all of the other interviewees have said, are far more experienced in interrogations, and aren't nervous and scared like the person being interviewed.

I was fairly certain that I was never even remotely considered a suspect. A couple of people had confirmed that they saw me leaving the club around quarter to seven, some neighbors had seen me walking Bozo Junior at around seven-thirty, and my neighbor across the street had apparently told the police that he had seen me putting out some recycling around maybe eight-fifteen or eight-twenty. All things that I had already told the investigators. No one had told investigators of any unusual interactions between me and Skye over the weekend.

I almost wished that the detective had asked if they could search my phone and computer, because I would have let them, and they would have found virtually nothing to interest them. No internet searches for Skye Brodie, no emails, calls, or texts, except for the one innocent phone call to her back in March thanking her for sharing her family tree, although they already knew about that call from Skye's phone records. No internet searches for "How do I get away with murder?" or anything stupid like that. No maps of Belfast. Not much other than curling research and genealogical research about Molly, which would likely have been of little interest to the police.

"Do you know of any reason why Mr. Scamman would want to harm Ms. Brodie?" the detective finally asked.

'No," I stated bluntly.

Detective Cunningham had been saving his next combination question-statement, perhaps to rattle me or to catch me off-guard. "Did you know that Mr. Scamman and Ms. Brodie were having an affair?" If his intention was to surprise me, it certainly worked. I had no idea that Rich and Skye had any relationship whatsoever, much less a romantic one. On the other hand, I didn't even know whether the police actually had evidence or were just fishing. Clearly, the investigator could see that I was surprised. I thought on how best to answer.

"I had no idea," I finally answered. "I'm not even sure that I believe you. How do you know?" Of course, I wasn't going to get an answer to that question. Murder investigators are in the business of asking questions, not answering them.

"Let's just say we know," he said, without elaborating. Cunningham asked a few more questions about the relationship between Rich and Skye, of which I knew absolutely nothing. Suddenly, Rich's decisions to stay behind after I left and watch the Nae-Sayers' final matches at the Pumpkinspiel and the Broomspiel made much more sense to me.

The final question about Rich was one which had already been asked, but the detective tried again, after telling me about the affair. "Can you think of any reason whatsoever why Mr. Scamman would want to harm Skye Brodie?"

I again answered with a simple, "No."

I thought that the interview was over, but it wasn't. I had, in fact, quite accidentally left a couple of breadcrumbs along the way for the police to discover. The first was the time that I had spent with Skye sitting alone at a table during the Broomspiel back in March. Apparently, someone had taken notice and mentioned it to the police, most likely one of the Nae-Sayers. "I understand that you and Ms. Brodie spent some time together at a curling tournament in Massachusetts a few months ago, is that correct?" the detective finally asked.

It was a question that I hadn't anticipated, and which uncomfortably shifted the focus off of Rich and onto me. At the Broomspiel, Skye and I had found an empty table where she could show me her amazing color-coded family tree. We sat there alone for some time as she explained what the various codes, colors, and lines on her family tree all meant. This, of course, was before I knew anything at all about her relationship to Cuthbert Urquhart. "Yes, we did." I answered.

"We were told that the two of you were looking at some kind of picture or chart or something. What is it exactly that you were looking at?"

The detective had succeeded in catching me off guard with a couple of his questions, so I decided that I would try to make him a little bit uncomfortable, too, as well as buy a little bit of time. "Do you know about my wife?" I asked.

"Yes, I do," he replied. "Officer Cutts told me. I'm sorry for your loss."

"Thank you," I said, although I really didn't care about complete strangers expressing their sympathies. In fact, when it didn't really seem sincere, I resented it. I then told the detective the story of how I had begun working on Molly's family tree a few weeks after her death, how I had started curling with Rich at the club, how we had gone to the Pumpkinspiel in New Hampshire and played the Nae-Sayers, how we sat together with them after our game, how Skye and I had talked about genealogy and family trees, how she had told me that she would bring her color-coded tree to the Broomspiel for me to look at, and that I had told Skye about Molly's passing. The detective made notes as I talked. "Aren't you going to ask me if we danced?" I added when I was finished, perhaps a little more sarcastically than I should have. I guessed that if someone had mentioned seeing me and Skye talking, someone had probably also mentioned us dancing.

"I was going to, but since you brought it up, why don't you tell me about it?" Cunningham suggested.

"I was getting ready to leave when she came up and asked me to dance. I hate dancing, and at first I said no, but finally I gave in. I think that she was just trying to be nice." I tried to move the interview along by elaborating. "After that, I went back to my hotel. I said hello to her on Sunday morning after my game and then I drove back to Belfast."

"And is that the last time that you saw her or spoke to her before the weekend she was murdered?" he asked. I'm not sure how stupid Detective Cunningham thought that I was. He already knew that I had called her from Skye's phone records. They had no doubt seen that I had called her on Monday, March 29th, the day after the Broomspiel. What the detective didn't, and couldn't possibly know, was what we had talked about. So I told him, mostly.

"As you no doubt know, I did talk to her one time. It was a day or two after the Broomspiel. I called her to say thanks for showing me her family tree and for being kind and understanding when I told her about Molly. I also thanked her for giving me a curling lesson. Other than that, we talked about the Broomspiel for a few minutes and said goodbye. That was the only time that I spoke to her other than at a bonspiel." All of that was true, but incomplete. I didn't tell the detective the part about saying that I needed some time to think about things or Skye's suggestion that I consider a visit to Canada. That would forever remain between me and Skye, I hoped.

At the time of that phone call, I knew nothing about Skye's relation to the Urquharts. I learned of their relationship later that same day. The investigators' focus seemed to be on Rich, not me, although I was quite nervous being quizzed about my own relationship with Skye. It is a dangerous, dangerous game, trying to outsmart the police, and one which I tried hard not to play. The police knew things that I didn't know, they were much more experienced investigating crimes than I could ever hope to be, and they had the vast resources of the State at their disposal. To the extent that I could, I tried hard to tell them the truth and to cooperate.

I had thought long and hard about what I would do if the investigators asked if they could look at my phone or computer. There was nothing incriminating on either, but, just on general principles, I didn't want to turn them over. They certainly couldn't have gotten a search warrant based on what they knew, which was virtually nothing, surely not enough to establish probable cause. On the other hand, why look like I had something to hide when there was nothing to be found there, anyway. Fortunately, they didn't ask and I never had to make that decision.

With that, I left the interview, promising to let the detective know if I thought of anything that might be helpful. I guess that Detective Cunningham was satisfied, because I never again spoke with the police about the murder of Skye Brodie.

Chapter 23

Another Trial

It had been nine months since Skye's murder. I wasn't even called as a witness at Rich's trial, since the prosecutor had no interest in calling one of Rich's friends and Steve Alexander didn't need me for the defense. All that I could do was sit and watch every day as my friend stood trial for a murder which he did not commit. I felt really guilty that Rich had to go through this, but I was certain that he would be acquitted.

The police seemed to have completely forgotten about me after our interview the day after I returned home from Scotland. The detectives hadn't found any holes in my statements. I had an alibi until 6:45 p.m. when I was at the curling club, and also from 7:00 until 7:30, when I was walking Bozo Junior, which some neighbors witnessed and confirmed for the detectives. I had logged onto Netflix around 7:45 to start watching the end of *Breaking Bad*, and I had made sure to put my recycling out noisily at the same time that my neighbors across the street were putting out theirs, at 8:15. At 8:20, I had logged onto my tablet to check email, which was nothing but junk. I stayed logged on until 10:00, doing searches and reading about all things Scotland, including Ailsa Craig, with *Breaking Bad* on in the background. Periodically, I turned lights off and on so that my neighbors or dog-walkers would know that I was home.

I had no experience with committing crimes, but I knew enough to know that one of the easiest ways to screw up was to leave a digital trail. I had come to know, in March, shortly after the Broomspiel, what Skye Brodie's fate had to be. How could it be anything else after I learned about her and the murderous Cuddy Urquhart? I never searched for her or anything related to her on my computer. I never emailed, texted, or called her, except for that one innocent time before I knew the truth. I never mentioned her to anyone. I didn't read anything about her murder online. I didn't take my phone or my car when I went to Eagle Road that night. Both could have been used to track my movements. On that fateful Saturday, I had put my cellphone on "silent" during my curling match, and had "forgotten" to un-silence it the rest of the day, so that I had an excuse in case I didn't answer any phone calls between seven forty-five and eight-fifteen on Saturday night. A forensic analysis of my phone would have confirmed that it was on "silent" all day Saturday. The only thing that was even remotely interesting on my phone or computer was my research into Molly's family tree, and that would likely have been of no interest to the police, even had they looked, since neither Skye nor the Urquharts are mentioned. No, as far as I knew, I had not let my digital life betray me.

Steve Alexander had been pushing hard for a quick trial date for Rich. He knew damn well that the State's case was flimsy, almost non-existent, and he had no interest in giving them more time to develop a stronger one. The trial finally started with jury selection on Monday, July 24, 2023, in the Belfast District Court. Jury selection lasted for two days. Above all else, Steve wanted jurors who weren't going to hold Rich's Friday night dalliance with Skye Brodie against him – certainly no evangelicals and no one who had been blissfully married for forty or fifty years. Both immediately before and after jury selection, the judge attempted to broker a plea deal between the

State and Rich. Judges want cases settled, not trials. Steve, at Rich's direction, flatly refused every offer, although the State would have gladly taken any of them.

It was awful, what I was forcing Rich to go through, but I had no choice. Making my friend stand trial for a murder that he didn't commit was cruel, but what else could I do? I once considered confessing and sparing Rich the ordeal and the possible consequences, but quickly decided that I could never do that. I wasn't going to spend the rest of my life in prison for a crime that was completely justified and righteous. What I did shouldn't even be considered a crime. Confession may be good for the soul, but not for its mortal consequences. Besides, I convinced myself, there was no way that a jury would convict Rich for something that he didn't do. If somehow he was convicted, I might reconsider, I rationalized. I don't think that I would have, though. I didn't deserve punishment.

The State didn't have much of a case to present. There were no witnesses to the crime, no motive for the crime, other than pure speculation, no murder weapon, and an uncertain window for the time of death. All that the State had were a defendant who had initially omitted to disclose his Friday night fling with the victim and his inability to verify that he had spent Saturday night alone after leaving the curling club. The State hoped to bolster its case by introducing a wholly novel and unproven forensic science. Steve looked forward to eviscerating it.

Not only was Steve Alexander a very smart and capable attorney, but he was also a brilliant trial tactician. When he knew that his client was guilty and that the State had an overwhelming case, he fought and clawed at everything the prosecution presented, the zealous advocate for a person wrongfully accused by a spiteful and vindictive State, looking to find any crack or flaw in their case. If he could find one – just one – he might be able to exploit it for his client. For Rich Scamman's trial, though, Steve would be calm and accommodating and would let the prosecution present whatever case it wanted, short of unvarnished speculation. He would object to very little, because jurors usually surmise that if you object to evidence, you are hiding something. In this case, the defense had absolutely nothing to hide.

After opening statements and the preliminaries, with officers describing the call informing them that Skye was missing and the first responders describing their arrival at the crime scene on Eagle Road, the more interesting testimony began. The prosecution called the medical examiner, who was questioned for more than two hours about her training and credentials, about processing Skye's body at the scene, and about the autopsy results and the cause and manner of death. Steve was polite and respectful in cross-examining her, focusing his initial questions on how long Skye might have lived after her injury, forcing the witness to estimate that Skye may have been alive for anywhere from ten to thirty minutes after the attack. He then asked questions about the examiner's conclusion that the estimated time of death was between 6:30 and 9:30 p.m. Steve used the word "estimated" in his questions a lot. The more uncertain that he could make the time of the attack, the better for Rich, both because he was seen at the club at seven-thirty and had arrived at his home at seven forty-six, but also because it demonstrated how uncertain the State actually was about some facts. All of this was mainly just for show and to plant in the jurors' minds the notion that the State was simply speculating about a lot of things, a notion which Steve fully intended to emphasize later. Skye was very much alive and at the club until seven forty-five, and yet the witness estimated that she could have been dead at six-thirty. Steve wanted to talk about that.

Reluctantly, the witness conceded that estimating time of death is part art as well as science. She was quite used to being challenged over time of death. No one, she said, could credibly pinpoint an exact time of death absent actually being there when it arrived. There are simply too many variables, such as the victim's age, overall health, ground temperature, air temperature, wind, precipitation, and the kind of clothing being worn. All of that being said, her calculations, following accepted scientific forensic standards, pointed to a time of death of 8:00 p.m. In order to account for known and unknown variables, the window of ninety minutes on either side was the generally accepted forensic guideline for estimating time of death for bodies discovered within twenty-four hours of death.

Steve's final questions went to the 6:30 p.m. estimate as the earliest possible time of death. "Are you saying that six twenty-nine would not be possible as the time of death?" Steve asked. "Possible, but not likely," she replied. "Six twenty-eight?" The examiner gave the same answer. "Six twenty-seven?" Same. By the time that Steve had reached six twenty-five, the witness was clearly tired of this game. "I can say that within a reasonable degree of scientific certainty that Skye Brodie did not die before 6:25 p.m." The words must have sounded almost funny to the jury, which is exactly what Steve was aiming for. He had made his point. Everyone knew that Skye was alive and well at the club at seven forty-five, and here was the medical examiner testifying that she was absolutely sure that Skye didn't die before six twenty-five.

"I'm a little bit confused about this estimated time of death, as I'm sure some of the jurors might be," Steve prefaced his final question. "First, you swore under oath that it was between 6:30 and 9:30 p.m. When pressed, you said maybe as early as 6:25. You said that it might have taken up to thirty minutes after the attack for Skye Brodie to die. If my math is right, that means that your testimony is that the attack could have occurred as early as 5:55 p.m. Yet, we know that she was alive and well at seven forty-five, almost two hours later. So, my final question is, how accurate, exactly, are these *estimates* of yours?" Steve knew that there would be an objection from the prosecutor, which he got. Before the judge could even rule on the objection, Steve withdrew the question. His point was made. There was no sense letting the witness ruin it by actually answering the question.

The prosecution next called a series of forensic investigators from the Maine State Police Crime Lab. They testified that fingerprints found in Skye's car matched those of the defendant Richard Scamman, that Richard Scamman's DNA had been recovered from both Skye's body and from her motel room, and that the GPS in Skye's car had been set for 2 Eagle Road in Belfast. The jury seemed particularly interested in the fingerprint and DNA revelations, because they were the first pieces of evidence that actually linked Rich and Skye. Steve probed a little bit about chain-of-custody issues for the evidence, which require the State to document and account for the evidence's whereabouts and security at all times. He asked about the investigators' credentials, lab certifications and reliability, and other innocuous and mundane details. He had no intention of disputing any of the evidence that Rich and Skye had a rendezvous on Friday night.

The big fight over the admissibility of evidence had come before the trial even started, where the prosecution was dealt a near-fatal blow by Judge Jeanne Brock. During discovery, the State had offered a report from the crime lab which concluded that some of Rich's fingerprints found in Skye's car were less than twelve hours old, which would have meant that Rich was in Skye's car not only on Friday night, as he had admitted to being, but also on Saturday, the day of the murder, which he had denied. If that fingerprint-aging evidence were to reach the jury, Rich's fate would be in much greater jeopardy.

The crime lab's conclusion about the age of the fingerprints was based on a single 2020 study from Iowa State University claiming that by measuring levels of triacylglycerols in fingerprint residue using *matrix-assisted laser/desorption ionization mass spectrometry*, the age of fingerprints could be determined. "Expert" witnesses usually try to use indecipherable language to make them seem smarter than everyone else, and hence, to be automatically believed. Steve filed a pre-trial motion to exclude all evidence regarding the alleged age of the fingerprints in Skye's car.

The standard for admitting scientific evidence at trial requires that its methods and results be reliable, relevant, and generally accepted in the scientific community. A mini-trial before only the judge was held on the reliability of the supposed fingerprint aging science. Steve had engaged a well-respected forensic scientist who gutted the State's argument for admission, noting that the "so-called" study involved precisely three sets of prints, that the results had never been replicated in any other study, and that the study had never been peer-reviewed. He used the phrase "junk science" a lot. Steve's expert concluded by noting that no court in the country – district, county, state, or federal – had ever admitted fingerprint aging into evidence. The Honorable Jeanne Brock informed the State that her court was not going to be the first. The jury would never hear it. A key element of the State's case was gone.

The next three witnesses were the ones that Steve was most interested in – Officers Danny Cutts and Susan Wells – who had conducted the initial interviews at the club on Sunday morning, and Detective Mark Cunningham, who had interviewed Rich, and who had also interviewed me upon my return from Scotland. Steve made an occasional mild objection to their testimony based on hearsay, but knew that they would all be overruled. He actually wanted the testimony to be admitted, but needed to preserve his objections in the unlikely event that there would be a guilty verdict and that he would have to file an appeal. Both Officer Cutts and Officer Wells recounted how they had questioned everyone at the club on Sunday morning twice, the first time when it was simply a missing person case and again after Skye's body was discovered.

The officers testified that Rich said he knew Skye Brodie, that he thought that the last time he had seen her was around seven-thirty on Saturday night, shortly before he headed home for the evening, that he had neither seen nor heard any arguments, that he didn't know if Skye had any plans that night, and that he was unaware of whether Skye had any friends in Belfast. During the second interview, Rich told them that he had left the club around seven-thirty on Saturday night and went straight home, arriving around seven forty-five. Both officers testified that Rich said nothing about being with Skye Brodie on Friday night. Steve asked the officers a few questions about their interviews and confirmed with the officers that they had asked the same questions of everyone. No, they said, they didn't develop what they thought were any promising leads on Sunday morning.

"Did you ask Rich specifically what he had been doing on *Friday* night?" Steve asked. Steve always called him Rich, while the prosecution called him Mr. Scamman. No, they hadn't asked Mr. Scamman specifically about what he was doing or where he had been on Friday night.

Steve's question about Friday night was designed solely to pique the jurors' interest. Up until then, they had heard exclusively about the events of Saturday night and Sunday morning, and Steve wanted to be the one who introduced Rich and Skye's tryst. The next witness would be Mark Cunningham, the lead investigator from the Maine State Police, a man who had investigated nine murders, leading to nine convictions, and who had an unimpeachable record of service. Detective Cunningham was the one who had interviewed Rich after learning from the crime lab about Rich's fingerprints and the DNA evidence. After meticulously recounting the investigation, following-up on the alibis of everyone who had been interviewed, the interviews with residents on Eagle Road, and all of the other investigative steps, the prosecutor finally got to the part that Steve cared about – the Thursday interview with Rich. Cunningham testified that he had asked Rich all of the same questions that he had previously been asked – did he know Skye Brodie, when had he last seen her, did she mention any plans, were there any arguments or disagreements, could he account for his whereabouts on Saturday night. Rich's answers were exactly the same as what he had told officers Cutts and Wells, and they were all absolutely true.

"What was the next thing that you asked the defendant?" the prosecutor asked. The prosecutor and the investigator had rehearsed the testimony extensively, and the investigator knew exactly how the prosecutor expected him to answer.

"During an interview, my main objective is to let the subject say whatever he wants and to get him to talk. After getting the particulars that I am looking for, in this case confirming what was told to officers Cutts and Wells, I like to ask an open-ended question. In this case, I asked Mr. Scamman if there was anything that he wasn't telling me."

"What was the defendant's response?"

"The defendant told me that he couldn't think of anything else."

"Did the defendant say anything at all about what he had been doing on Friday night?" the prosecutor asked. "No, sir," came the answer.

"Did the defendant say anything at all about having an intimate relationship with the victim?"

"No, sir, he did not."

"At that point, did you consider Mr. Scamman to be deceptive?" Steve could have objected to the question, but passed.

"Any time a witness withholds relevant information from me, I view that as deceptive. In this case, yes, I found the defendant to be deceptive."

"Did you then ask the defendant how his fingerprints got into the victim's car?" It was a leading question, but Steve was fine with it. He was studying the jury, which had suddenly become very interested in the testimony.

"Yes, sir, I did."

"What was the defendant's response?"

"Mr. Scamman didn't say anything for a few moments. He seemed reluctant to say anything, but finally confessed that he had been with the victim on Friday night. The defendant also admitted that Ms. Brodie had refused his suggestion that they get together again on Saturday night." "Confessed" and "admitted" were words which the State had obviously coached the witness to use. The investigator then recounted Rich's statement about his rendezvous with Skye – how there was a romantic spark, how they had snuck away from the curling club together in Skye's car, how they had spent a couple of hours together at the motel, and how Skye had driven Rich back to the club to retrieve his car around midnight. Rich's recounting of the events was confirmed by Skye's GPS and cellphone data, which showed their movements, as well as by the motel security camera footage and by the DNA evidence found in the room. Rich's cellphone confirmed the exact same movements and timeline.

"As a result of your investigation, did you form an opinion as to who murdered Skye Brodie?" the prosecutor asked.

"I did."

"And what was that conclusion?"

"Based upon all of the evidence – the fingerprints, the DNA, the fact that we couldn't confirm the defendant's whereabouts around the time of the murder, and his deceptiveness – our conclusion was that the defendant Richard Scamman killed Skye Brodie."

"And did you form an opinion as to why the defendant killed Skye Brodie?"

"I did."

The prosecutor then asked what he very-well knew to be a highly improper question, but he felt as though he had no choice but to do it. Jurors are much more comfortable returning a conviction, particularly in murder cases, when they can find a motive. Even though the State is not required to prove motive in a murder trial, things usually go much better for it if it offers one. The prosecution knew that it was extremely unlikely that Rich was going to take the stand and also knew that it had no evidence of motive whatsoever. The prosecutor had to somehow plant something that they could find as a motive in the jurors' minds.

Finally, the prosecutor asked, "Was your conclusion that Richard Scamman killed Skye Brodie because their affair had gone bad?" Steve was on his feet before the prosecutor finished the word "bad." He had suspected all along that the State might try to back-door some cooked-up motive.

"Objection, Your Honor! The question is leading, calls for nothing but pure speculation, and assumes facts for which there is no – NO! – evidence. I move for sanctions against the State and for an immediate mistrial." Steve knew that there would be no mistrial and that there would very likely be no sanctions against the prosecution, which he really didn't care about at all. He was speaking to the jury as much as to the judge.

"Objection sustained," Her Honor ruled without hesitation. Judge Brock immediately turned to the jury. "You are to completely disregard the last question by the prosecution. You are to strike it from your memory. Let me remind you again that statements made by counsel are not evidence in this, or in any case. They are not to be considered in any way in your deliberations." Turning to Steve, she said. "Mr. Alexander, your motion for a mistrial is denied, but noted for the record. We will continue with this trial." Glaring directly at the prosecutor, she warned, "The motion for sanctions against the State, which I can assure you that I will very seriously consider, will be addressed immediately after the conclusion of the trial."

Still glaring at the prosecutor, Her Honor said, "I believe that the prosecution has no other questions for this witness?" It was phrased as a question, although it was anything but. The prosecutor returned to his table and sat down. He had at least tried. It was Steve's turn to cross-examine Detective Cunningham. He wouldn't take long.

Steve was well aware that the jurors would pay the closest attention to the very first things that they heard on cross-examination, so he started with what he surmised was their biggest concern about Rich, his failure to initially tell the police about his Friday night fling with Skye. He asked the question that the prosecutor had intentionally *not* asked. "Did Rich offer an explanation about why he did not initially tell the police about his Friday night with Skye?"

"He did," Detective Cunningham answered.

"Would you tell the jury what his explanation was?"

"His explanation was that he was separated from his wife and that their divorce proceedings were 'contentious,' I believe is the word that he used. He said that he didn't want word of an extra-marital affair getting out and providing his wife with information that would not be helpful to him in the divorce proceedings."

"I presume that you confirmed that Rich was separated from his wife, that they were in the midst of divorce proceedings, and that it was not an amicable situation?" It was a compound question, but the prosecution was understandably reluctant to raise an objection with Her Honor.

"We did."

With that out of the way, Steve wanted the jury to hear, in concise fashion, everything lacking in the prosecution's case. "To be clear, the State never located a murder weapon, correct?"

"That is correct."

"The State never found any evidence that Rich has *ever* been to 2 Eagle Road, correct?"

"Correct."

"Or that he was there on the night Skye Brodie was killed?"

"Correct."

"The State found no records of any phone, text, or email communication between Rich and Skye Brodie, correct?"

"Correct."

"The State confirmed that Rich was at the Belfast Curling Club from at least 6:00 p.m. until 7:30 p.m. on the night of the murder?"

"We did."

"The State also confirmed that Rich drove directly home from the club and arrived at his house at 7:46 p.m. on Saturday night?"

"Yes."

"Did the State find any evidence whatsoever that Rich was anywhere other than at his home from 7:46 p.m. on Saturday until Sunday morning?"

"We could not confirm where Mr. Scamman was after 7:46 p.m. on Saturday night."

Steve didn't care for the investigator's attempt to fudge on his answer, and was going to let him know. "I understand that you have been on the witness stand for a while and may be getting tired, sir. Do you need a break?" Steve asked.

"No, sir. I'm fine," was the sheepish answer. Never let the witness control cross-examination, Steve knew.

"Good," Steve replied. "Now let me ask you the same question again. Please listen very carefully to the question." Very slowly and deliberately, Steve asked, "Did the State find *any* evidence that Rich was anywhere other than at his home from 7:46 p.m. on Saturday until Sunday morning?"

"No, sir, we did not," the witness answered. Steve went back to look at his notes, just so the answer had time to sink in with the jury.

Lastly, Steve would take one final shot at the State's feeble attempt to conjure up an affair gone wrong as the reason for Skye's murder. "During your direct testimony, the jury was shown some security camera footage from the motel on Friday night. Would you agree with me that the footage appears to show Rich and Skye Brodie smiling and laughing and having a good time as they left the motel that night?"

"I really couldn't make a judgment about that," Detective Cunningham answered. It was a stupid answer, better than Steve could have hoped for, because it insulted the jury. Jurors hate being treated like they're stupid. They had seen the motel footage at least three times during the course of the trial and had clearly seen Rich and Skye happily leaving the motel together. Steve could have pressed his luck and tried to get the witness to repeat the same stupid thing, but sometimes less is more. And with that, Steve returned to his chair beside Rich, but not before turning to the jury to make sure that they recognized just how bad the detective's answer truly was. The court dismissed the jury for the day before Judge Brock and the attorneys retired to chambers to haggle over some jury instructions. The judge tried one last time to broker a plea deal, to no avail. When court came back into session the next morning, the sides presented their closing arguments, the defense first and the prosecution second. Before the closing arguments began, Judge Brock instructed the jury that what the attorneys said in closing was *not* to be considered as evidence, but was merely the parties' attempts to summarize the evidence before them. Her Honor glared directly at the prosecutor while delivering the instruction.

The jury only took two-and-a-half hours to return a verdict, an extraordinarily short deliberation for a murder trial. It probably wouldn't have taken half that time had the jurors not wanted to be treated to one final catered lunch courtesy of the State of Maine. "Not guilty" was their unanimous verdict. No jury was going to pin a murder conviction on someone based on what the State had put forth. Justice had been served. An innocent man was set free. Steve, feeling magnanimous, threw the prosecution a bone by withdrawing his motion for sanctions. There would be other trials with the same prosecutors, so why not build a little bit of goodwill?

I had watched the entire trial from a bench in the courtroom, not exactly praying, but rather trusting, that the jury would do the right thing. No one seemed to take any particular notice of my constant presence, since I was a retired lawyer and Rich was my friend.

———◆O◆———

Steve knew what the verdict would be. He had been through enough trials and faced enough juries that he was rarely wrong. A couple of days before the case went to the jury, Steve had called me and asked if I would whisk Rich from the courthouse when the case was over. Of course, I agreed. I parked in the lot behind the courthouse, away from the press. Steve had already made the arrangements with courthouse security in anticipation of a quick verdict. Steve was more than happy to walk out the front door of the courthouse and address the media, but he didn't want Rich to have to go through that. And Rich certainly had no interest in answering reporters' questions.

I waited while Steve and Rich completed the paperwork. Finally, they emerged through the back door. Rich shook hands with Steve, climbed into my car, and we drove away. Steve went out the front door to meet the press and drum up business, since beating a murder charge isn't always easy, and a lawyer who can do it must be pretty damn good. Steve had probably just raised his hourly rate.

I drove to the curling club, which was closed and locked, but I had a key, as all members do. Rich and I were the only ones there. There were sure to be reporters staked out at Rich's house, and Rich had no interest in talking to them. So we went to the club, poured a couple of beers, and sat down on one of the pews facing the ice house. There would normally have been ice, but, it being August, there was just the floor. The last time that we had been together at the club was on the Sunday morning of the Broilerspiel, shortly after Skye's body was discovered. Neither of us were at all interested in talking about the Nae-Sayers or about Skye Brodie. Rich had no interest in talking about the trial, either.

We talked about the upcoming curling season, which would be starting in a few weeks. We even shared a few laughs. Rich was determined that he was going to resume his normal life, no matter the stares and whispers that he was sure to encounter. He had done nothing wrong, and he shouldn't have to hide.

While I was shocked at first to learn about Rich's affair with Skye, I didn't really care about it and certainly didn't hold it against him. Skye Brodie had long ago shown me who she was, and how evil and duplicitous she truly was. Bragging about her great family, even while knowing the evil they had perpetrated against Molly's, revealed the depth of her depravity. Having an affair with my friend while pretending that she cared about me was the least egregious of her many sins. Perhaps I had even saved Rich from Skye.

There would forever be a secret between Rich and I. I had forced him through a terrible ordeal, one that I could have prevented and which no one should have to suffer, being falsely accused of the most heinous crime. But what else could I have done? I had no choice, really. I could surely not be expected to confess and live out my life in a prison cell. No, I did the only thing that I could have done, which was to let Rich stand trial and wait for him to be exonerated. It all worked out in the end.

Rich was a good friend, for sure. If he knew what I had done, and why I had done it, he would understand. He would know that I couldn't sacrifice my life for his, not after all that I had done to bring justice to the world. He would understand and forgive. No, things turned out exactly as they were meant to. Sitting silently together on the pew, we both hoped to never speak of Skye Brodie again.

Chapter 24

Vengeance

More than two years after the Broilerspiel and the still unsolved mystery of Skye Brodie's murder, my book, *Roaring Stones: A Much Too Comprehensive History of Curling*, was released by a small Maine publisher, Dirigo Books. I had, in fact, been granted access to Scottish Curling's Historic Scottish Curling Places database by Bruce Andrews after returning home from Scotland, and had spent hundreds of hours pouring through it, looking for more details for my book. I also made a three-day trip to Ottawa to do some historical research into Canadian curling at the Library and Archives of Canada. It took me well over a year to write the book and to find a publisher for it. I did a few book signing events around Belfast, at the curling club, Marshall Wharf Brewing, Downshift Coffee, Left Bank Books, and Owl & Turtle Bookshop. For a few weeks, Left Bank Books even featured a copy of my book in the front window, which I delighted in seeing while I was out walking Bozo Junior. I attended a number of bonspiels around New England, setting up tables, talking curling, and hawking books. I was even invited to appear on *207*, a Maine television show featuring local-interest stories.

The trip to the Library and Archives in Ottawa was not the only trip that I made to Canada, however. Five years after the Broilerspiel, I attended the Scotspiel at the Heather Curling Club in St. Andrews by-the-Sea in New Brunswick, the club to which Skye Brodie had once belonged. Rich Scamman, for obvious reasons, elected not to go, but three other members from our Belfast club decided to join me in forming a team. We debated amongst ourselves whether it was an appropriate thing to do. I was the one who was most in favor of going, and we ultimately agreed that it would be OK. On a cold Friday in November, I made the drive into Canada, using the passport which Skye had once suggested that I use.

The Nae-Sayers were there, reconstituted without Skye Brodie. We were welcomed to the bonspiel, although not with a great deal of warmth or enthusiasm, as I fully expected and understood. The Heather Curling Club members did not have fond feelings for Belfast, and justifiably so. None of them had ever returned to Belfast to the best of my knowledge. Their reticence, while making our visit a little bit uncomfortable, didn't really bother me all that much. I didn't come to see them, or even to curl, for that matter. I came to see Skye Brodie one last time.

On Friday night, one of the Nae-Sayers approached and asked me if I had heard of any developments in the investigation into Skye's murder. I knew that it was bound to happen at some point during the weekend. Discussing the case with one of her friends made me pretty uncomfortable, although I didn't detect any real malice in the question. I had hoped that no one would be bringing the case up, but knew that I was unlikely to be that lucky.

"I haven't really heard of anything since Rich's trial ended," I answered, which was the truth. "As far as I know, the case is still open." It probably was still an open case, technically, but I doubted that there was really anything much happening. If there had been, I would have certainly heard something about it.

"We just never understood one thing," the Nae-Sayer replied. "It clearly wasn't just a random incident. Skye intentionally drove to that particular house. Why would she do that? She didn't know the people who lived there, and she didn't tell anyone that she was going there. Why she went there seems like the key to the whole case."

"It certainly does," I said. "If the police could answer that one question, I'm pretty sure they would find the killer." He was absolutely right, of course. Skye's inexplicable visit to 2 Eagle Road was the key to the case.

"Are there any theories floating around?" he asked me. Now he was clearly just fishing, and I was anxious to talk to anyone else about anything else. Five years later, I still could make a mistake and say something that I shouldn't. Who knows why, exactly, he was asking me all of these questions. I tried to end the conversation.

"I haven't heard a thing since the trial," I answered. I thought about saying that I knew that Rich didn't do it, but even that might lead to questions about how I knew. I didn't know whether the folks in St. Andrews had come up with any theories of their own, and I didn't particularly want to find out. I suddenly developed an immediate need to speak with one of my teammates, and excused myself. What I really wanted to do was to get the hell out of Canada and back to Belfast, but I had matches to play and a visit to make before I could leave.

The Scotspiel ended for us with a lopsided loss to one of the home teams on Sunday morning. I'm sure that the locals took some special pleasure in handily dispatching the team from Belfast. I was glad that the match was early in the morning, so that I could get going. I had intentionally driven up to New Brunswick by myself, telling my Belfast teammates that I would be making a couple of stops on the way home and that I might not be getting home until Monday.

On my way out of St. Andrews, I drove to the Greenock Presbyterian Church on Montague Street, a church whose construction was financed, naturally, by a Scotsman, Christopher Scott, in 1824. The church's steeple is adorned with a hand-carved oak tree in full bloom, the emblem of Greenock, Scotland, a town west of Glasgow on the River Clyde and Christopher Scott's hometown. Although it was Sunday morning, I had no intention of attending the church service. I went to Greenock because within the church's cemetery lies the final resting place of Skye Brodie. I parked my car amongst those of the worshippers inside the church and made my way to the cemetery.

The Greenock Presbyterian cemetery is quite small, unlike the enormous Glasgow Necropolis where Darcie Ross is buried. It looked just like any one of thousands of Protestant church cemeteries. It didn't take very long for me to find Skye. I stood over her, reading the inscription, "Skye Brodie, October 24, 1971 – November 6, 2022." Carved into her gravestone was the image of a curling stone. We were alone together for what would be the final time.

I stood there over Skye, silently, not prepared to speak just yet. I didn't sit with her like I had with Darcie, but purposefully stood towering over her. What could I say to a woman whom I had killed? What was it that I had to tell her? I certainly didn't owe her an explanation. In fact, I didn't owe her a damn thing. And I certainly had nothing to apologize to her for. No, I had come to gloat, to brag, to celebrate even. Five years had not diminished my hatred and had inspired no regrets.

It took a long time for the words to come, even though I had been looking forward to this moment for five years. Finally, I spoke. "Hello, Skye. Alone at last. You've probably been expecting me . . ."

I made one final trip to the top of Cadillac Mountain. Long after my visit to Scotland, the trial of Rich Scamman, and the Scotspiel, I climbed into my car and drove north to Acadia National Park. I once again sat on the pink granite where Molly and I had sat as teenagers, and the place where I had let go of her ashes. I told her everything.

I continued to curl at the Belfast Curling Club until I was eighty years old, when the cruelties of age and a general fatigue made it impossible. Rich Scamman had passed away a few years earlier, and his memorial service was held on the ice at the club. I spoke of what a true and kind friend he had been. I said nothing about the Broilerspiel or the trial, nor did anyone else.

Other than when I went out curling, I mostly sat at home and reflected on my life. Mostly, I thought about Molly and our very short time together. We were married for twenty-five years and I was a widower for thirty. Yet my memory of her was clear and recent. I remembered her face, her smile, and her voice, and I missed her every single day. I still had the pictures of Molly and Darcie side-by-side on my dresser, even three decades later, both now quite faded.

I thought about Skye Brodie, too, although I tried to vanquish those thoughts whenever they intruded. I thought about Darcie Ross, someone I never knew except through a single photograph, and I thought about the murderer, Cuddy Urquhart. I thought about the quarrymen and their conspiracy of silence. And I thought a lot about what I had done. I reflected on justice and what it might mean. And for some reason, I kept thinking of the feather which had fallen beside me atop Ailsa Craig.

Others might try to say that we were alike, Cuddy Urquhart and I. One no better or worse than the other. We had each killed in anger, although of quite different kinds. My anger and hatred were nurtured, cultivated, and embraced until they were irresistible and all-consuming. Cuddy's seemed to flash in an instant. Worse yet, some people might say, we had each gone on to live lives of freedom, privilege, and abundance. They would say that we were each spared the consequences which we surely deserved, at least in our mortal lives. But those people would be wrong, for I, unlike Cuddy, was surely justified in what I had done. Cuddy Urquhart most assuredly was not.

Although I remained agnostic throughout my life, I knew the words from the Old Testament which God had spoken to Moses, Deuteronomy 32:35, to be exact:

> *Vengeance is mine; and recompense; Their foot shall slip in due time; For the day of their calamity is at hand, and the things to come hasten upon them.*

Perhaps I *had* sinned by claiming that which was not mine to claim – revenge and another's life – and assumed for myself that which was not mine to assume. Although I did not regret any of it, and in fact was proud of what I had done, I still remembered what Confucius once said, "Before you embark on a journey of revenge, dig two graves." Confucius was wrong, I decided. Revenge felt good, because it was righteous and just and pure. The only grave which deserved to be dug was Skye Brodie's, and I made sure that it was.

On occasion, as my final days approached, I thought about finally confessing to what I had done. Confession is allegedly good for the soul. I elected not to. What good would it possibly do? I wasn't concerned for my soul, anyway. And, quite frankly, confession is for those who need atonement.

As I lay alone, eighty-one years old and dying in a hospital bed not far from my home, my final consciousness turned to Molly. I thanked her for the feather, told her that I loved her, that I hoped that she understood, and went quietly toward the light.

Epilogue

A ilsa Craig is also known as "Paddy's Milestone," due to its location approximately halfway between Belfast, Northern Ireland and Glasgow, Scotland. People looking for work in Glasgow or elsewhere in Scotland, particularly the Irish, often made the trip northward via boat through the Firth of Clyde and past Ailsa Craig. When they reached Ailsa Craig, they knew that they were halfway through the journey.

Many poems and songs have been inspired by Ailsa Craig. Below is a sampling, along with the traditional *Curler's Grace*.

Ailsa Craig

And o'er the swell our boat made way
As gallant as a gull in flight,
A rare excitement stirred my soul
To see that grey and naked height.

This far-flung Scottish island sings
Sweet siren songs of skies and winds,
No women wait, no children play
My heart extends, my head rescinds.

Gossiping groups of puffins clump

Gaudy paint-box beaks a gabble,
Guillemots, stacked on thin ledges
Greet us with peculiar cackle.

Peril awaits on craggy rocks
Stretched beneath great rugged shoulders,
Only wild feet there can venture
O'er the guano covered boulders.

Here nature spins the years around
And if I'm purposefully vague,
This place must stay remote and wild
This stunning island, Ailsa Craig.
-Elfin

Paddy's Milestone

Beyond Culzean's daurk cliff
Past Girvan Water's urge,
The black crag o Ailsa soars above
The wild Atlantic surge.

A seal head, thrust above the tide,
Clyde's rush to integration,
A stane tae mark in silhouette
The lang sea miles o emigration.

The passage o the dispossessed
As Glasgow bound they sailed
Never tae return tae the Roisin Dubh
When the tattie harvest failed.

For years men sailed across the Firth
Tae bring its granite treasures hame
Tae shape and polish them till fit
Tae grace the Roarin Gemme.

When, bloodied frae the tangled nets
Hauns sair frae cauld an rain
Thanfu, the skipper tirns the wheel
Heads back fur shore again.

A lightness fills his weary heart
When ther across the Firth
The licht oan Ailsa's soarin rock
Points the wey back tae his berth.
– George McEwan

To Ailsa Rock

Hearken, thou craggy ocean pyramid!
Give answer from thy voice – the sea-fowl's screams!
When were thy shoulders mantled in huge streams?
When from the sun was thy broad forehead hid?
How long is't since the mighty Power bid
Thee heave to airy sleep from fathom dreams –
Sleep in the lap of thunder or sunbeams –
Or when gray clouds are thy cold coverlid?
Thou answerest not, for thou art dead asleep.
Thy life is but two dead eternities –
The last in air, the former in the deep!
First with the whales, last with the eagle skies!

Drown'd wast thou till an earthquake made thee steep,
Another cannot wake thy giant size!
- John Keats

In the Firth of Clyde, Ailsa Crag

Since risen from ocean, ocean to defy
Appeared the Crag of Ailsa, ne'er did morn
With gleaming lights more gracefully did adorn
His sides, or wreathe with mist his forehead high
Now, faintly darkening with the sun's eclipse
Still is he seen, in lonely sublimity,
Towering above the sea and little ships;
For dwarfs the tallest seem while sailing by,
Each for her haven; with her freight of Care,
Pleasure, or Grief, and Toil that seldom looks
Into the secret of tomorrow's fare;
Though poor, yet rich, without the wealth of books,
Or aught that watchful Love to Nature owes
For her mute powers, fixed Forms, or transient shows.
— **William Wordsworth** *(during an eclipse of the sun)*

Curler's Grace

O'Lord wha's love surrounds us a'
And brings us a' the gether
Wha' writes your laws upon oor hearts
And bids us help each ither
We bless Thee for Thy bounties great

For meat and hame and gear
We thank Thee, Lord, for snaw and ice
But still we ask for mair
Gi'e us a hert to dae whit's richt
Like curlers true and keen
To be guid friends along life's road
And soop oor slide aye clean
O Power abune whose bounty free
Oor needs and wants suffices
We render thanks for Barley Bree
And meat that appetises
Be Thou our Skip throughout life's game
An' syne we're sure to win
Tho's slow the shot and wide the aim
We'll soop each ither in.

Appendix

To those who aren't intimately familiar with curling, a brief introduction to its origins, how it is played, the surface that it is played on, and the equipment that it is played with, will be helpful. Its spirit, too, is an important part of the game. Curling's nickname – *The Roarin' Game* – comes from the sound of the granite stones rumbling down the ice.

The very first thing that you are likely to notice is that almost everyone looks happy when they are curling. Whether they are learning to curl for the first time or are experienced curlers playing in a league, people are smiling and laughing. Curling is fun. How could it not be – playing on a team, sliding stones down a 150-foot-long sheet of ice, and watching and hearing the stones as they crash into each other?

Curling is most familiar to people from being prominently featured on television every four years during the Winter Olympics. To many, it is simply a curiosity. Although the overwhelming consensus is that the game originated in Scotland five centuries ago, there are still occasional heated and emotional arguments favoring the Netherlands as its true home. A quick primer on the history of the game is in order.

The earliest *physical* evidence of curling being played comes from a curling stone inscribed with the date "1511" which was discovered when a pond in Dunblane, Scotland, was drained hundreds of years later. It is the oldest known curling stone still in existence, although it bears little resemblance to the stones that are used today.

The earliest known *written* reference to curling comes from Scotland and dates back nearly 500 years. In 1541, a notary named John McQuhin recorded a challenge made by John Sclater, a monk at Paisley Abbey outside of Glasgow, to Gavin Hamilton, the lay governor of Paisley Abbey. It seems that Gavin Hamilton was thoroughly and rather intensely disliked by nearly everyone, but because a monk could not possibly challenge a governor to a duel, the monk decided to challenge him to a curling match instead. It is not known whether the challenge was accepted, or who may have won the match, but the monk had nonetheless made his point.

The first *artistic* depiction of curling comes from 1565, when Flemish artist Pieter Bruegel the Elder completed two paintings, *Winter Landscape with Ice Skaters and Bird Trap* and *The Hunters in the Snow*. Each of the paintings depict outdoor curling scenes and represent the oldest known visual representations of curling.

The first reference to curling in *literature* is found in a 1639 poem by Henry Adamson. Adamson wrote in *The Muses Threnodie*, that James Gall "was much given to pastime, as golf, archerie, curling; and Joviall companie." Scottish poet David Gray wrote of whiskey-drinking curlers at the Luggie Water, a stream in Kirkintilloch.

The first formal curling society, or club, was established in Kilsyth, Scotland in 1716, although, as with most things related to curling, that honor is disputed by others claiming to have been the first, including curling societies in Kinross and Muthill. The Kilsyth Curling Club, at more than 300 years old, is still in existence today.

The earliest known written description of the game itself is found in Thomas Pennant's 1772 book, *A Tour in Scotland and Voyage to the Hebrides*:

Of the sports of these parts that of Curling is a favorite; and one unknown in England. It is an amusement of the winter, and played on the ice, by sliding from one mark to another great stones of forty to seventy pounds weight, of hemispherical form, with an iron or wooden handle at top. The object of the player is to lay his stone as near to the mark as possible, to guard that of his partner, which has been well laid before, or to strike off that of his antagonist.

Just as they have done with Ailsa Craig, poets have long celebrated the sport of curling, including Robert Burns, the 18th century Scottish poet, in 1786's *Tam Samson's Elegy*:

> *When winter muffles up his cloak,*
> *And binds the mire like a rock;*
> *When to the loughs the Curlers flock,*
> *Wi' gleesome speed,*
> *Wha will they station at the cock?*
> *Tam Samson's dead!*
>
> *He was the king o' a' the Core,*
> *To guard, or draw, or wick a bore,*
> *Or up the rink like Jehu roar,*
> *In time o' need;*
> *But now he lags on Death's hog-score*
> *Tam Samson's dead!*

Curling, by the early 1800s, was also claimed to have definite medical benefits. Dr. Alexander Pennecuik wrote:

To Curle on the ice does greatly please;
Being a Manly Scottish Exercise,
It clears the Brains, stirs up the Native Heat,
And gives a gallant Appetite for Meat.

On July 25, 1838, the Grand Caledonian Curling Club, which would become the national governing body for the sport in Scotland, was founded at the Waterloo Hotel in Edinburgh. It was granted a royal charter in 1843 by Queen Victoria, who was fascinated by the game after viewing a curling exhibition on the wooden floor of Scone Palace in Perth. The Queen even tried to throw a stone, but it "proved too heavy for her delicate arm." After the exhibition, Prince Albert was presented with "a splendid pair of Curling Stones, made of finest Ailsa Craig granite." The Grand Caledonian Curling Club was formed to nationalize the sport and to create some uniformity in how it was to be played, since various clubs throughout the country were playing with widely differing kinds of stones and with quite different rules. Renamed the Royal Caledonian Curling Club after receiving the royal charter, the first formalized set of curling rules was adopted.

Prior to 1838, there had been few serious attempts to unify or codify the rules of curling, although the Duddingston Curling Society had drawn up a set of regulations several years prior. Each club played by their own particular rules, and matches between different clubs required extensive negotiations over how the game would be played. With the formation of the Grand Caledonian Curling Club as a governing body, a uniform set of rules was finally adopted. With a uniform set of rules now the standard, the modern sport of curling rapidly evolved and grew in popularity.

Curling was brought to North America, primarily to eastern Canada, by Scottish emigrants, in the eighteenth and nineteenth centuries. The first Canadian curling club was established in Montreal in 1807.

To understand modern curling, it is necessary to understand both the surface on which it is played and its specialized equipment. Curling is played on a much different kind of ice surface than hockey or figure skating, which require smooth ice. Curling is played on "pebbled" ice, which is created and maintained through a meticulous combination of art and science. While hockey and figure skating ice is smooth and renewed using a Zamboni, curling ice is a different animal altogether. First and foremost, curling ice must be completely level. A variation of one-eighth or one-quarter of an inch would make a curling sheet virtually unplayable. A Zamboni is *never never ever* used on true curling ice. Curling ice also requires a specific temperature, controlled by thousands of feet of piping or tubing a few inches below the surface of the ice, through which a very cold brine or glycol is pumped. Most curling ice is only around two inches thick.

Once a level sheet of ice at the proper temperature is laid down, the real process of making curling ice begins. "Pebbling" is what makes a curling stone travel as far as it does and enables it to curl, or turn, by reducing the area of the stone actually touching the ice and thus reducing friction. Ice technicians use purified, deionized water with as few dissolved solids as possible to pebble the curling ice. Pebblers walk backwards down each sheet, with a tank of warm water on their backs, heated to around 120 degrees Fahrenheit, while waving an attached wand, similar to the aspergillum used by priests to sprinkle holy water, dispersing tiny droplets of water onto the ice.

The droplets freeze almost immediately, creating tiny bumps on the ice. It may take several passes to apply sufficient pebble to the ice.

When the pebbling is done, a scraper is pushed up and down the ice. The scraper is a large, expensive piece of machinery with what amounts to a four or five-foot wide razor blade attached to the bottom. As the scraper is pushed down the ice surface, it shaves off the top of the pebble so that the remaining pebble is of a completely uniform height, creating consistency in how a stone behaves as it slides down the ice. Uneven pebble would cause the curling stone to wobble and misbehave as it slides down the sheet. After the ice has been shaved, a soft, wide, dry mop is pushed across the length of the sheets to remove the bits of ice which were shaved off of the top of the pebble by the scraper. At last, the ice is ready for play.

Curlers use two kinds of specialized equipment unique to the game – curling shoes and brooms, which really aren't very similar to what are commonly thought of as brooms, although they once were. Curling shoes have a different sole on each shoe. When curlers push out of the hack, they push off with their dominant leg. The shoe that is used to push out from the hack has a gripper on the sole, enabling the player to walk on the ice without slipping and to maintain the traction needed for sweeping. The gripper resembles the skin of an orange, only made out of soft rubber. On the sole of the shoe on the other foot, which remains flat on the ice, is a slider, usually made out of Teflon. Teflon has an extremely low coefficient of friction, so that it can slide down the ice without slowing down the curler. Teflon on ice is an extremely slippery combination.

The broom, or "besom" in old Scotland, is like a sponge mop. Attached to a handle made of lightweight fiberglass or carbon fiber is a cloth brush, which is the part of the broom which actually touches the ice. By applying downward pressure on the broom and sweeping it back and forth in front of the sliding stone, the sweeper warms the ice, which reduces friction and allows the stone to travel farther and straighter. Through the use of sweeping, players can guide the sliding stone to its desired location. Sweeping can add as much as eight or ten feet of distance to a shot if done properly. What a sweeper may never do is touch the stone with the broom.

Yet another bit of curling equipment, not often seen on the ice in modern play, is noted by John Kerr in his 1890 *History of Curling*:

> *An indispensable equipment, according to a majority of curlers, is a flask . . . A flask is useful, but not indispensable. It is certainly dangerous to the feet if it affects the head . . . [E]very skip must take special care to keep this equipment in its proper place.*

With the ice prepared, curling shoes on, broom in hand, and stones in place, the game can begin. Curling rules are fairly simple, although execution is quite complex, much like chess. In fact, curling is often referred to as "chess on ice." The ability to envision two or three shots ahead is critical to success at higher levels of competition and helpful at lower levels.

A curling match is generally scheduled for eight or ten ends, similar to innings in baseball. In a normal match, each team consists of four players, who alternate taking shots. Each player – lead, second, vice, and skip – takes two shots per end, meaning that a total of sixteen stones, eight per team, will be thrown by the two teams in each end. The skip stands in the house, which consists of a twelve-foot wide circle, within which are smaller four-foot and eight-foot circles, as well as the button, or bulls-eye, which together comprise the scoring area. The skip directs the shooter as to what kind of shot to attempt and exactly where the skip wants the stone to come to rest.

The skip may want a shot to land in the house, but might also want the shooter to place a guard in front of a stone that is already there. A guard protects the stone which is in the house from being "taken out" by an opponent's stone. The end continues with teams alternating shots, setting guards, knocking opponents' stones out of the house, and tapping their own stones closer to the button, trying ultimately to get the highest number of stones closest to the center of the house. Players control how their stones behave by gently turning the stone's handle either clockwise or counterclockwise upon release. A clockwise spin will make a stone curl from left to right, while a counterclockwise spin will make it curl from right to left. The sound of the forty-two-pound stones rumbling down the ice, and they are noisy, gave curling its nickname of *The Roarin' Game*.

There are two competing theories as to how curling got its name. The one which is most often told is that the name derives from the way that shooters can make the stones turn, or curl, by turning the handle upon release. The other theory is that it derives from the Scottish word "curr," which describes a low, rumbling sound. The first theory makes for a better story, but the second is probably more accurate.

Once all sixteen stones have been played, the score for that end is tallied. Scoring begins with the stone that is closest to the button, or the center of the house. If a red-handled stone is closest to the button and a yellow-handled stone is the second closest, the red team gets one point. If a red stone is both the closest *and* second closest, red gets two points, and so on. In theory, therefore, one team could garner as many as eight points in an end, although I have never seen that happen. A three or four point end is a significant score.

Obviously, it is a big advantage to be taking the final shot in an end, which is known as having "the hammer." The hammer goes to the team which lost the previous end. Teams with the hammer would like to score two or three points in an end, while the team without the hammer would prefer to limit their opponent to one point, or even to "steal" a point for themselves when playing without the hammer.

———◄○►———

In a nutshell, that is the modern game of curling. It wasn't always played that way, of course. For years, centuries even, there was an earlier "Points Game," which entailed executing a number of specific shots in very specific ways. That, however, is a story for another time.

The most important piece of equipment, of course, is the granite curling stone itself. To learn about the modern curling stone, we need to travel back in time sixty million years to the birth of the volcanic island of Ailsa Craig in the Firth of Clyde, ten miles off the west coast of Scotland.

About the Author

DAVID S. FLORIG is a member of the Maine Writers and Publishers Alliance as well as a member and past-president of the Pine Tree Curling Club in Portland. *The Stones of Ailsa Craig* is his debut novel and is an homage to Belfast, Maine; the glorious Maine coast; and the ancient Scottish sport of curling.

David grew up and lived in South Jersey before retiring to Maine. Adopted by Charles and Marjorie Florig, he has seen a single picture of his birth mother. Subconsciously, that picture may have inspired this story.

For years, David practiced law in Pennsylvania and New Jersey. Following his legal career, David was the Executive Director of two nonprofits – *Court Appointed Special Advocates of Burlington County* (New Jersey) and the *West Philadelphia Alliance for Children. WePAC* recruited and trained volunteers to open shuttered elementary school libraries in Philadelphia, and for his work on behalf of Philadelphia's children, he was honored as one of the inaugural *GameChangers* by KYW Newsradio in celebration of Black History Month.

He lives in Maine with his wife of thirty-five years, Nancy, and their ill-mannered rescue dog, Molly Malone.

davidflorig.com
Facebook.com/david.florig.5

To inquire about booking David Florig for a signing or speaking engagement, please contact david@davidflorig.com.

Thank you so much for reading The Stones of Ailsa Craig. *Gaining exposure as an independent author depends mostly on word-of-mouth. If you have the time, please consider leaving a review on Goodreads, Amazon, IngramSpark, Barnes & Noble, or wherever you purchased this book. Please know that I truly appreciate reviews and take each one seriously.*

Printed in the USA
CPSIA information can be obtained
at www.ICGtesting.com
JSHW020525221123
52397JS00001B/1